THE
LOST
SAINT

RACHAEL CRAW

Published by 8th Note Press
Text Copyright © 2025 by Rachael Craw
First edition published 2025
All rights reserved.

ISBN: 978-1-961795-29-7

Manufactured in the United States

Cover and map design by Marcus Pallas
Typeset by Typo•glyphix

For my dad, Tony Gorman

Also by Rachael Craw

THE LOST SAINT

CHAPTER ONE

He was watching. Ana could tell, but she swallowed against the lump in her throat and pretended not to care. She crouched in the shallows at the edge of the Namen River, her waders bunching at the backs of her knees, and attached the specimen container to the end of her extendable pole. She looked up, sending a quick prayer to Saint Ansel.

This was her river, after all. Surely the best place to ask for help. Though Ana doubted a saint who split a river to save her people was much concerned with broken hearts. Or a failed student trying to win free beer in their tour guide's daily challenge.

She blinked at the blue sky, vaulting high and bright above the forest with a little red mark in the center, like an eyebrow drawn in fading red chalk.

A comet.

Exciting for the first five minutes. Boring after a week.

The ancients thought comets were omens of blight or impending doom. As far as Ana was concerned, the warning had come too late. She was already blighted — crops failed, prospects dashed. No word from the dean on her submission for exemption after missing two exams in one day and failing to meet the deadline for her last assignment. Her place on London's Queen Mary University theater program lost. Her mum ropable about her *wasting an opportunity on account of a boy.*

Worry burned in her chest like a hot stone. She breathed and pushed it down. *Stay in the moment.* At least the sun was shining overhead, promising a molten afternoon. She only wished she could fully relax and enjoy it, but Stefan waited on the bank, judging her. She could tell by his sigh; it made the muscle in her jaw cramp.

Ana hated beer but she refused to give him the satisfaction of screwing up their chances to win.

With a firm grip on the lever, she extended the pole across the water. A quick dip and she lifted the canister from the icy flow. Morning light dazzled her eyes, refracting on the veins of quartz in the submerged rocks. Her head spun and she faltered.

"Careful," Stefan called.

She swung the pole around, water sloshing on his trainers, and he stepped back, a knot forming in his brow. Ana's stomach gave a little twist. He took hold of the canister before she could do any more damage, and she released the lever but did not apologize.

Gwen watched from her seat on the rocks, the muddy bank too slippery for her prosthetic leg. Twice, yesterday, she'd nudged Ana and whispered she was being "a bit snippy" or "trying a bit hard." The memory chased heat into her cheeks.

The awkwardness between Ana and Stefan polluted the atmosphere, tainting every interaction. While it made him cold and distant, it made her irritable and oversensitive. She couldn't help but read into every word, look, or gesture, as though she needed to keep score. As though she couldn't let him win.

Which was ridiculous. He'd won over two months ago, the balance of power sliding into his hands when he said, "This. Us. It isn't working. Not for me. Not anymore." And dumped her. Two days before exams.

He dipped a testing strip. "This time."

Ana collected the control strip from the tour guide's kit to compare with the newly dipped sample. "No signs of bacteria or contaminants and pH levels look ... almost perfect."

"No such thing as perfect," Stefan said.

Gwen looked up from her perch, clipboard balanced on her knees as she collated data for their team. "Saint Ansel's Tears, baby."

Stefan gave her a flat look. "It's fresh water from a natural spring, fed from the roots of a mountain glacier; of course it's pure. And not because some medieval fantasist with a God complex sobbed over the water."

"Not an ounce of wonder in that body, Stef." Ana meant to tease but it came out brittle.

He turned his back on her and passed the dipstick to Gwen. "Better than blathering on about miracle tears."

Gwen shot Ana a look and she bit the inside of her lip. The three of them had signed up for the week-long summer tour six months ago. Back when love was grand and the future golden with possibility. A last hoorah for most of their graduating class from Hamburg's Brightwater International School. Only a few hours' drive from Hamburg to the quaint medieval village of Tauber, six nights at the famed *Heilige Preisen* (Saints be Praised), Tauber's seediest accommodation for backpackers.

The tourist company was cheap and cheerful, which appealed to most of the class. The holiday package promised beer tasting, tours of historical landmarks, castles, monasteries and such, thermal springs, and a series of sometimes silly, sometimes loosely educational daily challenges with the prospect of beer-related prizes. To top it off, the week would end with a literal bang—fireworks, bonfires, food trucks, and live bands for Luft's Solstice Festival.

What none of them had anticipated was Stefan and Ana breaking up right before finals. Thanks to a combination of nonrefundable tickets, Stefan's refusal to admit fault, and Ana's blistering pride, neither of them had canceled. Now they had to suffer through small-group activities every day of the trip.

No one would swap. No one would save her.

Ana's sole survival plan was to preserve her dignity by appearing indifferent. She might have lost her place on the theater program but she was a good actor and by the end of the week she planned to be a master of her fucking craft.

"And yet," Gwen said, nudging Stefan with the toe of her boot, "here you are in the land of Saint Ansel, on the eve of the summer solstice, with signs and wonders in the heavens."

Stefan frowned at a gap in the tree canopy, where the tail of the rusty red smudge seemed frozen in the sky. He'd been tracking the comet's progress on his stargazer app for days.

"The Eldi Comet is neither a sign nor a wonder," he said. "I mean, it's undeniably cool. But, at the end of the day, it's a giant ball of dusty space ice, orbiting the galaxy once every seven hundred years. Not an omen."

Gwen wrinkled her nose. "Keep your dusty space balls and let me have my celestial wonder."

He shook his head and hoisted himself onto the rock beside her. "We'll have a better view tonight if it stays clear."

Stefan was Gwen's cousin, tall and dark-skinned with firm lean limbs and a sharp jaw, his close-cropped hair hidden beneath a designer beanie. People said he looked like a runway model. Mainly because he rarely smiled and looked bored and superior. Really, he was just shy ... and superior. More so since he won an early scholarship for Queen Mary—a full ride, to complete an undergraduate degree in Biomedical Engineering.

It's not something Ana should have cared about, his looks, but she had. Deep down, she had never quite believed that someone as beautiful as Stefan could truly want her, yet for eight giddy months she had been the "chosen one."

Gwen was beautiful too. Not like Stefan, who made you feel like you needed to try harder, but a warm beauty that drew people in. She was petite with dark curls, light-brown skin, and freckles on her sweetheart face.

When Ana and Gwen had met in their first year at Brightwater, they'd bonded quickly. Sure, Ana was pale and gangly but they both had freckles, green eyes, birthdays three days apart, and, remarkably, matching She-Ra phone cases. They loved the same books, movies, and music. Practically twins.

Still, she couldn't compete with cousins—couldn't drag Gwen away and make a "besties only" pairing to exclude him. It killed her that Gwen and Stefan would go to London without her. Be in the residential halls at Queen Mary *without her.*

If they could dip-test Ana's blood, they'd find pollutants. Bitterness. Envy … Lust.

That was the worst part, the part that filled her with self-loathing. She couldn't turn it off—wanting him, loving him. Not that she had ever said the words aloud; she'd been waiting for him to say it first. It was her only comfort, in the shitfest of heartbreak, that she hadn't compounded her humiliation by giving him the power of those words.

She dumped her waders on the gear rack and dug her phone from her pack.

"You're wasting your time," Stefan said. "There's too much interference."

"Too much magic in the air," Gwen said, wiggling her eyebrows.

Stefan gave her a droll look. "This is electromagnetic interference. Magic is for superstitious peasants."

"Perfect for a drama student." She gestured at Ana.

"Gap year," Ana said, sticking with her cover story.

Gwen ignored her. "Perfect for an English major like me."

"Peasants indeed." Stefan nodded. "How you two will get jobs is beyond me."

With no help from you, Ana thought, but she kept her mouth shut for Gwen's sake. Besides, she had taken more than her fair share of digs from Stefan about the pointlessness of her future degree and she wasn't about to give him an excuse for more. It would only draw attention to her abject failure. He didn't know about her missed exams and Gwen had promised not to tell him. As far as her class was concerned—Ana had missed graduation because of flu.

"I just had service." Ana opened her camera app and managed to snap a couple of shots before the screen glitched and turned black. Her shoulders slumped. "How are we supposed to collect evidence for the scavenger hunt without taking photos?"

"Or make people jealous if we can't post?" Gwen shook her head. "You'll have to ask Will to come and sketch you, if you want a permanent record." She nodded at the hunched figure sitting at the base of a tree, his hand sweeping across his sketchpad in ferocious arcs. Will Han was intently focused, his kohl-lined eyes flashing like lasers.

Ana turned her back on him and glowered at Gwen. It was a mistake pointing him out at the bus depot. Tall, square-shouldered, and serious, Will had had a major glow up from his weedy start at Brightwater. He'd filled out, finding his chiseled jaw, biceps, and style. Goodbye basketball shorts and jerseys, hello corduroy pants, waistcoats over vintage band T-shirts, and cherry Doc Martens. Stefan called him a poser—which was what he said about anyone prettier than him.

A white woman with wiry gray hair and a National Park polar fleece vest came down the bank, jangling her lanyard. "Our next lecture starts in twenty minutes in the clearing. There are thermoses if anyone would like to make some tea."

Stefan grimaced. "This is the lecture for the art students?"

"For everyone," she said, spreading her arms. "We'll be covering the Great Northern Purge and Saint Ansel's first recorded wonder."

The guide slipped into the trees. Ana gathered her pack and Gwen jumped down from the rock. "Taking credit for an earthquake?" Stefan shook his head. "Saint Ansel was a con artist."

Railroad sleepers nestled against the hillside, forming a shallow amphitheater overlooking the Darmish valley. Sunlight lanced through the trees, hazing the air in shafts of gold. Awed, the students fell quiet. Half dazed, Ana took her seat on Gwen's right. Stefan on the left.

It struck her anew. This was the way it went now. Gwen in the middle. On the bus, at the dining table at Saints be Praised, walking down the street. A buffer. To keep Ana at bay. It loosened something dangerous in her chest. She clenched her teeth and breathed through her nose; she couldn't lose it over a sunbeam.

A guide set a thermos beside Ana's knee. She kept her eyes down and dug out her camp mug from the side pocket of her pack. Gwen administered teabags from her stash, peppermint for Stefan, blackcurrant for her and Ana. Ana poured the hot water and cupped her mug like she was brewing salvation, drawing the steam deep into her lungs, each breath a tamping down.

Stefan sighed, leaning back on one elbow.

"Have an open mind," Gwen said.

He lowered his sunglasses. "Give me a nudge if I start snoring."

Ana gritted her teeth and pulled a baseball cap from her pack to shield her eyes. She grabbed the daily challenge sheet and a pen. There was a gap to include a quote from the lecture for number 4. Ana needed a win.

A middle-aged woman with brown skin and a braided skein of black hair stepped onto the flagstones that denoted the stage. She wore the same vest as the other guide but her feather earrings and colorful muslin skirt signaled a creative spirit.

"*Guten tag*, scholars. We trust you have gathered all you need from the Namen River." She had a strong German accent and her voice was rich and carrying as she gestured beyond the trees. "This is the first of Saint Ansel's landmarks, where an earthquake so sudden and violent changed the shape of the hillside and the course of the river in an instant."

Ana wondered if Stefan would soften at the guide's nod to science, but she didn't check to see if his lips remained pursed. He wouldn't be won over that easily.

"Where you sit today," the guide went on, "is in the middle of the original path of the Namen. The gentle undulations of the land are overgrown now but you would not have to dig far before you found the stony riverbed."

Ana pictured the path through the forest filled with rushing water and a prickling sensation tickled her spine. Movement at the corner of her eye made her turn. Will was in the row above them, his elbows on his knees, absorbed by the guide's words. The muscles in his forearms shifted as he laced his fingers together, sunlight refracting from the blank face of his smart-watch. She blinked against a muzzy feeling in her head and forced herself to sit up.

"There are varying accounts of *Herren der Säuberung—the Lords of the Purge*," the guide said. "Some believe the company was formed by a coalition of Germanic feudal lords who sought to seize the fertile fields of Darmlund and Luft. Though some lesser sources mention shadow hordes and legions of the dead." Chuckles rose around the amphitheater and the guide smiled knowingly.

"Here we go," Stefan muttered.

"Based on archaeological findings, it is more likely the region fell victim to Viking raiders. Whatever the case, Ansel escaped the scourging of her village with a handful of survivors, described in Truman Schreiber's *Book of Heralds* as 'the very old, the very young, and the infirm.' Raiders chased them to the edge of the flooded river, where desperation drove Ansel into the water. It is said she wept and cried out to heaven and a living wind filled her with prophetic unction. Given breath, she cried aloud the word '*Aperio*,' which loosely translates to...?" She paused, inviting the students to share their knowledge.

"Abracadabra?" Stefan muttered under his breath.

Gwen snorted but lifted her hand. "'Open,' or 'make way.' It's a command."

"Someone's been reading their Schreiber," the guide said, delighted.

Several classmates looked at Gwen, impressed.

Ana pulled the color-copied brochure from the pocket of Gwen's pack. *The Story of Saint Ansel.* Gwen snatched it and muttered, "Let me have my moment."

Ana shook her head and Gwen laughed.

"The account records the ground shaking," the guide forged on, relishing her retelling. "Then the opening of a great crevasse, which diverted the course of the Namen River behind the fleeing villagers, cutting them off from the raiders, who were swept away.

"Ansel, caught in a state of spiritual ecstasy, seemed not to see nor hear. The survivors lifted her onto a donkey and led her from the dried riverbed into the forest of Eadin." She opened her palms and gestured at the surrounding forest. "The concentration of unusual phenomena in the region is well documented. Nowhere more so than Eadin and none more often than the periods of the summer and winter solstices."

As if on cue the wind rose with an eerie moan, barging through the treetops and barreling down upon their heads, like the beating of hundreds of wings. Ana ducked and Gwen clutched her arm, while Stefan nearly spilled his tea. "Bloody hell," he muttered.

Ana laughed but it was a skittering reflex that cinched her throat. Her skin prickled with a charge of adrenaline and the wind whipped her baseball cap from her head. She lunged to catch it, but it flew high out of reach, then fell as the sudden gust died.

The cap dropped, smacking Will on the top of his head, and he flinched.

"Sorry." Ana gestured for it back. Instead, he adjusted the clip, put the hat on, and pulled the bill down to shield his eyes from the sun. She scowled. He winked.

Gwen grinned and nudged Ana but she flushed and looked at Stefan; she couldn't tell if he was watching from behind his glasses.

"I don't know if we have any meteorologists in our midst," the guide said, untangling her earrings from her hair, "but that was an excellent example of the type of 'unusual phenomena' that might have caused medieval folk to wonder."

"Pfft. Changing air pressure," Stefan whispered.

"You were spooked," Gwen said.

He patted his mouth, pretending to yawn.

The lecture continued without further interruption from wind or seismic activity but Ana could feel her nose and cheeks beginning to burn and cast an irritated look at Will. A soporific heaviness was filling her head, filling her bones, as the sun rose above the trees. She found herself blinking in languid sweeps, struggling to stay focused as the guide teased the students about the curious timing of the comet converging with the solstice.

Resting her chin in her palm, she propped her elbow on her knee.

Her boots slipped in the mud, rain and wind pummeling from above. The flame at the end of her torch whipped in the storm, threatening to extinguish. She kept looking back, but the path through the trees was grotesque with shadows. The cries of children pierced the air. Mules brayed, protesting the pace and the load. Wheels groaned as their wagons jolted over the stones. Ahead of them, the roar of the Namen crushed her hope. What if the bridge was flooded? What if they couldn't cross? What was she leading them to?

Behind them, howls rose, high and close. A fresh bolt of terror gripped her, followed by a scalding pain, spreading across her thigh.

Ana jerked back, squinted against the sun. "Shit," she hissed. Her mug of tea had spilled across her leg.

Gwen gave a soft yelp and yanked her pack out of the way.

The guide paused at the disruption, her expression kind but concerned.

"Sorry," Ana said, mortified as people leaned to see what the commotion was about. "Clumsy. It's fine. I'm fine." But her leg burned, her head swam, and her heart pounded like she was being chased.

It was a dream. She had fallen asleep. That's all. Caught up in the guide's excellent storytelling. Her mind had simply conjured the scene of Ansel's escape from Luft. But it was the vivid detail that shook her, the smell of mud and soaked hemp linen that lingered in her senses, and the prickling sensation behind her ears.

CHAPTER TWO

Ana waited with the others in a dank alley behind Saints be Praised, tuned out among the excited chatter of her friends. An overflowing dumpster reeked beside them and the cobbles were slick and oily beneath their feet. A neon sign with a cheery Benedictine monk, holding a tankard of beer, flickered blue and pink across the street.

It was late and she still felt off-kilter after the weird dream. Her thigh was tender from the spilled tea and she had a bad feeling about going out tonight—like she was tempting disaster.

Gwen nudged her. "You're frowning."

"I can hear rats." She shuddered. "Scurrying."

"Cheer up. It's the medieval experience."

"The grime is too authentic."

"Think of the caves, the glowworms, the hot pools."

It was the main reason she had signed up for the trip in the first place, the chance to get cozy with Stefan in the hot pools. Now she'd spend the night trying not to stare at him in his swim shorts. She deflected the thought with a shrug. "Shouldn't we be out in the woods, leaping bonfires for the solstice?"

"You little witch," Gwen said, linking her arm through Ana's. "We could put in a request?"

Ana peered up at the narrow slice of sky above the alley. "Too bad it's so cloudy tonight. Stefan wanted to see the comet."

"We're stopping at Eadin Palace on the way; it might be clearer up there."

Two vans pulled in with Metzger's Cured Meats logos. Ana shot Gwen a look that promised *if we die, tonight, it's all your fault.*

"They run cave tours as a side hustle," Gwen said.

"If there are carcasses hanging from hooks..." Ana muttered.

Her classmates squashed into the vans with their swimsuits, towels, beer, torches, and party snacks. Gwen nabbed the front passenger seat and Ana found herself crammed between Olly, Brightwater's head boy, and Will, stealer of hats. The door slid shut with an ominous clang and she fought a brief claustrophobic urge to escape. Boisterous singing filled the van and Will patted the back of the driver's seat with the signal they were ready to roll.

"Smells like ham," he said, grimacing.

She smiled tightly and tucked her arms in. The van rumbled into gear and the momentum sent Will bumping into her. He didn't pull away or ask her to move, so she tried to relax her shoulders and ignore the close press. After all, she wasn't worried about Olly bouncing against her arm, why fuss over Will?

She wondered who Stefan sat with in the other van. Her insides gave their trademark dumped-girl twist.

Will dug a pack of gum from his pocket and offered her a stick.

She raised an eyebrow. "Does my breath smell?"

He shook one into his palm, unwrapped the wax paper, and popped it in his mouth. "Blocks the *eau de* ham."

The scent of mint wafted nicely from him, so she took a stick for herself.

"You're kind of surly," he said.

She looked at him sideways. "You stole my hat. Now I have a burned nose."

"It walloped me."

"It was the wind and I said I was sorry."

"In a surly way." He grinned. "You should wear sunscreen with skin like that."

"I *had* a hat."

"Oh, yeah."

Olly swiveled next to her and offered her a bottle of vodka. She didn't take a sip. The last time she'd touched alcohol it ended with cutting her hair and drunk-dialing Stefan at two in the morning, sobbing incomprehensibly. Thinking about it made her flush with shame. She passed the bottle to Will, but he shook his head and held up his palm. "I don't drink."

She shrugged and passed it back to Olly, who began to lead the others in the school song.

"You're not going to ask me why?" He cocked his head and Ana took note of his skin, his eyes, his lips, and jawline. Objectively, she knew Will was very attractive and while they had never been close at school, she could tell he had a sense of humor and might even be flirting with her.

Was that what this was?

It struck her as a colossal wasted opportunity. If she was over Stefan, she would get into the banter, the shoulder brushing, the whole bit.

"Does there need to be a reason?"

"You wouldn't think so, but people like to make a big deal about it."

"I tried drowning my sorrows." Like a bad teen movie. She'd shut herself in her bedroom and hacked the dark lengths of her hair to her nape with blunt craft scissors. Gwen called it "The Butchering" and had coaxed her out of her wardrobe to salvage the remains.

When Stefan saw her, on the first day of the trip, his stricken double take had given her a brief thrill of triumph. He had loved her long wavy hair, loved to run his fingers through it. When they made out, he would roll her onto his chest and slide the band from her ponytail just to feel it tumble around his bare shoulders.

Of course, she was the one who suffered true regret. She didn't recognize this version of herself; it was like playing a part. Short-haired Ana. Single Ana. Ana 2.0 but full of glitches.

"It didn't work?"

"I'm trying this new thing," she said. *"Dignity."*

He raised his eyebrows, a smile stretching his lips. "How's it working out?"

She swiveled her hand, *so-so*, and he gave a soft laugh.

As promised, they paused in the visitors' lot for Eadin Palace. The air was warm and lush and there were breaks in the clouds. Many of the students scanned the sky, trying to spot the comet. Ana was more interested in the ruins reaching above the trees, turrets like broken fingers crooked at the stars. Beneath the moon, the silhouettes were eerie and the plunging forest blurred into a dark green sea.

She turned to see if Gwen needed a hand but her friend had come prepared in her hiking boots. Conor, a stocky Ukrainian rugby player from their English class, was smiling beside her with a gas lantern at the ready. Gwen looped her arm through his and bounced her eyebrows at Ana. Ana bounced hers back and they both grinned.

Her heart squeezed for her best friend. If anyone deserved to have a fun summer holiday, it was Gwen. Caught in the middle of her and Stefan's drama, she had put up with weeks of Ana's chaos and ugly tears. Expressed nothing but kindness and love after her academic meltdown. Even though her screwup ruined Gwen's plans too; they were supposed to room together at Queen Mary.

Ana had promised herself she would pull her shit together for the trip, for Gwen's sake. Stop making everything about her. Stay in character. Indifferent and unbroken. She drew a deep breath and whispered to herself. "No moping. No pining. Just fun."

Her resolve was instantly put to the test when she spotted Stefan standing by the other van with two Asian girls from their biology class. Kendra and Sun-yu, with their long smooth ponytails and gloss-shiny lips. They seemed to find everything Stefan said funny and charming. A grinding sound interrupted her thoughts and she unclenched her teeth.

"Only twenty minutes, you guys," one of the Metzger brothers called in a thick German accent. "Then everyone back in the vans, if you want to make the caves before midnight."

With the Metzger boys leading the way, the group trailed into the forest. Ana hung back to take the rear. It was like stepping into black velvet, the sounds of the night dampened by a hush. The group seemed to feel it, the close press of shadows, and they kept their voices low. Lantern light splashed gold on the stony path. Will looked back to see that she was keeping up. "You all right back there?"

She gave a small wave but kept her focus on her feet.

What if Will tried something tonight? Cozied up to her in the hot springs? Went in for a kiss? Her mind spat images of Stefan and the ponytails. Trouble was, if Will's flirting turned into something more and she went along with it, Stefan would see right through it. He'd *know* she was trying to make him jealous but he wouldn't care—wouldn't say anything. He might be annoyed it was someone as good-looking as Will but really, he'd be relieved to have the burden of her broken heart taken from his hands.

The path curved and they stepped out of the trees. The ruins of Eadin Palace eclipsed the horizon and her angst receded against the rush of wonder, tingling up her neck and behind her ears. The clouds had parted and the moon glowed like a great pearl, hazing the stonework in silver.

"Wow," Gwen murmured, pointing at the bright red streak arcing above the palace.

"Yeah," Ana breathed. Even she had to admit, it was an impressive sight. So much brighter in the night sky.

The whole group had stopped still, awed by the spectacle of the comet and the ruins together. Eadin Palace was immense. They had come out at the top southwest corner, where the remains of a turret soared high overhead. An outer wall crumbled to the north and east. She'd seen the illustrated maps and the Google Earth images. From above, the original structure was a great rectangular frame of buildings built around an ancient grove of trees, as big as a football stadium.

Most of the palace was inaccessible now, fenced off for safety, though they could hear a tributary arm of the Namen River running beneath it. An ache gripped Ana, deep in her chest, a visceral longing to know it, to belong to it.

The palace had once housed guilds of great knowledge. Seers and saints and scholars. Or, as the guide had joked that

morning, heathens, heretics, and holy men. There had been a
hospital, library, and school. An observatory, stables, an
armory, and foundry. Saint Ansel had lived here, somewhere,
establishing the guild of saints.

She was tempted to let the group go back to the vans
without her and sit right there on the grass to soak in the
wonder of it. If her delusion at the amphitheater hadn't been
so frightening, she could almost wish to slip into another
dream right here. Something set in the palace. Perhaps wandering the colonnades. Exploring the Sacred Grove. She sighed.

The Metzger's Cured Meats boys called them all to order
and they headed back to the vans. It would be a slow 45-
minute drive from here to the caves around winding mountain
roads. The thought of making conversation with Will seemed
daunting but once they were back in the van, he launched in
unfazed.

"Is this your first visit to Eadin?" he asked.

"I've never been across the Darmish border."

"My parents brought us when we first moved to Hamburg."

She cocked her head. "Are both your folks at a
consulate?"

"Dad's in finance. Mum's a translator. She works for six of
the consulates."

"Six? She knows six languages?"

He laughed. "Dad, only three. She gives him shit about it."

Ana shook her head. "That makes me feel like a slacker."

"She makes everyone feel like a slacker."

"Do you know other languages?"

He hunched into his shoulders. "Three. And a bit."

"That doesn't make me feel better."

"Well, Dad's Korean and Mum's French, so I grew up with those. I only had to learn English. I've picked up a little German now too."

"Your accent is quite posh."

He cringed. "That's because I went to an English boarding school before my folks got their posts and I was enrolled at Brightwater." The van swerved tightly and she found herself pressed hard against his arm.

"Sorry," she said, sitting up when the path leveled out.

He smiled with a look to say he didn't mind, and she bit her lip and stared at her feet.

"What about your family?" he asked.

"It's just me and Mum. She's a lawyer. A policy auditor for the US Consulate. Mainly immigration stuff. Helps people with their applications."

"Where were you before Brightwater?"

"All over. Mum's English, Dad's a Kiwi. I grew up in New Zealand until I was eight, then Mum and Dad got divorced and we hopped around embassies—Ireland, Scotland, and the States. Then Mum was all about settling so I'd have high school in one place. I've been at Brightwater since I was thirteen."

"Brightwater's okay."

"It's the international thing," Ana said. "We're all desperate outsiders, so people are keen to make friends."

He chuckled and Ana tried not to let her mind race. Talking to Will was easy. He wasn't the too-cool guy she'd thought. He was making an effort and she didn't know how to feel about it.

Will kept up the flow of conversation all the way to the cave reserve. He even waited for her when they climbed out of the van. Again, she looked for Gwen and Stefan, but her friend was with Conor and her ex was chatting with one of the pony-tail girls. The hollow feeling in her chest intensified. She ignored it and fell into step with Will.

The cave reserve was much lower in the valley than Eadin Palace, almost halfway between the spot where they'd collected river samples and the palace itself. The path was flat and easy to follow, though the trees were tall and the moonlight struggled to pierce the canopy. All Ana could see were torches and lantern lights winking among black shadows.

"The cave entrance is up ahead," a Metzger boy called. "Mind your step."

Gwen looked back over her shoulder and half smiled, half grimaced.

Ana gave a thumbs-up but she touched Will's wrist and leaned to whisper. "Is this really safe?"

His close gaze flitted over her face. "I guess we'll find out."

Mint lingered on his breath, and she caught the scent of soap and cologne on his skin and pulled back. She didn't want to notice how nice he smelled.

CHAPTER THREE

The cave entrance was a trick. Almost impossible to see until you found yourself swallowed by the gap. A sharp right turn and they stepped into a natural corridor. Inside, it was easier to see as the lantern light reflected on the slick stone like the wet corrugations in the roof of a mouth. Chatter echoed off the walls but apprehension tightened Ana's chest. She tried not to think about the tons of rock above her head, seismic fault lines, or being eaten alive.

The sound of water reached them and the air temperature rose. The corridor opened into a vast cavern where steam curled from glittering pools that lapped a pebbled shore. Water spilled from one to another, disappearing where the cavern twisted out of sight. It was magical and murmurs of awe rose around the group.

A Metzger's Cured Meats boy climbed up on an out-jutting rock, holding up his lantern so they could see his ruddy face. He grinned like he owned the place. "Here we are, then," he said. "Number one piece of advice for staying alive: do not be an arschloch."

Several people laughed and the Metzger boy winked before

barreling on. "There is only one place where it is safe to dive or jump in the wasser. The pool by the right bank where the rock forms a ledge. Anywhere else and you will likely crack your skull or break your bloody neck. Sooo?" He waved his arm for someone in the audience to supply the correct response.

Olly piped up, "Don't be an arschloch?"

Everyone laughed and the Metzger boy pointed at Olly. "There's a gut lad. Now, stick together. Do not go wandering alone. There are a lot of caves leading off the main corridor and if you get lost, we *will not* find you."

Nervous chuckles rumbled around the assembled students.

Metzger boy lifted his hand in warning. "There are many stories about people entering these caves and never being seen again."

"Bloody hell," Ana muttered under her breath.

"So, we must take care of each other. Obviously, leave the glowworms alone. Do not touch them, do not splash them, and…" He gestured again, conducting the group.

"Don't be an arschloch!" they called back to him.

"That's right!" he said with a laugh. "And finally, this is a bloody natural wonder, so treat it with respect. If you need to use the bathroom, piss off into the woods. Any bottles or cans, food wrappers, whatever, you take your trash with you. And once more for luck?"

"Don't be an arschloch!" everyone cried.

The group dispersed, finding places to sit and open their packs. A couple of girls from Ana's music class had even lugged guitars on their backs. Several boys kicked off their shoes, peeled their shirts off like ripe fruit, and splashed into the water, whooping at the heat. Ana took a seat on a rock next to Gwen, keeping the corner of her eye on Will. Would he sit with them?

He dropped his pack next to Olly's and wandered further along the bank, craning his neck to spot glowworms.

"So?" Gwen said, bumping shoulders. "You two were getting chatty."

"We were just talking."

"I heard banter."

"Don't start."

"He's hot."

"Gwen."

"I mean hawt."

"Keep your voice down," Ana whispered, but it was hard not to laugh. "How was *your* trip with Billy Biceps? Anyone get handsy?"

"I tried."

"The night is young."

There were several torches and camp lanterns and some girls had bought candles from the village that afternoon. Soon there were golden pockets of light all around the cavern, glowing against the shimmering rock.

The two girls with guitars made their way gingerly across a path of stepping stones and clambered onto a flat rock, feet dangling in the water. A sweet, soft strumming filled the cavern, and their voices rose in harmony. The acoustics were beautiful.

Of course, Ana couldn't help looking for Stefan. She told herself it was a strategic check rather than a pining check. He was already in the water with the ponytails and Simon, a Turkish boy from their biology class. Determined to keep her vow to give Gwen a break, she waited until the boy with the biceps returned, trying to look casual with his can of beer. She left them to it and wandered down the bank to the next pool and undressed. She stood there long enough for Stefan to spot her in the emerald-green bikini he used to love.

She slipped into the water, savoring the brief combination of spite and heat—pure bliss. She made her way to the far side of the pool, where it was deeper. There was a shelf of stone to rest on and she leaned back to stare into the cave ceiling. Glowworms clustered in the crevices, forming soft galaxies of bluish light. Again, she felt a tingling sensation behind her ears and fluttering in her chest.

Keira, a Somalian girl from her drama class, tiptoed into the pool with two bottles of vodka mixers. "These are yours, Ana. Gwen paid for them in the whip-round."

"She didn't have to do that," Ana said with a sigh.

"I'll leave them here, then?" Keira propped them on the ledge beside Ana. "Don't want them getting hot."

"Thank you," she called as the girl waded back to shore.

She couldn't deny she was tempted to drain a bottle. The idea of forgetting herself had huge appeal but she knew it wouldn't work like that. She'd just get morose and weepy and likely debase herself at the altar of Stefan.

Others joined her and she smiled in welcome but turned her back on them, resting her arms on the ledge, so they'd think she was busy watching the jumpers in the main pool.

The heat, the water, the late hour lulled Ana into drowsiness and she laid her head on her arms. For a moment, she closed her eyes, letting the sounds of the cavern wash over her. The girls had stopped singing, content to pluck notes in ribbons of melody. Soft laughter and the intimate hum of conversation added to the dreamlike buzz.

In the low firelight, the cave was bleak with shadows. A woman glowered before a central hearth in a rough linen dress; it was pale and soot-smudged and hung loose from her shoulders, the frayed neckline revealing a prominent collarbone. The tattered hem brushed at her ankles, where dust had turned her bare feet gray. A fine spatter of blood stained the fabric in a diagonal slash from breast to thigh.

Ceremonial paint masked the woman's face, a thick white daub that crackled around her mouth and caked her eyebrows, making it impossible to guess her age. Her ashen hair hung woven with small bones, pale beads, and yellow thread. Her eyes flashed blue, sharp as needles. Before her, a man with a golden circlet on his brow knelt before the flames. Tattoos covered his shaved head and countless black marks ringed his throat. A man of power, bent in humiliation and rage.

The pair were not alone; a crowd of witnesses stood close, some shackled and cowering in filthy rags, eyes downcast. Others stood watchful and silent, warriors tall and blond, clad in animal pelts, tattooed and menacing. But there were women, too, a line of women behind the kneeling man, dressed in finer garments, with braided gold circling their brows. Each seemed bowed with unknowable grief, hugging their arms, hugging each other.

The priestess scooped a handful of tiny bones from a basket and whispered over her cupped hand. Something like fear tightened her eyes, curling her shoulders as though she were bracing before a blow. Then she held her fist aloft, gritted her teeth, and squeezed, hissing through her teeth, until red drops dribbled between her fingers and dripped into the flames.

The scene warped with the hiss and sizzle of her blood, grew hazy and lost its definition; images tumbled into shadows, flashes of indistinct detail throbbed with malice before clearing again. The scene had shifted in time, skipped ahead, and now a body lay crumpled at the priestess's feet and dark mounds smoldered in the hearth. The still kneeling man stared unseeing at the smoking heap, lost in some deep inner darkness, while the women behind him wept.

The priestess brought something to her mouth, swallowed it, then licked her fingertips and shuddered. A stillness settled over her and the cave fell silent. She drew a long, rattling breath and closed her eyes.

No one moved.

When she finally exhaled and opened her eyes, something new stared at the supplicants that wasn't there before, like a nocturnal creature peering silver-eyed through the dark. A muscle shifted in the priestess's jaw and a voice issued from her open mouth, a guttural chorus. She spoke slowly, her words heavy and bruising, judgment twisting her lips, baring her teeth, driving into the marrow of her congregation until they lowered their heads and fell to their knees as though shoved.

The fire crackled and a red spark sprang from the hearth, floating slowly upward, then another and another until seven had spiraled up through a hole in the ceiling. She appeared grimly satisfied until the fire crackled and spat and a bright blue spark shot from the flames. The woman hissed, grasping to extinguish it, but a sharp wind blew, catching the spark and whisking it through the hole.

Several things happened at once. Ana became conscious of herself as a spectator and the vision shifted perspective so that she now watched the scene from above. The blue spark spiraled out of the hole and flew at her face. She gasped, heat searing her throat, and started to choke on a mouthful of warm water. She coughed and thrashed until a large warm hand caught her under the arm.

Will pulled her upright. "Shit, are you okay?"

Ana coughed and hacked some more, eyes running, heart racing in the aftermath of the dream. Vision? Whatever it was— it was too real. Her throat burned like she had swallowed fire.

"Did you fall asleep?" He kept his hand on her arm.

She cupped her cheeks. "I must have."

Will stood shielding her from the curious looks of the others in the pool and her face flushed hot. He was a gentleman and she was humiliated.

"You're shaking." He offered her a bottle. "It's just water."

"Thank you," she croaked, taking tentative sips. "I don't know what happened."

Once he seemed confident she wasn't going to sink, he released his hold. "It's late. We had a big day."

She didn't want to admit it was the second time she'd fallen instantly asleep and had a bad dream. Another word slunk in the back of her thoughts—*hallucination*. Was she so broken that she was losing her grip on reality? But this one wasn't like the first dream, where she was swept up by the guide's story about Saint Ansel. This had been random but weirdly detailed, still with the medieval vibe. Maybe that's all it was, the influence of too many history lessons.

"I'm okay," she said. "I should probably get out of the water. It's making me sleepy."

Will looked disappointed, then his eyes cleared. "We could check out the caves?"

Careful to collect the bottles Keira had left her, she waded for the bank. Images from the dream—or hallucination—swam in her mind, the kneeling man, the white-faced woman, and her animalistic hiss. Goose bumps shivered across Ana's skin. She pressed her palm to her neck, where her throat still burned. Will followed her out of the water.

"I don't want to keep you from enjoying the springs," she said, grabbing her towel.

"It would be cool to explore."

She turned to face him, careful not to stare at his torso. He was in impressive shape and she was flustered and giving off a less than relaxed vibe. She darted a look around the cavern to find Gwen. She was in the pool with Conor; they were close and smiling. Ana couldn't drag her away—to what? Babysit her after a bad dream?

On automatic, she scanned the pool. Stefan was with a ponytail girl. Her insides shrank and she turned to Will. "Yes. We should. Can't let you go wandering by yourself. Don't want to be an arschloch."

He glanced in the direction she'd been looking, realization making him nod and flatten his lips. "Look, it's no sweat. I'm not trying to make things complicated."

"No." She took hold of his arm. "I'm not—it's not about that. I want to. When do you get a chance to explore a natural wonder? We should make the most of it. Grab a torch or something, I'll get dressed."

He cocked his head, his dark eyes probing. She gave him a shaky smile and he went, not looking entirely convinced, to find a light. She turned her back on the cavern, pressure mounting in her head. She touched her burning throat again. Was it the memory of the blue spark? Or the aftermath of swallowed spring water? Or the result of suppressed emotion at the sight of Stefan and the ponytail?

She told herself they weren't making out. Not yet. They were just bobbing in the water. Close. Face to face.

Screw dignity.

She grabbed a bottle, twisted the lid, cutting the base of her thumb on the metal tab. "Shit." A bright-red bead of blood welled up and she sucked the flesh, squeezing to stop the flow. She dug her fist into her bundled towel and took a long drink. It was a fruity vodka mixer with a kick that irritated her already burned throat. She paused to cough, eyes watering, then drained the bottle. She checked her thumb. It stung but it wasn't too bad.

She yanked on her denim shorts and punched her arms through the long sleeves of her thin white shirt. Her wet hair dripped on her collar and she tucked it behind her ears, then opened the other bottle with more care. When Will returned with a little gas lantern, he cast an uncertain look at her face and the bottle she was draining.

"Listen…" he began, his chest filling with a sigh. "We can just hang here…"

When she bent to grab her sneakers, the cavern spun. She swung her butt around and landed on the rock ledge. Determined to make it look deliberate, she brushed the gravel from her toes and jammed her feet in her shoes. With a forced smile, she sat back, bracing hands on her knees, giving her head a moment to stop spinning.

"You drank that pretty quick."

Warmth shimmered in her stomach, spreading heat up

through her chest. She shoved the image of Stefan and the girl from her thoughts and shrugged.

Will was gorgeous and, apparently, a genuinely nice guy. He wanted to spend time with her. It was … nice. When was the last time she felt remotely desirable to anyone? She was not going to ruin the evening. She was not going to fall apart. She was going to explore a cave with a hot guy and if it led to some fooling around, she was bloody well going to let it.

She held out her hand. He bit his lip and helped her to her feet and she swayed into him. She splayed her hand on his chest, steadied herself, and laughed. "You smell good."

"Are you drunk?"

"Barely tipsy." It felt super weird holding another boy's hand. "Shall we?"

A small war seemed to be going on behind his eyes and he dragged his lip through his teeth. He didn't want to take advantage of the situation. He was a good guy. If he backed off now, she really would start crying. She turned toward the path, tugging him after her. She smiled at him over her shoulder, not looking beyond him.

The passage stretched back into the hillside off the main cavern. It was broad and the ground fairly even. Ana worked to stay inside her body and not let herself be dragged into the sucking vortex of despair. She concentrated on her steps.

The glimmering rock. Her breathing. Will beside her. She kept
her fingers loosely wound in his. Put her energy into noticing
the simmering tension. The unspoken question in that touch:
What did it mean?

She knew what it meant.

It was evidence of the truth she had left behind in the main
cavern. A haunting proof more tangible than her cut hair. It
was over. She and Stefan were truly over.

"Hang on," Will said, squeezing her hand. The passage had
narrowed. "Let me go in front with the lantern."

She stopped but didn't lean back for him to pass by. A test.
For him? For her. He would have to brush against her, chest to
chest. If she let it happen, it was more proof and she needed
proof because denial was a fist in the middle of her rib cage,
bruising her with every heartbeat.

Understanding hooded his eyes and he paused, wary, like
he was approaching something dangerous yet compelling. She
waited, the velvet rush of alcohol warming her blood, loosening her joints, smudging her senses in a dreamy haze.

He took a step, brushing against her, his eyes fixed on hers,
a close reading. *Is this what you want?* Was it? His focus
moved down to her lips and she saw the counter-challenge.
Another test. For her. Did she mean this?

He blinked, the moment ending, and the slight transfer in
his weight, from one foot to the other, told her he was about
to move past. She stopped him with the smallest touch, her
hand at his waist, and decided.

Pulse hammering, she slid her arm around him, finding the hollow of his spine, and rose on her tiptoes. Slowly, she leaned in, closed her eyes, and kissed him. At first, he stood stock still, only tipping his head to meet her lips. The shock of nearness rang through her, the startling newness of someone else's body. The fist tightened in her chest but she didn't pull away. She would stay in the moment.

Something shifted between them, as though Will's caution gave out, and he brought his hand to her cheek, slipping his fingers into the damp hair curling at her nape. Goose bumps flashed down her neck. He was good at this. She parted her lips a little, inviting a deeper kiss. He responded with the softest brush of his tongue and drew her closer.

But her mind's eye kept looping back to Stefan in the water, face to face with the ponytail girl, triggering a fresh flood of grief. To counter the hollowed-out feeling, she tilted her hips to find friction with Will. His breath caught in his throat and she stroked her tongue against his, willing her body to wake up.

He was in the moment. She could feel it, thrumming in his skin. He was thinking about *now, here, her*, but it was like her body refused to recognize the sensory input, programed for someone else's touch.

Unbidden, a memory surged to the foreground. Her back pressed to Stefan's chest where she sat between his legs on his bed. They would pretend to watch some Netflix show, while he kissed her neck and let his hands roam and slowly wind her tight and loose at the same time.

He had strong hands and molded arms and she was always mesmerized by the beauty of his muscles flexing beneath his skin when he touched her like that. She couldn't resist the sight of those sculpted arms surrounding her body. She had to run her fingers from his bicep to his wrist, tracing his knuckles as he tumbled her into bliss.

A tear slid down her cheek but she ignored it, determined to push through the ache.

Will pulled back a little and wiped the tear from her skin. "Ana."

"I'm fine," she said, pressing her stomach to his. "This is nice."

"We can go back."

"I don't want to go back." She brought his hand to her breast. "Not yet."

He lowered his head and she touched her forehead to his.

"Just because I'm sad doesn't mean I don't want to be happy," she said.

He groaned and squeezed his eyes closed, brushing his thumb slowly across the swell of her breast, like he was trying to convince himself.

"I can feel both things at the same time." But her voice broke over the lump in her throat.

He gently pulled his hand away, parking both on her hips, and looked into her eyes. "I don't think this is making you happy."

She bit the inside of her lip. "It might."

He sighed. "Maybe … you need time."

"I don't want time. I want…" She couldn't say *you*. "This."

He stepped back and tucked his hands in his pockets, a rueful smile curving his lips. "I'm not your rebound guy."

She blinked at him through her tears.

"But … I can be patient."

"Wait. What?"

"I've waited this long."

Her brain ground to a halt.

He wrinkled his nose. "Since first year. When I was short and skinny and you didn't know I existed."

"Will, no. That's nearly five years—"

"Look, I haven't exactly been pining away. I've been dating. I just thought, if you were ever single and I was single and we were in the same place and, you know, if the stars aligned." He pointed at the roof of the cave and the Eldi Comet marking the sky somewhere high overhead. "Let's give it a couple of months. Next time I'm back in Hamburg, if you're up for it, I'll take you out for dinner like normal people. Probably just a kebab because I'm quite poor."

She snorted and wiped her eyes. "We could pack our own sandwiches."

He raised his eyebrows and nodded. "After that, I'll follow you into any cave you like and you can have your way with me."

She cringed. "God, I'm so sorry, Will. This was really out of line—"

"Hey, I got to touch your boob. So…"

She dropped her face into her palm and they both laughed softly.

"You know, if you want me to spread a rumor that we banged each other's brains out, it might get back to Stefan and piss him off a bit."

She groaned.

He chuckled, scooping her free hand to kiss her knuckles. Her cut thumb stung but she didn't care; for the first time in weeks, she felt lighter. Will frowned and opened her palm; a line of blood dribbled from her cut and dripped on the cave floor.

"Oh shit," Ana said. "Did I get blood on you?"

He wiped his hand on his shorts. "It's fine. What happened?"

"I cut it on a bottle cap." She rolled her eyes and sucked on the wound. "A cautionary tale."

"I think Keira has a first-aid kit," he said, turning to pick up the lantern, when suddenly the warm breeze in the cavern turned cool. The lantern flame flickered and they froze, staring into the darkness. The gleaming grooves in the rock made Ana think again of the roof of a gaping mouth before a deep, black throat.

Goose bumps prickled over her skin. Suddenly, the walls felt too close. The jagged ceiling too low. She wanted to duck and run until the night sky was the only thing above her head.

"Has the weather turned?" she whispered. Why was she whispering? Her inner ears crackled and she flexed her jaw to clear them with a pop. Stronger than before, tingling bloomed up the back of her neck and her head swam. "Whoa, did you feel that?"

"Feel what?" Will said, holding her steady.

"Something … weird…"

A boom echoed beneath their feet. Ana's knees buckled and Will dropped the lantern. The glass cracked and the flame whipped wildly. Screams rose from the main cavern and the sound of falling rock reverberated through the passage. The need to escape crashed in on her and she saw the same terror etched on Will's face. "Come on," he said, grabbing the lantern and pulling her behind him.

They just made it into the main cavern before the passage behind them began to collapse. Ana screamed and leaped away from the falling debris. Will stumbled to one knee. The ground surged and the pools splashed choppy waves onto the bank.

The cavern was in chaos. The sound of rumbling below and screaming above compounded Ana's terror. She hauled Will to his feet and dragged him along the path. Rocks tumbled from the cavern ceiling, splashing into the pools like thunderclaps. Against the far wall, boys and girls huddled on the jumping ledge. In the candlelight, Ana saw their horror unfolding. How would they make it across?

Bodies floated in the water. Ana clamped her hand over her mouth. She couldn't make out who the bodies were. Where was Gwen? She couldn't see her. "Gwen!" she screamed. "Gwen!"

"We'll find her," Will cried, colliding with students scrambling out of the pool.

"Come on!" a Metzger boy cried, pressed against the sheer rock face near the entrance corridor, holding his lantern high, his face a mask of fear.

Another boom shook the ground, knocking everyone off their feet. Water splashed Ana's elbows as she landed on her hands and knees and joined the chorus of screams. She lost hold of Will, who was struggling to keep the lantern above the flooding water. A wind blew sharp and sudden, barbed with ice, stirring panic as the candles that hadn't fallen into the water flickered out.

"Gwen!" Ana cried, clambering back to her feet.

"Ana!"

A sob cut from her throat as she turned toward her best friend's voice. Conor was helping her up the bank, her arm around his neck. She hopped, blood trickling down the side of her face. Beyond Gwen, Ana glimpsed the girls who had been playing guitars, kneeling on their rock in the middle of the pool holding each other. A terrible cracking from the cavern ceiling made everyone duck. Then a huge dark mass fell onto the girls and Ana screamed, her hands clamped to the sides of her head. People surged around her, scrambling to escape. She fought the tide to get back to Gwen.

"Ana!" Will called.

Conor was crying, looking back over his shoulder at bodies in the dark water. Gwen scrambled for her prosthetic, ramming it onto the bottom of her leg. Ana skidded to her knees beside her, scooping up Gwen's clothing and grabbing their packs as the earth shook. Gwen looked pale, her eyes wide and wild, like she was outside of her body watching the disaster happen. "Don't leave me," she gasped.

"I won't leave you," Ana cried, attempting to haul her up.

"Come on!" Will stumbled beside her. He thrust the now broken lantern at Ana and scooped Gwen's other arm around his shoulders. "We've got her!" he shouted. "We've got her. Ana, hold the light."

Dizziness hit her, a flood of tingling, and her ears crackled again. She drew the shoulder straps of their packs over her arm and grabbed the lantern, yelping at the heat burning up from the broken glass. She staggered toward the entrance corridor, where people lurched through the bottleneck, screaming as the world quaked around them, threatening to bury them all.

They made it into the tunnel as booms echoed behind them, a gale of cold wind thrusting at their backs, with the reverberation of falling rocks. The cavern quaked. Ahead, a milky light filled Ana with desperation as the students fought to stay on their feet, hauling each other up the path.

The crackling in her ears intensified, pressure building in her head like she was being squeezed through a rubber tube. All around her people clamped their hands over their ears as they ran.

Finally, they reached the turn and confusion reigned.

It was daylight.

Pain drilled Ana's temples, and her head spun with a deep

sense of wrongness. At the threshold, the burning in her throat came back, a surge of heat that made her picture the blue spark from her dream. It scorched its way down and, just as she took a step into the light, dropped like a naked flame into her chest. The pressure lifted from her head so suddenly, it sent her sprawling on the ground, grazing her knees and smashing the lantern completely.

The survivors spilled out onto the path, a cloud of dust billowing behind them. Ana coughed, gasping at the transformed forest, the patches of snow, the bare branches, and the icy bite of winter in the air.

A great cry rose from the trees.

At first, it looked as though the ground itself surged upward, mud, moss, and rocks sprang to life. But when her eyes cleared, her mind still failed to grasp what she saw.

A wild horde.

Tall, light-skinned men, clad in animal pelts. Shaggy-haired. Some blond and braided. Some with the sides of their heads shaved. Tattooed, teeth bared and shouting. They seemed shocked, delighted, gripped by vicious joy.

One man stood out among the rest, his shaved head marked with tattoos, the black marks coating his neck, the vicious grin as he lifted a huge black axe. The man from her dream.

Was she dreaming now?

The horde ran toward them, unleashing axes, knives, crossbows, ropes, and spears. Then the students started screaming again. Ana scrambled to her feet, slamming into Will as others slammed into her, but there was nowhere to run. The cave was demolished and the hillside steep and rocky.

They were going to die.

Then a new noise pierced the air, cutting through the shouts and screams. A high, bright horn that caused the wild men to skid to a stop, turn and brace for attack. The horn blew again and then came the thundering of hooves. A new group of armored men charged on horses from the left, mowing down the wild men.

Metal rang and the men in armor swung their swords. The wild men responded with bloodcurdling screeches, raising their axes. Heavy bodies collided in battle. The horn blew again and a sharp whining filled the air, and all around Ana students began to fall.

Gwen's scream cut through the noise and Ana whirled around. Conor had an arrow sticking from his forehead; the feathers at the end of the shaft fluttered in the wind. He sank to his knees and fell dead.

Wide-eyed, Will opened his mouth to cry out, but he was cut short as a whine pierced Ana's ear. A hot, burning sensation seared her cheekbone and then Will, too, had been pierced by an arrow, right in the corner of his left eye. His lips formed a final word before he collapsed. "Run."

CHAPTER FOUR

On her knees beside him, Ana screamed and gasped, struggling for air to scream again. Gwen, too, had fallen to her knees, her hands fluttering, her face stark with shock. Around them, their classmates wailed over their fallen friends. Ana was stuck in a loop of impossible things: the arrow in Will's eye, the wash of milky daylight, the stench of blood and burning, the arrow in Will's eye, the snow beneath her knees, the shriek of clashing metal, the arrow—

"Gwen!" a desperate voice called. "Ana!" Stefan almost tripped over Conor's body to get to his cousin. "We've got to go." He scrambled to haul Gwen from the dirt. "Now!"

"Will," Ana choked, her hand splayed on the boy's cooling chest.

"He's dead," Stefan barked, his eyes wild. "We can't help him. Come on."

A handful of students were still on their feet, dragging their injured friends down the hill and into the trees. Ana staggered upright, almost careening into Gwen. The world was tilted. A nightmare. A hallucination?

The backpacks still dangled from her arm and she hugged

them tight to her side as she stumbled away. Nauseating dizziness forced her to keep her eyes on her feet. In her peripheral vision men fought on, roaring, slashing. The incomprehensible sounds of slaughter.

They followed the others, reaching tree cover, where the snow had barely settled. The terrain grew less rocky as they moved away from the cave but thick tree roots threatened to trip her every step. Stefan half lifted Gwen, keeping up a constant stream of words. "It's okay. I'm here. I won't leave you. Watch your step. It's okay. Keep going. We got away. We're okay." But Gwen wasn't screaming or sobbing or speaking at all. Then she paused and pulled away from him, holding her hand up to signal she didn't need his help. He blinked, nodded and let her be. From here, she kept her eyes on the path, taking care with her feet. Silent.

Ana was still lost in her impossible loop, her ears crackling and popping. The flame in her chest had eased. Even as the sounds of battle grew more distant behind them, she could feel her mind recoiling from the evidence of wrongness. Her brain wanted to hurl every sound, sight, and smell away from her body. This couldn't be real. Any moment she would wake. Like last time. The last two times. She would wake. She would wake.

But the nightmare dragged on as they staggered deeper and deeper into the forest. They let the slope pull them along, finding narrow tracks forking left then right. It didn't matter, as long as it was away. Ana had no sense of time, no sense of direction. The sky was overcast and she couldn't guess the position of the sun or which way was north or how long they'd been tramping through the woods. She became aware of pain in her body, and the cold. Shivers seized her joints.

None of them were dressed for hiking. A couple were wearing nothing but swimsuits and had bare feet. Stefan's back gleamed with sweat. He had no shoes. Gwen was in a bikini; her foot was bleeding.

"Wait," Ana whispered, then a little louder, casting a glance over her shoulder at the empty forest. "Wait."

Stefan stopped. The others, further down the track, stopped and turned, all of them looking to see if they were being followed.

"People need clothes," Ana said helplessly. "Shoes."

The group gathered in a clear patch of dirt. Ana counted. There were seven of them. Stefan, Gwen, Keira, Olly, the Metzger brothers, and her. Only four of her classmates? Again, that nauseating dizziness gripped her. Were the others all dead?

"We can't stop," Olly panted, his brown face pallid and drawn. "There's bloody Vikings chasing us."

"Don't say that," Keira snapped, a gash glistening on her cheek. "Don't say *Vikings*. They can't be Vikings. Because that's—that's…"

"Axe-wielding monsters?" Stefan offered, helping Gwen sit. He rested his hands on his thighs to catch his breath and looked around the group.

"The blokes on horses?" Olly jutted his jaw. "Are we allowed to call them knights?"

The Metzger brothers stared at the others, wide-eyed.

"There's a rational explanation," Keira insisted. "There must be…"

Olly blinked rapidly and started to nod. "They could be larping? But like messed up."

"Larping?" Stefan shook his head.

"Live-action role play," Olly said, chasing the idea. "But for rich arseholes who pay to kill people in real life."

"Rich arseholes who import snow, strip the trees of leaves and fake daylight?" Stefan straightened, hands on his hips. "That's more believable than time tra—"

"It's getting colder," Ana blurted out, to cut him off. It was too much—too much to consider, and if she let herself think about how and where or … *when* they were, she had to think about the people they left behind. In the cave. In front of the cave. The tattooed man from her dream. No. She needed to deal with what was right in front of her.

She dug in Gwen's pack, struggling to hide the trembling in her fingers. She pulled out clothes and pushed them into her friend's arms. Gwen hugged them to her chest, staring into the middle distance.

"Gwen, get dressed," Ana prompted gently, but Gwen didn't move. She gestured to the others. "Come on, we need to bandage wounds—" A painful crackling in her inner ear made her wince and she stretched her jaw.

Stefan watched her. "Your ears popping?"

She frowned and nodded.

"Same," Keira said, wiggling her finger in her ear.

Olly swallowed. "Me too. Is it an altitude thing? We're not that high up."

Gwen said nothing, still staring.

"You all speak German?" the taller Metzger brother said, shivering in his swim shorts.

Wrong-footed, Ana shook her head and shrugged. "Only a few words and not very well." She covered her ears and pressed against the strange crackling. She didn't know if it was a comfort or concern to be sharing the same sensation as the others. At least the pressure she'd felt in the mouth of the cave hadn't returned. She unzipped her own pack and tipped the contents onto the ground.

"I'll keep watch," Stefan said, studying his cousin with worried eyes before flicking a meaningful look at Ana. She didn't know what to do about Gwen either. Her silence was frightening.

They had four packs and a tote bag between them. Clothes, snacks, mobile phones, tissues, tampons, wallets, pens, note-books, a towel, and a small toiletry bag. Gwen had a long muslin skirt, boots, a T-shirt, and cardigan, but still hadn't put them on. Ana was already wearing her clothes, except for a mint-green oversized sweatshirt with the rainbow logo *Love is Love*.

Ana took Gwen's muslin skirt and shook it out. "Lift your arms," she murmured, pulling it over Gwen's head and down to her hips, the fabric falling to her ankles. Then, irritated, Gwen snapped to attention and took over dressing herself, jamming her T-shirt over her head, tugging on an ankle sock and the other hiking boot not attached to her prosthetic. She wrapped the fluffy cardigan around her shoulders. It was hot pink and outrageously bright in the grim monochromatic light.

Gwen pulled it close around her body. Then she found the protective sock. Then she found the protective sock for her amputated leg and removed her prosthetic. The skin was red and she winced, rubbing the muscle below her knee.

The girls had made out better than the boys, having grabbed their bags, but still the clothes weren't winter forest hiking material. Olly at least hadn't gone swimming and was fully dressed in jeans, a plaid shirt, and a purple sweatshirt, but the Metzger brothers had nothing but their swim shorts, and their pale bodies shook with cold. Stefan had nothing either. Ana offered him her sweatshirt.

Stefan looked at her thin shirt over her bikini and denim shorts and shook his head. "You're not wearing much more than me."

"I'm okay for now," she lied. "I can fit in that cardigan with Gwen when we rest."

With a shaky exhalation, he took the sweatshirt and pulled it on. On him it looked regular size and he suited the color.

Olly offered one of the brothers his sweatshirt but he was much smaller than them and it barely reached the navel of the boy who pulled it on. Keira had her pack and a tote bag. She pulled out a big towel with a watermelon design and passed it to the other Metzger brother. He wrapped it around himself, tying the corners over his shoulder toga style, his bright blond hair standing on end. Several of the group were bleeding, but all they had left was Ana's towel.

"We can rip this up for bandages," she said. "There might be enough for you guys to wrap your feet if we're economical about it."

"I have this," Keira said, unzipping her pack all the way and folding out the edges. Ana exhaled, forgetting the crackling in her ears for a moment. Set into the lining of the pack was a small first-aid kit, a manicure set, a packet of tampons, a make-up bag, hairbrush, and an entire packet of muesli bars.

"Keira," Ana said breathlessly. "You are a genius."

The girl offered a shaky smile, her eyes watering. "I have these too." She pulled a lighter from her back pocket and upended the tote bag. Candles dropped onto the dirt.

Overcome, Ana gripped Keira's shoulder. "Genius."

A sob broke from the girl's throat. "I don't know why I grabbed it," she laughed weakly. "It's not even mine. It was sitting by the tunnel entrance and I just scooped it up in case it was something important."

"It is," Olly said, nodding his head.

"We find somewhere to hide," Ana said. "We light a fire. We pull our shit together and figure things out."

"Figure things out," Stefan said. He gazed back up the hill, wiggling a finger in his ear, scowling as he tried to make it pop. "Why it's daytime? Why it's winter? Who those men were, killing each other? Killing us?"

She swallowed and nodded. "Like I said."

CHAPTER FIVE

They settled in a mossy hollow beneath an overhanging ridge. The sky had grown dark and iron-heavy with unspent rain. At least they'd have some shelter if it poured. There was a grassy area before the hollow and then the ground fell steeply away, offering a view of the valley below. An ocean of trees. No sign of a town in the distance. Just trees.

No one had said anything about the lack of signs of civilization. They focused instead on foraging for dry wood and rocks to build a campfire, like they'd seen in movies and survival shows. Olly and the Metzger brothers had some camping experience but dry wood was hard to come by. It was winter. Apparently. The ground was damp with leaf mold. It took much longer than Ana could have anticipated to find what they needed and longer still to get the fire going, even with a lighter.

Keira checked wounds. A lot of the toweling bandages had soaked through and crusted dry. They had three bottles of water and didn't want to waste it cleaning cuts but they were worried about infection too. The little tube of antiseptic cream from Keira's first-aid kit was half empty. Worrying about infection poked at much greater, confronting worries. They didn't know where they were. Or *when* they were. Or if there was any way to get back.

They huddled close, the frigid air banishing any bashfulness about cuddling up to strangers. They kept those with fewer clothes in the middle. The poor Metzger brothers shivered between Olly and Stefan. Then Gwen, Ana, and Keira stacked next to them. They kept a pile of firewood close to the fire to help it dry. The heat was intense on Ana's face and shins where she kept her legs tucked up in front of her, but her back was freezing against the moss-covered rocks, an aching cold.

She couldn't imagine sleeping here. She couldn't imagine closing her eyes for more than a second. Every creaking bough made her heart jolt. She strained for the sound of hoof beats or distant voices.

What if they were followed by the men from the cave? It's not like they had thought to cover their tracks.

"What if they see the smoke?" Keira whispered.

Ana rubbed her eyes. She had been worrying about this too.

"At this stage, I'd say our greatest threat is hypothermia," Olly said.

"Perhaps," one of the Metzger brothers said. "A sword-swinging murderer might top that."

They fell silent.

"We should introduce ourselves," Ana blurted out, not ready to face it. "I don't know your names."

"Nikolas," said the boy wearing Olly's purple sweatshirt. He was the one who had given the rules about not being an arschloch. He was stockier than his brother, with darker blond hair. "This is Conrad." He nodded at the boy with the watermelon towel, whose teeth chattered audibly. Conrad stared at the flames, his mouth pressed in a tight line. "Sorry, I did not pick up any of your names."

"I'm Ana," she said. When the others remained silent, she added, "This is Keira, Gwen, Stefan, and Olly."

"Well, I am very sorry we got you into this mess."

"Oh?" Stefan said flatly. "You knew you were taking us to a hole in the space–time continuum? That an earthquake and medieval knights would kill three-quarters of our class?"

Silence rang like a struck anvil. Nikolas rolled his lips in tight, his eyes glistening as he looked at each one of them. "Is … is that what we think is happening? Medieval knights?"

Stefan shook his head. "Unless Olly's right about larpers hunting people for sport, how do we explain the swords and crossbows? The literal chain mail or the feral bastards wearing animal pelts and the actual murder of our friends?"

"And the daylight," Keira added.

"The snow," Olly said.

Gwen said nothing, she simply stared at the flames. She'd let Ana crawl inside the huge cardigan with her but she hadn't answered any of her questions, if she was all right. Of course she wasn't all right. None of them were.

"Your German is very good," Nikolas said, as though looking for the bright side. "All of you."

"What are you talking about?" Olly said.

"You are speaking good German."

Olly frowned. "I'm not speaking German."

Ana stared at Olly's lips as he spoke and saw a mismatch of shapes to sounds. An eerie prickling sensation flashed across her skin. "Are ... you guys speaking English?"

Nikolas frowned. "I am not."

"Don't," Keira sobbed. "This isn't the time—it isn't funny."

"I am not trying to be funny," Nikolas said, looking to his brother for support. "They are speaking German?"

Conrad nodded but his eyes were wide and he looked nauseous. "Their lips do not match the words."

Nikolas sat bolt upright and stared around the group as though he'd found himself in sudden danger. "Say something."

"Like what?" Ana said, but she was staring at his mouth now and her heart was thudding behind her ribs. "Your English is clearer? Your accents are barely noticeable and I'm not speaking German? In fact, I only know how to order coffee and ask for directions in German, maybe a little vocab, but that's about it."

Keira gasped and shunted against the back of the hollow. Nikolas, Conrad, and Stefan shot to their feet. Olly clamped his hands over his mouth, but Ana was trapped in the cardigan with Gwen, who wasn't reacting at all.

"What the hell is going on?" Keira's fingers trembled at her lips. "What the hell is going on?" she said again with a little sob. "What the hell is going on?"

"Stop that," Stefan snapped. "What are you doing?"

"That was Somali, then English, then German," Keira whispered.

Conrad turned and puked on the grass. Nikolas gripped his brother by the shoulders and looked back at Keira like she'd grown antlers.

Ana thought she might vomit too. "Do it again. Move your hands. I want to see your lips."

Keira swallowed and faced her, repeating the phrase again three times in a row. Ana's ears crackled as she watched the girl's lips moving, the slight mismatch, not like bad dubbing in a low-budget movie but subtler. Tears welled in her eyes. "I hear English."

"I hear German." Conrad sank to his knees by the fire and Nikolas crouched beside him.

"I hear English," Stefan said.

"I hear English," Olly whispered. "But ... if I think about it, I could be hearing Hindi."

Keira nodded, tears tracking her cheeks. "It makes me feel dizzy."

"Same," Olly said.

"What the hell?" Stefan murmured, visibly shaken and pacing now before the fire. "That's impossible. There are centers of the brain that control language. There's hardwiring, synapses—"

Olly clamped his palm to his forehead. "What about those stories you hear where people who survive car crashes wake up fluent in French or they can suddenly play piano or do advanced mathematics."

Keira buried her face in her hands. "This can't be real. Maybe we're still buried in the cave. Maybe a rock hit my head and this is a—a delusion. I'm losing oxygen and my mind is…"

Dizziness made the forest swoop around Ana's head and nausea rose in her stomach. She inhaled, dragging freezing air into her lungs, willing it to clear the fog. Should she tell them about the hallucination she had at the river and what happened in the thermal pool? That she dreamed about the guy with the tattooed head and the black marks on his neck? Then he was there … waiting outside the cave? But her throat closed over the words. Admitting it aloud was too frightening. What could it mean?

"We're going to need food." Conrad broke the silence. "Water … more clothes."

"We know," Nikolas said, wrapping his arm around his younger brother.

"I don't think I can do this," Conrad said, his teeth chattering again. "It's cold, Nikolas. I'm so cold."

"Shivering is a good sign," Stefan said. "If you stop feeling it, that's bad."

"Then I must be really good," Conrad said, and Nikolas gave a forced laugh, rubbing his brother's arm, but there was no humor in his eyes. He looked … desperate.

Slowly, darkness swallowed the forest. They added wood to the fire and divided the muesli bars and water. No one suggested rationing either. There was no point. They talked for a long time about the strangeness of their changing speech; testing each other, staring at each other's lips, listening so hard Ana felt like her brain was turning to mush. Finally, they fell silent, staring at the flames.

"Someone should keep a lookout," Stefan said.

"Not apart from the group," Ana said. "We need to stay warm."

"What if someone comes?" Keira said.

"Do you really think you'll be able to sleep?" Ana asked, but the girl didn't reply. No one did. "I think we should spoon."

"Spoon?" Nikolas tucked back his chin.

"We need body heat," she said. "Put your arms around each other and get as close as you can." She tugged Gwen, rolling her friend behind her, and held out an arm, inviting Keira to be the little spoon. The girl was wearing jeans and a thin floral bomber jacket of shimmering silk over a T-shirt. She looked at Ana, her big brown eyes gleaming, but turned on her hip and wiggled back into her. Unashamed, Ana wrapped her arm around the girl and pulled her in close.

Gwen slipped her arm around Ana's waist, inside the shared cardigan, leaving her the sleeves, and buried her face between her shoulder blades. Her silence frightened Ana as much as the prospect of the frozen night and not knowing what lurked in the forest. There was grunting and jostling as the boys did their best to burrow in close. Conrad swore as he tucked his towel around him and complained about Nikolas's hair tickling his nose.

Eventually, she felt Stefan's arm hook over Gwen, brushing

against Ana's back, and that finally triggered her own tears. She wasn't in Stefan's arms. He didn't want her. She wasn't in Will's arms. He was dead. They were lost. More lost than any one of them could comprehend. They were freezing. How would they last the night?

The strange crackling in her ears was growing faint and she didn't know what it meant. She kept touching her mouth and whispering random words under her breath to feel the shape of the sounds, but exhaustion was making it harder to concentrate.

The image of Will forced its way into her thoughts, his body splayed on the ground, the arrow in his eye. She tried to remember their brief closeness in the cave but she couldn't hold on to it. She couldn't stop it from flipping ahead to the horror outside the cave. The arrow. Over and over. The look on his face, lips parted in shock. His rasping whisper as he fell, "*Run.*"

"What if—" Gwen finally spoke, her voice little more than a rough whisper. "What if they're still alive? The ones we left in the cave?"

It was like a punch to the solar plexus and Ana squeezed her eyes shut. She didn't want to think about it. The girls with guitars. The kids huddling on the jumping ledge. Bodies floating face down in the water. Flailing limbs and hands grappling as they scrambled to get up through the rock passage.

"Who did you see?" Keira finally replied for all of them. "I think Raphael made it out but he must have been shot."

"I thought Kendra and Sun-yu made it out," Stefan said, his voice haunted. "But they can't have survived the crossbows ... or they'd be here."

"Conor was shot," Gwen said, her voice breaking. "The boy who helped me."

Ana scrunched her eyes closed and sobbed, "Will. Will was shot."

Keira wept too, and at least a couple of the boys behind them.

"Who was left in the cave?" Olly said, his voice thick with emotion.

Keira sniffed and cleared her throat. "The girls from Mr Hill's music class. Priya and Antoinette. They were caught beneath the falling rocks."

Gwen moaned and sobbed anew. Ana's throat ached, trying to keep from bawling, terrified of making too much noise.

They guessed eleven hadn't made it out of the cave, but they couldn't say for sure. They thought maybe six lay dead before the cave entrance.

"Should we go back?" Keira said. "Should we check?"

"The tunnel caved in," Ana said, suppressing the guilt rising in her belly. "How would we clear it?"

The group fell silent again, contemplating. Was she being a coward? She couldn't bear to go back. To see their friends lying dead on the ground. The thought of stepping foot in the cave opening made her insides shrivel. But then she imagined what it would be like if she was left behind, stranded in the pitch black, injured, terrified, and alone.

"Do we even know the way back?" Stefan said, his voice low. He sounded exhausted. He was right. They'd zigzagged, following any path that seemed clearest on the way down the slope. They'd walked for hours before they found the hollow.

Aside from up, what other direction could they be confident about? She felt a wave of gratitude for Stefan's common sense, letting her off the hook.

"I can't stand it," Gwen choked. "I can't stand thinking of them trapped in there."

"Don't," Olly said, his voice rough. "We have to focus on surviving."

"When the sun comes up, we head down to the bottom of the valley," Ana said. "That's the most likely place for us to find water at least."

"Then what?" Gwen said, shuddering.

"We look for help?" she said. "A town. A village or farmhouse."

"Try to rest," Stefan said. "Conserve our energy. We'll sort it out in the morning."

They fell silent and the sounds of the night amplified. The wind haunted the trees, with long, cold moans. The hiss and crackle of the fire was Ana's only comfort, the orange flicker through her eyelids. She concentrated on the sounds of her friends breathing, and after a while the weeping stilled and exhaustion dragged her down deep into darkness.

CHAPTER SIX

Leon wiped blood and sweat from his eyes, panting and half dazed in the aftermath of battle. They had prevailed, only just, but the casualties dismayed him. He held his flaming torch aloft, searching for injured Eadin Palace soldiers they might have missed.

He shook his head, surveying the carnage. Oleg the Butcher. Not random trespassers trying their luck on the borders of Eadin Forest. But Oleg *himself*, leading a full company of blooded warriors. One hundred? Two hundred?

In the chaos, it had seemed an innumerable host.

The notorious Northern lord was a figure from nightmares. Leon had not dreamed of ever facing him in the field. Neither did he get the chance tonight. The Butcher, with his shaved head and distinct tattoos, had been deep in the heart of the fray, causing the most damage. The way he'd swung that obsidian axe, letting the blood of Leon's men. Leon had fought to reach him but his way had been blocked.

He balled his fist to hide the trembling in his free hand. It was simply the ebb of battle rage being displaced quickly by a different sort of rage.

Truman Schreiber had delivered the order late last night, knowing it would irritate Leon to receive instructions from the craven prick. An obscure order based on an obscure prediction from the Council of Eadin.

Had he not despised Schreiber, would he have prepared more diligently? If he had put stock in the prediction, might he have driven his men to ride faster? Taken more care with his scouts? Anticipated the Northmen's resistance?

Leon and Micah, his fellow lieutenant, sought confirmation from Captain Wulfryn, then rallied the men without question or complaint. Dutiful, yes. Wary, always—especially this close to the border. But the nature and timing of the prediction and the delivery by Schreiber … Leon was ashamed to admit, he had dismissed it as little more than Eldi-induced hysteria.

In the days since the red comet appeared in the sky, there had been a slew of wild prophecies, and matters had only escalated as the solstice drew nearer. Mystics falling into trances, clerics claiming to see visions, ecstatics emerging from the Sacred Grove, delirious from fasting, delivering riddles in the tongues of angels. Eadin Palace attracted an eccentric sort. Leon was hard put to hold *every* revelation in earnest.

It wasn't that he lacked faith. There were several members of the council he held in high esteem, but Leon was a practical man, his duties were physical concerns, not wrestling with the mysteries of heaven.

Yet here they had found Northern wild men camped in the very spot the council had predicted. *Beware the trespassers*

*lying in wait for pilgrims to emerge from the sacred caves.
Pilgrims marked for heathen desecration.* That was the prediction, according to Schreiber.

"Lieutenant!" Oakin came panting up the rise, a young
soldier with hair like dandelion floss and a raw wound on his
forehead. The blood stood stark against his pale skin, drib-
bling all the way to his chin, staining his teeth a violent red.

Leon raised his eyebrows and clamped his gloved hand on
the boy's shoulder. "You're alive."

The boy ducked his head. "I made a point of staying so."

"There's a lad."

"Micah wants you by the caves, sir." The boy darted a
harried look over his shoulder. "There's some mischief among
the pilgrims' bodies."

Leon patted the boy and nodded. "Help the medics and
send messengers to Ulmenholz and Reinwald. We'll need
wagons for the wounded. Tell them what … this was. Burn the
dead Northerners."

Oakin grimaced. "Aye, sir."

In the clearing before the cave, Leon spotted a cluster of his
men surveying the pilgrims under torchlight. When they had
approached the encampment, the battle had been so fierce Leon
had barely registered the people stumbling from the caves.

He eyed the moss-covered rocks with wariness. This place
was sacred. They should not be there with blood on their
swords.

Micah seemed to agree. The tall lieutenant stared at the

blocked cave entrance, his warm brown skin looking slightly pallid. When Leon joined him, the other soldiers rose from where they had been crouching, examining three bodies. Two young women and one boy killed by arrows. Bundles lay in the dirt beside them, their strange contents half spilled. Other peculiar objects lay scattered in the grass.

The bodies were mostly naked. The young women's female parts were barely concealed by small triangles of brightly colored fabric, laced together with string of the same hue. The boy was covered from waist to knee in breeches made from a patterned fabric that shimmered like silk. The patterns were like nothing he'd ever seen before, depictions of muscular men bedecked in red, blue, and white, poised for battle, one with bared teeth and green skin.

Yet the boy himself did not possess the bearing of a soldier. Nor did he look like a farmer's lad; his hands were smooth and unmarked. His teeth were white. The girls, too, had no calluses on their fingers, their nails rendered with tiny, shimmering works of art. Could they be nobles?

"They do not look like pilgrims," Leon said.

Micah nodded, raising his eyebrows. "Pilgrims are generally robed."

"I thought there were more." Leon scanned the faces of the men. Their expressions ranged from bemusement to fear.

"Several escaped," Micah said, his voice a deep bass, gesturing down the slope at the trees. "Some were taken by Oleg's men, back toward the Namen."

Leon studied Micah's face. He was an exceptional soldier, scout, strategist. When Micah worried, Leon worried too.

"What can explain this?" Micah posed the question in his usual steady style, casting his gaze around the assembled group. Not an arrogant demand but an invitation to collaborate. He crouched and gently turned the middle girl's face. She had black hair pulled into a glittering band, the upturned eyes and light brown skin of a people from lands far south and east.

"Perhaps they were slaves?" Edwin suggested, raking dirt-caked fingers through his long hair. His usually ruddy cheeks were pale as milk. He was feeling the deep strangeness of the place and the problem at their feet. Born in Modeh, a village south of Eadin, Edwin had gone through training with Leon and Micah when they were lads. He was a sensible young man, uneasy with marvels or what he'd term "devil's nonsense."

Micah crossed his arms, biceps smeared in someone else's blood, and responded without scorn, "Well fed, clean, with white teeth and smooth, unmarked skin?"

"Pleasure slaves?" Edwin said, frowning.

"Oleg the Butcher takes the left eye of all his slaves," Micah said. "Even if he had favored these ones and shown uncharacteristic mercy to leave them unmarred, would he bring his slaves across the border simply to bathe with them in the sacred pools of Eadin?"

"The Butcher fears our sacred sites," Leon said, his focus turned inward as he grappled for meaning in the puzzle of it all.

"Perhaps it *was* an act of desecration," Tabor said, an

Ottoman with huge round shoulders. "Oleg has desecrated temples. Held orgies in gutted churches and razed druid groves to ash. That was the nature of the prediction, yes? Pilgrims marked for desecration?"

Before they could consider further, a snarling cry rose behind them. They turned to see Oakin standing over a captive tied to the trunk of a tree, waving for them. A clanswoman, raging in the Northern tongue.

Leon knew some of the language but he lacked Tabor's fluency. He looked to the man but did not have to ask; the Ottoman fell into step beside him.

They reached the tree, and Leon dismissed the worried-looking Oakin to his duties. The woman sat with her legs splayed, and wore animal skin breeches and a vest. Her neck was tattooed and one side of her head was shaved to the skin. Blonde braids hung from the other, knitted with small bones and yellow thread. She snarled and launched into a fresh diatribe.

Tabor's brow furrowed as he listened. "She says, we are rutting fools ... interfering in matters that do not concern us."

"If it happens on our land, it concerns us," Leon muttered.

"They were ours," Tabor translated. "A gift from ... the Kjálka?"

"Kjálka?" Leon wondered aloud. "Teeth?"

"Mouth?" Tabor scratched his beard. "Maybe jaw?"

"Speak plain, witch." Leon crouched beside her, keeping beyond kicking distance. She bared her teeth, releasing a stream of boiling hate.

"The Kjálka is hungry," Tabor said. "She sent us to harvest an offering for her ... plate, I think. Seven. She's saying the number seven. Seven to ... placate or appease. Seven to ... mend. Seven to sow. Seven to ... tear, rend?"

Seven? Leon glanced back at the fallen by the cave entrance. There were three dead. How many had been taken? And some had escaped.

"Now you have interfered," Tabor translated, "Oleg will not rest. He will find them. His scouts will not stop until they are found. He will ... scour this land ... no mercy for those who stand in his way."

She bared her teeth with a final declaration. Tabor stepped back and crossed his thick arms. "The Kjálka is hungry."

"God save us," Leon muttered, crossing himself. "Oleg wants this lot to feed a hungry mouth?"

Micah approached; he'd heard most of it. "I'll form a search party."

Leon rose and gripped his friend's forearm. "Let me. This is my fault."

Micah frowned. "I received the council's order, just as you did."

Leon lowered his voice, ashamed for Tabor to hear his confession. "I let Schreiber taint my judgment."

"None of us were expecting the Northern Butcher." Micah rested a hand on Leon's shoulder. "We'll take a dozen men. They will not have gotten far."

CHAPTER SEVEN

Aloud cracking jolted Ana from a fitful sleep. A flare of light with it, the flames of their campfire leaping as a fresh log was added to the little blaze. She cricked her neck turning her head too fast. Olly was sitting up from where he'd been the last spoon in the set. His brown face wan and hollowed out in the firelight.

"I was worried it might go out," he whispered. He hadn't slept.

Incredibly, the others were sleeping. Incredibly, she had been too. Fatigue and spent adrenaline must have done its work.

"My ears have cleared," he said, and she blinked at him, listening. Hers too.

"What does it mean?"

"That if we're out of our minds, at least we're out of them together?"

She gazed up at the trees, overhanging the ridge, but the sky above the canopy was an impenetrable black. Out through the gap in the trees, across the valley, blackness. "How long have we been out?"

Olly shrugged and dug his phone from his pocket. The screen lit up. 6:11 pm. Just on dinner time back home? The idea scrambled her brain.

"How's reception?"

He didn't laugh. Those who hadn't left their phones behind in the caves had all checked reception at different points during their flight through the forest. No bars. No reception. But none of the interference they'd experienced the day before.

"Do you think the school knows we're missing?" Ana whispered, picturing the teachers checking rooms at Saints be Praised and finding empty beds. Olly shook his head but she couldn't resist reaching for hope. "They might have notified our folks. They might be searching for us, right now." But the idea deflated her. What would they find? A cave-in?

Her bladder was full. She hated the thought of leaving the hollow. While she was still cold, she had at least stopped shaking. Going out into the freezing dark to pee would have her teeth chattering again in a heartbeat. But there was nothing for it. With a soft groan, she unbuttoned Gwen's cardigan and slipped her arms free. Careful to avoid jostling her friends, she rose to her feet, staggering away from the flames to find her balance.

"Don't listen," she said to Olly, wrinkling her nose. He shook his head again; he didn't care. She slipped her phone from the front pocket of her backpack and turned on the little torch. The last thing she needed was to twist an ankle or plunge from a precipice. With hesitant steps, she shuffled away to the right of the hollow, until she was out of sight of their camp.

She kept the light low to the ground, half bent as she made her way through the trees. The idea of being seen, squatting in the woods, wasn't just mortifying, it frightened her silly. She imagined eyes in the dark, a foreboding presence in the trees. Watchful. Malicious. Calculating.

The image of the wild men lunging across the clearing toward them made her want to burrow beneath the frozen earth. Their contorted faces, smeared with lines of red or black paint, teeth bared, axes raised, murder in their eyes. The men in armor had seemed no less terrifying. The merciless strokes of their swords, war cries splitting the air. She stifled a small sob, propped her phone against a fallen branch, and fumbled her shorts down to her ankles.

When she was finished, she caught the sound of crunching leaves. That wasn't her.

As though a switch had been thrown, noise burst through the forest and burning torches flickered beneath the trees. She clamped her hands over her mouth to stifle a scream but screams were already rising from the campsite.

She struggled to her feet, yanked up her pants, and buttoned her shorts. She scrabbled for her phone, accidentally kicking it into the leaf mold, flipping it over and obscuring the torch. She fell to her knees, her fingers flailing through the dirt and leaves.

Stefan's voice rose from the campsite. "Stop!" he cried. "We've done nothing wrong. You can't just attack us!"

Nikolas swore and Conrad shouted.

"Stop!" Stefan cried again.

A horrible thud preceded Gwen's scream. "Leave him alone! You're hurting him!"

Ana couldn't find her phone. Tears sprang into her eyes. It seemed vitally important. She had to find it. Because why? What was she going to do? Call the police? Call her mother? Get someone to pick her up and take her away from what? The fucking dark ages? But she patted the ground anyway, her hands shaking with cold and terror, trying not to picture what might be happening to Stefan.

"We have six," a brusque voice declared. "Are there any more?"

Ana froze, spinning in a crouch to face the campsite, heart hammering in her chest. She had no single clue what she should do. Charge back to her friends? Or run into the night, alone, clueless, without her pack, nothing but the clothes on her back. She had no idea where she was, how she would survive the night, let alone men with swords hunting her in the dark.

"You can't do this," Keira cried. "You can't just attack people."

"Hold your tongue." Another male voice, a low bass.

"Search the surrounding woods," the first man said. "Bind the rest and load them on the horses."

Flaming torches swayed out from the campsite and with a terrible inner wrenching, Ana turned to flee. Then her foot caught her phone once more, flipping it several times, torch side up. She gasped and grabbed it and ran, as fast as she could, the tiny light slashing left and right.

"There!" a man bellowed, and Ana's throat burned with a half-strangled scream. "It's just a girl," he called back to his group. "I've got her."

Heavy boots pounded after her and she ran, arms out-stretched, catching scrapes and nicks from sharp branches, terrified of rough hands behind and the possibility of a cliff before her. Her phone light was no match for the deep black of the forest. She could hear the long gaps between her pursuer's footfalls. He was running at full stride.

She forced herself to tap her light off but instantly regretted it, colliding with an unforgiving branch, the impact loosening her grip and sending her phone spinning once more into darkness.

Winded, she couldn't cry out in dismay, or pain. And when the hand gripped her shoulder and yanked her around, she had no air to scream.

The man was huge. His flaming torch cast the side of his face in harsh gold. He panted through his teeth and his black eyes glittered in hooded shadows. The reek of blood and sweat and horses hung about him and his fingers bruised the muscle in her arm. Power and threat rippled from him and she felt in her gut he could so easily kill her.

One blow to the head and she'd be done.

Instinct made her wild. She thrashed aside, windmilling her arms, and the soldier's eyes flared wide. "No!" he shouted, dropping his torch and lunging for her with both hands.

Ana's back foot stepped into nothingness and she realized it was fear in his eyes, not rage. Her stomach dropped as she began to fall but he grasped her forearms with desperate cruelty, almost wrenching her shoulder sockets.

Their eyes locked. Understanding knifed through her and she knew, in that split second, his mass and their doom. He was huge because he was wearing armor. Huge and heavy. And her momentum was dragging him with her. Right over the edge.

CHAPTER EIGHT

Ana woke and immediately regretted it; she was freezing and pain wailed through her body like a siren. Her consciousness recoiled, and she kept her eyes closed, as though she could burrow back through the threshold of sleep to safety. But there was light beyond her eyelids, the distant sound of gurgling water, birdsong, and the shushing forest.

Her back was arched and agonized, her head suspended above the ground by an unyielding form, rasping beneath her shoulders. Wet susurrations. The soldier. The knight. Beneath her. *Shit.* She blinked and cracked open her eyes. Above her, the slope rose and rose to the overhanging tree canopy.

How was she alive? How had she not broken her neck or smashed her brains out?

She remembered then her friends, their panic. Stefan's pleas. Gwen's sobs. Violent thuds. Oh, God. Were *they* still alive? How would she find them? Could she even walk?

Teeth gritted, she hauled herself up onto her elbows, the movement causing her to slide off the soldier's armor, her numb ass hitting the cold ground. She wiggled her toes and lifted her shoulders. Everything hurt. Her palms were raw.

She was covered in scrapes, bleeding from shins, knees, wrists, elbows, and chin.

She struggled to her feet and looked down her body. Incredibly, her bikini top had stayed in place, but the white shirt was in tatters. Only one button had survived the plummet. She opened the flaps to grimace at her stomach. No deep cuts but impressive gravel rash and her ribs were bruised to hell. It felt like her skin was burning, the sensation at odds with the shivers racking her bones. Her denim shorts were covered in dirt and her beautiful white sneakers were filthy and scuffed. That really pissed her off. "I just bought these," she muttered to no one, and produced a tearless sob.

She shuffled around, tripping on a sword in its scabbard. It must have torn loose from the knight's belt. She righted herself and paused to look at the fallen man. A jagged stick protruded from his body below his arm, his legs splayed before him. She clamped her hand over her mouth at the pool of blood.

She was shocked to see he was much younger than he had appeared last night. Her terror had added age to his size and ferocity. While he was big, it was the breastplate and shoulder guards that had made him seem like a terrifying brute.

He might still be a brute. Hadn't he tried to kidnap her? Kidnap her friends?

A moan issued from the knight and she stumbled back, fumbling to draw the sword from its scabbard. The blade was so cumbersome, she needed both hands to lift the tip from the ground. The pommel was smooth and pale, carved from bone, with a silver crest stamped with an image of the sun.

She wasted no time marveling but held the sword before her. His head rocked from side to side, his breath coming in shallow rasps, but he didn't open his eyes. He couldn't be much older than her. He had a continental look about him, copper-colored skin, deep brown curls, and thick girlish lashes.

A familiar note chimed and she swung around, the momentum flinging the sword from her grip. Her phone alarm trilled its brief melody somewhere above her head. Her phone! A small cry of wonder burst from her lips and she whirled toward the immense slope, peering at the rocks and shrubs, trying to spot it.

There! Almost twelve feet above, caught in a bramble, her phone was lit up, repeating its melody, waiting for her to hit snooze.

With a whimper, she started to climb. Careful to find firm handholds and sure ledges for her feet. She moved slowly, blinking through the pain in her body, toward a lifeline.

Music called Leon up from the deep. A series of queer notes, cycling in repetition. A harp? A lute? But the growing awareness in his body told him this could not be so. He was lying flat on his back, numb with cold.

Light seeped beneath his lashes and every half-drawn breath brought stabbing pain beneath his left arm. A bright, searing pain that eclipsed the many other pains in his aching body. His skull felt as though it had been removed from his neck. The straps for his breastplate dug chain mail into his spine. Breathing was hard, a sawing labor, rasping as he tried to fill his lungs. His jaw felt like it had been struck with a flail. His entire body felt like it had been struck with a flail.

He groaned and opened his eyes. The pale sky spun slowly overhead. The strange music kept trilling and movement in his peripheral vision dragged him fully awake. Through the fog of his breath, he saw the girl.

She was splayed six feet up the slope, her tiny blue breeches bunched tight around her buttocks, her thighs trembling with the effort to climb. Her skin was grazed and bleeding and she was reaching with all her might for a small rectangular object. A box?

Impossibly thin and dully gleaming, it was lodged at the root of a bramble bush. His foggy brain struggled to comprehend how such a thing could produce such a sound or how it might come to be here on the slope. Had the girl been holding it when she fell?

"You need a stick," he croaked.

She yelped, losing her footing, and skidded back to the grass with a strangled cry. She grabbed his sword and whirled toward him, struggling to bear the weight of the blade.

He blinked at her bizarre clothes and winced at the blood

and dirt staining the shreds of her flimsy overshirt. Nothing about her fit inside his head.

"I seem to have one." He gestured, flapping his hand at the horrible branch stuck in his side. "It might do the job."

Her eyes darted to the wound. "I should drive it all the way in and this sword too."

He screwed his eyes shut and grimaced. "It feels quite ... painful ... as it is." When he opened his eyes again, she had cast his sword aside, well out of his reach, and was unlacing one of her unusual white boots. He tensed, fearing she might intend to beat him about the ears with it.

"You understand me?"

He frowned, at a loss as to how to respond.

"My words!" She waved the shoe at him and he flinched. "You understand what I'm saying?"

"I ... yes?"

"My lips match the sounds?"

"Ah ... yes?"

Her brow crumpled. "What language is this?"

"What ... language?" He blinked at her. "We ... we speak the common tongue of Alemannic."

"Like old-school German?" She brought trembling fingers to her lips, her eyes welling as she stared at the ground, nodding and muttering, "Right ... why not medieval German? If we're losing our shit, we may as well go the whole way."

Leon eyed her warily. Was she mad? It would explain her near nakedness.

She turned away and threw the boot at the bramble bush. Remarkably, it landed right in the middle, lodging in the branches above the musical box. "Are you fucking kidding me?" she shrieked. Leon jolted.

Still the box trilled on, its melody growing irritating as it looped. "How does it play without a crank?"

She shot him a scathing look. "A crank?"

"Your musical box. It is some manner of hurdy-gurdy? A symphonia?" He rotated his wrist, to demonstrate the turning of a crank. He'd seen a minstrel play such an instrument at a festival in Modeh, though it had been a much larger contraption.

"Are you for real?" she spat.

"I have never heard such a hurdy-gurdy as this, nor seen one so small. It is surely a marvel."

She tipped her face into her hands, indulging a brief hysterical sob. "A hurdy-gurdy."

"Have I … misspoken?"

"*Misspoken?*"

"I seem to have offended—"

"*Offended?* You beat the shit out of my friends and ran me off a fucking cliff!" She took a step toward him, spittle flying from her lips. "You murdered innocent schoolkids—you shot them with arrows!"

Leon's lips parted as he absorbed the girl's response and reconsidered his next words. She was staring at the stick wedged in the soft skin of his underarm. He feared she might, indeed, kick it deeper if his diplomacy failed. It also triggered a deeper fear, one he had been ducking even as consciousness returned to his body. Where were his men? It struck him as ominous that not one of them had come searching for him and the girl.

A dark possibility swept in. Had Oleg's scouts been on their heels? Perhaps his men were all dead. He pushed the horrible thought down. "I swear, that was not our men."

Tears sparkled in her pale-green eyes, pressure building in her face.

He held her gaze. "We would never kill innocents."

"But sneaking up on them in the dark, assaulting them, tying them up and dragging them away—that gets the green light?"

"What is … the green light?"

She fixed him with a poisonous glare. "Green means go."

"Go … where?"

"Listen to me, Sir Jerks-a-lot," she snarled, gesticulating at the musical box. "I'm getting my phone and my shoe and I'm going…" She straightened up, her eyes widening. "I'm going and I'm not staying *here*. I don't want to *be* here. I don't even know where here is. I don't know *when* this is. Or *how* this is. But I can't be here. I can't be here with a—" A bout of soft, unhinged laughter rocked her shoulders. "A medieval knight in shining armor."

His thoughts tumbled and failed to find a firm place to land. "I am not a knight," he said tightly. "I am a palace guard.

And while I am not entirely sure that I understood most of what you said, I promise you, we mean you no harm. Your companions were killed by Oleg's warriors. We fought Oleg's men. We knew we had to reach those of you who escaped the battle at the caves before he sent his scouts to round you up."

"Round us up?"

"You're not safe out here alone," Leon said. "Oleg's men will return. They hunt you."

"Hunt us?" she cried. "That makes no sense. Who is Oleg? We don't know any Oleg. Besides, how did he know we were there? *We* didn't know we would be there!"

Leon frowned.

She stared at him, a slow and dreadful realization creasing her brow.

"He was waiting for you."

"Waiting? For us? For—for schoolkids?"

He was not sure what she meant by "schoolkids." There was no local university and certainly none that would allow girls to attend. "He had foreseen your arrival."

She lowered her chin, her face screwed up. "What?"

"His seers. They foretold your arrival. 'Seven to appease. Seven to mend. Seven to sow. Seven to rend.' He intends to offer you to his gods."

Her eyes narrowed and her voice grew airless. "Bullshit."

"The only place where you will be safe is Eadin Palace."

She gave a mirthless laugh, her eyes welling anew. "The last time I saw Eadin Palace, it was a ruin."

He balked at the words and shook his head. "Ruin? Eadin Palace is impenetrable."

"Not according to the eight-foot chain-link fence surrounding the broken walls or the health and safety warnings about crumbling stonework."

He struggled to lift his head. "Watch your words. Threats against Eadin Palace will not be taken lightly and those that make them rarely have opportunity to speak again."

She turned away with a small shake of her head, as though it was not worth the effort of a retort. The incessant musical box chimed on and she scanned the ground, finding a long branch not currently embedded in his side, to try again. When she started to climb once more, her legs spreading wide for a foothold, Leon flushed and looked away from the seam of her thighs, astonished by the girl's audacity.

"What happened to your clothes?" he croaked, trying to reach across his breastplate to pull the stick from his side, but the buckled curve of the armor made it impossible. The movement jarred the wound and he hissed.

"I fell down a bloody cliff, didn't I?" she snapped, breathless as she struggled.

"I mean…" His face infused with heat. "Where are the rest of your clothes?"

"The rest of my clothes? You mean at the hostel? Stefan has my sweatshirt. I didn't bring anything else. Ah—nearly!"

He swung his head to see her reaching with all her might,

the end of the branch grasped tight in her fist, the tip smacking the brambles holding her musical box and boot.

"We were … just … going," she grunted, swinging her stick, "for a swim." Finally, she dislodged her belongings, the boot tumbling, the box sliding to the ground.

With a small gasp of triumph she jumped away, landing heavily in the grass, and scrambled for the still chiming device. She tapped one side and it stopped. She wiped it on her grubby sleeve, her expression etched in a strange mix of relief and agony. "Fifty percent," she muttered, swiping her finger over the surface.

"That is not a hurdy-gurdy," Leon whispered.

"It's my phone." She turned it toward him, jutting out her jaw. "It's for texting my friends and scrolling the internet."

He stared at the small rectangle, unable to fathom its dimensions or the bright wonder of the images it depicted. Like a tiny mirror, but clearer than any he'd ever seen. Clearer than glass or still water.

"Cool, huh?" she said flatly, the edge of her wrath softening. "Check this out." She swiped the screen a few times and Leon jolted on his back with a bark of pain, as the image changed again and again. She studied his reaction with obvious dismay.

His thoughts slowed to mud. "I … I have not seen such a thing before."

She gave a shuddering sigh and slipped the box into her back pocket, sucking on her tooth as she regarded him. "I guess not." Then, exhaling sharply, she turned away and retrieved her white boot, pulling it back on her foot.

Leon felt as though he was being dragged backwards into deep water; his mouth parted but no words took shape. The girl tied the small lace, then froze over the bow, turning her head slowly toward him.

"I'm not a witch."

He snapped his mouth closed, his eyes widening.

"That's a thing, right? Back in ... whenever this is?" She blinked at him. "People were always freaking out about witches, right? Like women who knew things or had ideas or opinions. They got burned at the stake."

Leon made no reply, his heart beginning to hammer in his chest as she crouched beside him, her bright, pale eyes round and fixed on his. Had she read his thoughts?

"I'm not a witch. I'm just a girl. In the wrong place. In the wrong time. I don't want any trouble. I just want to find my friends and go home."

CHAPTER NINE

Ana pleaded silently with the knight who was not a knight, willing him to see the truth. Willing him to stop frowning like she might sprout horns and hex him at any moment. There was a sickly sheen to his copper skin and a glazed look in his eyes. He must be in terrible pain. She turned her attention to the wound beneath his arm.

"I'll help you," she said. "If you help me."

The words snapped him into focus and he hardened his jaw. "I *was* helping you."

"Well, you did a shitty job."

He clacked his teeth. "You claim not to know where you are or how you got here. You want to find your friends and go home?"

"Yes. I want to go home."

His dark eyes roved across her face, settling into fierce resolve. "Then remove the stick."

She grimaced and balled her hands into fists. "We need water and bandages and antiseptic…"

The knight raised his eyebrows.

She swallowed hard. They had nothing. "How deep do you think it is?"

"Deep enough. Make it quick."

"Don't look."

He turned his face aside, the muscle in his square jaw bunching as he braced himself. She wrapped her fingers around the stick. Even that small motion made him grunt. She steadied her other hand on his armor, closed her eyes, and yanked the branch free.

He let out a bark and pulled his arm against his body. More blood seeped from the wound. "Help me take this off," he patted his breastplate. "There are buckles in the back." With an agonized groan, he tried to roll onto his side but the effort was too much and he flopped back.

"This time." She heaved with him and he rolled, shuddering. What followed was an ordeal for them both, and she swore her way through it, wrestling complicated straps to remove the breastplate and shoulder guards. Leon passed out when she peeled the chain mail free from his body, his head flopping back against her chest. The absurd intimacy of it made her skin flush.

When he grunted, confirming he was once again conscious, they dealt with his leather tunic and linen shirt, and by the end of it they were both sweaty and shaken. Awkwardly, she helped him lie down and tried not to stare at his chest and stomach. She supposed wearing all that armor and wielding a giant sword was quite the daily workout.

"How do you fight in all that?"

He cradled his arm against his body and panted. "You swear a great deal for a lady."

She shrugged. "I'm not a lady."

"Not a witch and not a lady. What are you?"

"Are they my only options?" She gestured for permission to inspect the wound and gently lifted his arm away from his body, making him wince. "Oh man."

His brow bunched. "You have the strangest manner of speaking."

"You don't say," she muttered. "Your wound is … messed up."

"Check for splinters."

Her eyes widened. "I don't think that is something that will be happening."

"If the wound turns putrid, it could kill me."

"I—I can't."

"Simply feel around for anything sharp."

She held up her filthy hands with dirt caked beneath her nails. "It's not sterile."

"Sterile?"

"Germs. Invisible bacteria that will make you very unwell if I go digging around in your open flesh with dirty fingers."

"Are you a healer?"

"No." She gave him a despairing look. "It's just … a thing that everyone knows … where I'm from."

"Where are you from?"

She exhaled sharply. What was the point of trying to explain? "A bunch of places."

"I have water." He patted his right hip, fumbling to unhook

a leather pouch sealed with a cork. When he couldn't manage it, she leaned across his torso to help free it from its tether. He watched her, his eyes dipping then looking pointedly away from the view down her shirt.

"Drink first," she said, tugging her shirt off and ignoring the biting cold prickling her bare skin.

He balked. "What are you doing?"

"I can rip up your shirt to bandage the wound, it's cleaner than mine, but we need a sling or something to take the weight off your arm."

"You need something to cover your…" He pressed his lips together, not looking at her chest.

"It's a bikini and it's quite normal where I come from—if it were warm and you were going for a swim. Which it was. Which we were. Back home. So, you don't have to be weird about it. They're just boobs."

"I cannot allow you to—"

"Give it a rest. You're not in a position to be *allowing* anything." She sat back on her heels to think. "I heard a stream nearby. Drink. I'll go wash my hands and refill it."

He shook too much to open the pouch one-handed. So she snatched it up and gripped the cork with her teeth, pulling it free with a pop. She took a swig herself; it was a little brackish but she was so thirsty she didn't care. She bent to support his head and he gulped the water down, spilling plenty down his neck.

"Hurry," he said, starting to shiver anew.

She darted into the trees, following the sound of babbling water, her panic in freefall. It was so cold. Her body ached. Her skin stung all over. The guy's wound looked awful. How was she going to poke around for splinters without passing out or puking all over him? He was losing blood. They had nothing, no useful supplies. Where were his men? Why hadn't they come searching for him? Each thought arrowed through her, perforating the remaining shreds of her courage, and she let herself sob.

The forest was full of gnarled trees, black bark, and creeping moss. The path between them was slippery with dead leaves. She watched her feet, taking care not to trip on rocks and roots, following the sound of water. It didn't take long to find the shallow stream. She knelt on the bank and plunged her torn hands into the water, hissing at the icy flow.

She scrubbed her hands for as long as she could bear, digging the dirt from her nails, but without soap it seemed fruitless. What about the open cuts on her fingers? Was she really going to inspect his wound with bleeding fingers?

The stream gurgled over the rocks and she told herself it must be an offshoot of the Namen. The purest water in the world. Ansel's tears. Now her tears too. A dizzy swooping sensation made her head spin at the thought.

What if she was trapped in another hallucination? All the stuff she'd heard at the lecture—what if this was her brain building a medieval dreamscape? Sadistic Northmen. Eadin Palace knights.

But the guy said the man from her dream was hunting them. That he'd been *waiting* for them outside the cave. Knew they were coming. The thought made her nauseous. Oleg. She pictured him too easily, his tattooed head and the black marks ringing his neck. Seven. He wanted seven for a *sacrifice*.

What an incomprehensible word. *Sacrifice*. She had no real framework for it conceptually. And yet the white-faced woman from the cave loomed in her mind's eye, the memory of that unnatural, multilayered voice—like many voices gathered in one throat. She shook her head and dipped the water pouch in the flow, letting it fill, swilling it round and tipping it out before filling it again.

The pale sky was reflected in the water, rippling with the flow over the rocks. Awareness prickled at the back of her neck. She went rigid at the soft scuff of footsteps and turned her head slowly to look back over her shoulder. A man stood on the boulder bank close behind her. Her insides recoiled; he was staring at her butt.

She turned, spinning up from her crouch, and his eyebrows rose as he beheld her bikini top and acres of scratched skin. She took a step back and scowled, gripping the water pouch as though it were a weapon, but she was keenly aware of how very not a weapon it was and crossed her arms over her chest.

The man was tanned, tall, and broad-shouldered, or at least gave the illusion of being broad-shouldered, for he wore a long thick cloak of midnight blue and a luxurious brown pelt of some dead creature about his shoulders. His dark hair was long to his collar, half pulled back in a knot with a few loose strands framing his face. He looked to be in his early twenties.

He might have been terrifically handsome, with those hazel eyes and thick lashes, if he wasn't so intimidating, glaring at a defenseless girl, lost and mostly naked, in the woods.

His clothes were rich in texture and hue, his boots sturdy leather, mud-spattered but thickly heeled. His cloak was held with a fancy silver buckle, embellished with a tower and tree design. He'd flung back the swathe of the fabric behind one hip to display the jeweled hilt of his long sword, where he laid a gloved hand with equal parts ease and menace.

"My companion is waiting for me," she said with a level calm that impressed even her. He arched a droll eyebrow, trailing a lingering gaze down her body. Outrage trumped fear and she snapped her fingers in the air between them. "Hey! Don't be gross."

His mouth tightened. "Will your *companion* disapprove?"

"*I* disapprove." She must have knocked her head on the fall. *Shut up, Ana.*

"Then perhaps you should reconsider displaying yourself in such a fashion, if you do not wish to be admired."

"That look has *nothing* to do with admiration." God, why couldn't she stop? "I was refilling my … water pouch thing, and minding my own business. Maybe you should mind yours."

With an expression that indicated he was losing patience, he dropped down from the boulder. She took a step back to keep some distance between them, but the rocks almost turned her ankle and she didn't want to get her shoes wet. He noticed the stumble and gave her feet a quizzical look. Not a Nike fan? His eyes roved again, noting her denim shorts and the shimmering fabric of her bikini, and she knew her strangeness, her otherness, was stirring questions in him that she would not be able to satisfy.

"Everything below this hill is my land and every person who passes through it is *my* business."

"I wasn't intending on stopping long." She lifted her chin. "Like I said, just a refill."

He narrowed his eyes. "What are you?"

She blinked at the clipped landing on *what*. Not who but what. A thing. "What do you mean, 'what'?"

"You heard me, wench."

"Wench?" It wasn't a smart stalling technique but she had to find a way to hold him off and get past. She debated running for it but he had her hemmed in against the stream and it would require scrambling over boulders, and she wasn't confident about the strength in her legs after plummeting down a cliff. She rubbed her frozen arms, keeping them folded over her chest. "Who are *you*?"

"Have I not said that I am the lord of this land?" He was growing annoyed and took another step toward her; she edged to the side but he positioned himself again to block her path. "Answer the question."

"I don't know how," she said, her voice rising. She willed the injured knight to notice the delay, to find the strength to rise and search for her. "I don't understand the question."

He flung his arms open. "Declare yourself, girl."

"I'm nobody," she snapped. "A traveler. A girl. Does it matter?"

"A traveler?" Fresh calculations met the irritation in his eyes. "In the middle of winter. Dressed so, with hair like that?"

"We were attacked … by bandits."

"They took your clothes and cut your hair?" He gave her a disdainful look. "I do not suffer bandits in this territory."

"Northmen," she said, too embarrassed to say Vikings because it sounded silly in her head. How could she be anywhere where Vikings were a thing? It was too ludicrous. "My group was attacked by Northmen."

"Your group?" He crossed his arms. "I thought you had a companion."

"We were separated from the others." There was no point clarifying the particulars. She gave the man an assessing look. "A gentleman might offer help."

"A gentleman might," he said coldly. "Northmen do not trespass in these lands any more than bandits."

Panic made her reckless and she took a step toward him. "Then you best beef up security. Now, if you wouldn't mind, my companion is injured. We're freezing our arses off. Clearly, I need help. Will you help me? Help my friend?"

Wariness hardened the man's jaw.

"We can pay you." She was making things up now.

"Do I look like I need coin?"

"We're making our way to Eadin Palace," she said, throwing herself at hope. "If you help us, perhaps they can be of service…"

His expression shifted from suspicion to something dangerous and knew she'd made the wrong play.

"What business does a wench like you have with saintly Eadin Palace?"

"Forget it," she said, her throat drying. "It doesn't matter. Please, let me pass."

For a moment, it looked as though he might lunge at her, but something flickered behind his eyes and he stepped aside. Pulse galloping, she clutched the water pouch and stalked past him, resisting the urge to bolt into the trees.

A high-pitched ding echoed from her mobile phone in her back pocket. A calendar notification? She cringed, but before she could cover up yet another oddity, the man grabbed her by the hair and yanked her back against his chest, his free hand pawing at her shorts. She yelped and made to tear herself away but he forced her head back and held up the phone.

"What is this?" he growled in her ear.

Eyes running, she thrashed, straining to grab her phone back. "Give it!"

He released her hair only to clamp his arm about her middle, driving his hip bone into her lower back. "Be still, witch, or I'll—" He broke off as her phone lit up on the lock-screen image of her and Gwen, faces pressed side by side. A photo from the summer; they looked sun-kissed and happy, hair wet from the ocean. Gwen had one eye closed and her nose screwed up, and Ana was grinning.

"Give it back," she cried, lunging over his arm, grappling for the phone. The camera activated and their fumbling clicked a photo.

The bastard gasped. "It is my face!"

"That's right, arsehole." Inspiration landed. "Now I have your soul. If you want it back, let me go!" She rammed her elbow into his stomach, making him release a loud gust of air, but he didn't let go and he didn't relinquish her phone.

"My soul?" he rasped. The photo disappeared as he groped at the screen one-handed. "Where did it go? What is this, you little bitch?"

A thud preceded the man's collapse. He dropped the phone and fell on top of her, pushing her to the ground in a painful spread-eagle. All her bruised bones collided with the stony bank and the air was forced from her lungs.

A grunt signaled the presence of another person, confirmed by the sudden removal of the nobleman from her back. With a choked sob of relief—the knight must have found his strength and come for her—she twisted around.

She inhaled the stench of unwashed skin, blood, and excrement as a white man with blackened teeth bent over her. His skin was leathery, his face scarred and mottled, and his pale-blue eyes shone with malice. Half the side of his head was shaved and roughly tattooed. The rest of his dirty blond hair and beard hung in matted braids, threaded here and there with small bones.

The nobleman lay face down on the bank, blood seeping from an abrasion on the crown of his head. She scrambled on her hands and knees, a scream bubbling in her throat, but the cry was cut short as the wild man rammed his knee into her back and looped a noose around her neck, yanking her backwards, slamming her into the grass. Her skull thudded so hard on the frozen ground that her vision darkened as she scrabbled at her neck, winded and choking.

"Oleg is waiting for you." He grinned at her and spoke with a thick accent that crackled in her ears before clearing. She instinctively knew he wasn't speaking German. Whatever it was, there was no syllable of kindness. "Pretty little demon."

She cried out but he clamped his reeking hand over her mouth and hauled her upright. Deep in the trees, a horse released a rough squeal, and the man swore under his breath. He dragged Ana toward the sound, keeping her off balance. She struggled to find her feet, struggled to haul air through her running nose and bruised larynx. Reeds of air. Not enough. Not enough. She thrashed against him, her burning scream trapped by his hand.

The black-toothed man rammed a savage punch in her stomach, the last atoms of air forced from her lungs. Darkness swept in at the corners of her vision. Her limbs slackened and she drooped in his arms, no longer seeing the forest.

Again, she heard the squealing of a horse, the stamping of hooves on frozen ground. Distantly, she realized she was likely going to be thrown over the saddle, that this stinking, vile man was about to gallop away with her to some hellish place. Oleg's men, the knight had warned her. This must be one of Oleg's warriors come to feed her to a dark god. She prayed her friends had escaped, that the knight's men had gotten them to Eadin Palace.

He dumped her on the ground, her limbs clacking together. She pawed at her neck, sliding a finger beneath the rough rope, and gasped for air.

"Lie still, devil," the man hissed.

A sliver of vision opened up, allowing her to see him tie the end of the noose around a tree. The squealing horse stamped, barely six feet from her head, its hooves reverberating through the ground. It was huge. Glossy. Black as the void. Nostrils flaring. It tossed its head, the whites of its eyes showing. The silken mane shimmered as it quivered all over.

Ana blinked, struggling to focus. The horse wore a gleaming saddle, studded with silver. The quilted blanket beneath was green velvet, an emblem of a turret and tree stitched in silver thread. Its bridle bore the same silver studs. The animal was pristine. Majestic. Furious. It must have been the unconscious nobleman's horse.

The Northman edged around it, muttering dark, unintelligible words. He pulled a fistful of dirty yellow fabric woven with bones and beads from his tunic, and rattled it at the horse.

The horse reared and pawed at the air, jerking away from the rattle. Tethered to a tree, it had little room to maneuver as the man hissed and chanted and shook the bones. Suddenly, the horse crashed its hooves down, as though struck still, its head tucked sharply back against its neck. The eyes rolled and nostrils flared but it didn't kick or scream. The man kept the object raised and spat in the earth at the horse's hooves. The horse stayed frozen, only the rippling of its flanks betraying its terror.

With her fingers looped through the rope at her neck, Ana staggered upright but the tether was too short, making it impossible to stand at full height. Even so, some combination of fury and fear made her determined to fight. She sucked as much air into her lungs as she could and screamed, teeth bared. *Let somebody hear. Let somebody come.*

He sneered and swung so fast she couldn't avoid the back of his hand thwacking across the side of her face. The momentum rammed her against the tree, giving her a sickening dead arm. Her teeth cut into the inside of her cheek and she tasted her own blood. Something came loose inside her.

She'd never been hit by anyone in her life. Not once. She felt shaken to her core.

"Get away from me!" she screamed, eyes watering from the blow. "Don't touch me!"

He leered, letting his repulsive gaze rake down her body—he understood her. She resisted the urge to touch her mouth; it wasn't the time to test the language differences. He pulled a dagger from his belt and licked his lips. Desperate instinct seized Ana and she roared at him again. He'd called her demon, hadn't he? Called her devil?

She willed herself still, rising as tall as she could muster, the rope keeping her neck bent. She pulled her shoulders back, bringing her arms slowly out from her sides, curling her fingers into claws. He wanted a demon? She would be a demon.

She bared her teeth and hissed, letting blood fill her mouth, letting it dribble down her chin.

He stopped where he was, still clutching the bundle of yellow fabric with its rattling bones and beads. His leer faded to caution, a lick of fear behind his eyes.

It was the spur she needed. If he didn't like what he was seeing, if he was nervous, she had to go all in and really sell the performance. Make him believe she had power. Make him believe she could hurt him.

Slowly, she cocked her head and widened her eyes. She shook her shoulders and groaned as though she were being overtaken by a dark power. She let her spittle foam with her blood, making it slip over her teeth, gurgling in the back of her throat. Meanwhile, her thoughts flipped in frantic loops; she needed words, something ominous and deadly, to keep the superstitious prick from laying another finger on her.

"Stay back," she growled, letting her voice drag roughly from her throat, seizing on an outrageous idea, scrambling for the lines she'd learned last year in drama class. She gasped and dropped her voice to an unearthly whisper. "Double, double, toil and trouble … fire burn and cauldron bubble."

A sudden sharp wind blew through the trees and blasted Ana's face. Like the wind she had experienced in the amphitheater before her dream of Saint Ansel, the sound of many wings. The man sucked air through his blackened teeth and ducked into a crouch.

She rolled her head on her bent neck and altered the lines, spitting, "*I* will drain you dry as hay: sleep shall neither night nor day hang upon your penthouse lid; you shall live a man forbid…" *Hell. What next?* "You! You … shall dwindle, peak and pine, something … something…" She was butchering it but the bastard's eyes were round. In a reckless rush, she abandoned the rhyme and snarled, "Your cock shall wither, your—your balls shrivel, and your tongue shall turn to ash—"

Movement in the corner of her eye stalled her mid-curse and the wind died. The knight was leaning against a tree, struggling to stay upright. His sword trailed by his leg, blood coated his left side, and his other hand gripped a small silver cross to his chest, his eyes fixed on her, wide with dismay.

The black-toothed man sprang to his feet, lunging at the knight with his dagger. Ana screamed, nearly strangling herself as she jerked upright. The knight barely managed to raise his sword and block the strike.

The Northman threw the bundle of yellow cloth and bones at the knight's face but the knight swiped it away, kicking it into the dirt. The feral bastard was much smaller than the knight but the knight was weak with pain and blood loss. Ana couldn't believe he'd made it this far. He'd heard her screams. He'd come to help.

She dared turn her back on the fight to grab for the rope but it was tied too tightly to the tree. She scraped her torn fingers on the rough fibers, trying to loosen the noose at her neck. The knot gave a little, then a little more, until she could slip it over her head. Grunts and bellows made her whirl around.

The knight swung his sword in a lethal overarching blow, but too slow to wound the black-toothed man, who ducked away and swung his leg low, catching the knight's ankle.

Ana didn't pause to watch the knight crash; she scanned the ground for something, anything, she could use as a weapon. A broken branch lay to her right. She scooped it up and ran at the Northman, who had slammed his knee into the knight's stomach, his dagger angled for the throat.

Without a second thought, she swung the branch like a base-ball bat. The damp, moldering wood shattered against the side of his head, sending him skidding across the mud-packed earth toward the horse.

Instantly, the horse shook its head as though a spell had been broken. With a ferocious neigh, it pawed the air and brought its hoof down on the black-toothed man's face, smashing his jaw. The man jerked beneath the impact, then lay still. The horse backed away from the body, stamping its feet as though disgusted by what it had felt.

Ana dropped the branch and rushed to the knight, falling to her knees beside him, but he jerked away, rasping, "Do not touch me!"

CHAPTER TEN

L eon's vision blurred and pain lanced his side. His boots skidded through dead leaves in his efforts to move away from the girl. Her hands trembled before her but she sat back on her heels, her expression fraught. Her eyes were red-rimmed, the pressure of the noose having left her freckled cheekbones blotched with color. A raw burn from the rope lashed across her throat. She wiped the blood from her chin on the back of her forearm and held up her hands as though she were surrendering.

When that first scream had echoed through the forest, Leon had lurched to his feet, stars popping behind his eyes with the rush to his head. He'd nearly toppled again, sweeping his sword from the ground, before he staggered through the trees.

When he reached the stream he couldn't find her and panic made him desperate. He'd let her be taken, naked and defenseless, while he'd been lying useless in his blood.

The gouges in the dirt told him she at least had not been taken without a fight. Her screams had risen again, driving him on, praying he wasn't too late. If she was screaming, it meant she was still alive.

But when he'd found them, the girl bound by the neck and Oleg's scout cowering before her, his balls shrank.

She looked possessed. Her voice, her eyes, her foaming mouth, that voice from the pit. He had not understood all the words but he knew she was uttering foul curses in the Northern tongue. His skin crawled with goose flesh and his hand sought the cross at his chest. God help him.

"It wasn't what it looked like," she stammered, her voice rough from the damage to her throat. "It was a bit from a play we studied last year. I'm not a witch."

"Your eyes."

"Anyone can roll their eyes," she said, wrinkling her brow. "I was trying to scare him. He kept calling me a devil and I didn't know what to do, so I just…" She rolled her eyes and clawed the air with her fingers.

Leon frowned and she slapped her hands on her thighs. "Come on. Don't be like that. He had a knife. I was half strangled and I had *nothing* to defend myself with. I thought if I could frighten him, it might give me a chance."

He narrowed his eyes. "It did."

Her shoulders bowed. "You believe me?"

"I believe you were successful … in delaying your abduction."

"But you think it was real? Me cursing him."

"I think you were … convincing."

With a moan, she flopped her face into her hands. "This place. I can't do this. I can't be here. I can't…"

He closed his eyes and sucked air into his lungs, straining his wound with the effort. Whatever the case, whatever the truth, his duty remained. The girl must be taken to Eadin Palace. Let the saints make their own assessments; they were more qualified than him to judge the state of her soul.

But it was impossible to resist that seed of fear burrowing into the back of his thoughts. What if the girl and her companions *were* dangerous and bringing them to Eadin Palace threatened the safety of its halls? Had she not spoken of Eadin as a ruin? Was that a curse? A threat? He would be a fool to trust someone simply because they seemed beautiful, defenseless, and lost.

She was beautiful. Despite her outrageous clothes and foul mouth, the jarring strangeness of her shorn head, her manner and speech, she was beautiful.

"What did you do?" he croaked, gesturing at her hair. It was horribly cropped to just below her ears.

She sniffed and combed back the damp curls hanging on her brow and gave him a narrow look. "You too?"

"What crime?"

"Crime?" She ran a lock through her fingers. "Are you being rude about my hair?"

"It is not uncommon, in some villages, for a girl to be punished in this way. Unless it was treatment for the sweating sickness?"

She shook her head, then seemed to change her mind about whatever snide remark she had brewing and fixed him with her pale-green eyes. "I cut my hair to punish the boy who broke my heart."

He didn't know what to say, but then realization landed. "What do you mean, 'you too'?"

"You didn't see the arsehole sprawled in the mud by the stream?" she said bitterly. "He was rude about my hair too—right before he attacked me."

He frowned and blinked at her. "What man?"

"Sir Benjamin Brandt," a low voice said.

Leon jolted backward, his sword beyond his reach.

The girl swung toward the voice and there came, staggering between the trees, a mud-smeared yet finely dressed nobleman, blood dripping down his forehead, his long sword drawn and dragging at his side. His eyes glazed in and out of focus and he swayed dangerously as he stepped around the fallen body of the Northman. "One of your bandits?"

The girl scrambled for Leon's sword and struggled to raise the blade before her.

"Wait," Leon warned. "Get behind me." But he could barely muster the strength to stay sitting upright.

She ignored him, positioning herself between the two men as though she could protect him. "Don't you come anywhere near me."

Brandt extended his hand and wiggled the girl's musical box. "Give me back my soul, witch."

Leon stiffened and glared at the back of the girl's head. She muttered over her shoulder, "It's not what you think."

"Release my soul," the lord hissed, as he stumbled, then
crumpled to his knees.

Ana yelped and jumped out of the way as the man collapsed, sprawling face first in the mud. With only a brief
hesitation, the girl whipped her strange box from his hand and
hugged it to her chest with a little sob. "We should get out of
here before he wakes up."

"What did he mean, give him back his soul?" Leon
demanded.

"I can explain," she said with a sigh.

He stared at her, too addled with pain to comprehend yet
more dark evidence of unnatural behavior. He was supposed
to trust this person? What if it was a ploy to get her to Eadin,
where she could rob the entire palace of souls?

These alarming thoughts were interrupted by the horse
blowing air through its nostrils as though demanding attention. The girl swiveled on her toes, hugging her arms against
the cold. "There are saddlebags and stuff," she said. "Looks
like a rolled-up blanket too. There might be food. Supplies."

"We cannot steal the man's horse," he said. "It is a hanging
offense."

"He attacked me," she said. "He dragged me by my hair."

"Perhaps he thought you were for sale." As soon as the
words came out of his mouth he regretted them.

"Fuck you," she said softly, and took hesitant steps toward
the horse.

"Careful," he warned. "He looks skittish."

She took a wide berth around the barely breathing body of the black-toothed man. The horse tugged against its tether and stamped its hooves, and the girl stopped still and stared up at it.

Leon watched, drawing shallow breaths. It was a warhorse, an exquisite beast. Why a horse bred and trained for battle would be so agitated struck him as unusual. Unless the Northman had harmed the beast in some way.

The girl approached it slowly, her palms cupped before her as though in offering. He suspected her trembling might be more fear than the frigid cold, but he could not help admiring her courage. The top of her head barely reached the horse's nose. One bite, one kick, and it could kill her.

Shamefully, he wondered if he would be relieved if it did. A problem solved. But he knew he could not make it back to Eadin Palace without her help. He was too weak. He'd lost too much blood. He doubted he could even make it back to his feet without her help. Even now, his vision blurred and he realized he had stopped shivering. He knew that was something to be very concerned about. "Talk to him," he said, panting. "Let him hear your voice. Reassure him."

The horse was huge. Ana felt keenly aware of the bareness of her skin and her defenselessness as she approached. She pictured its teeth clamping her shoulder, its hoof snapping her clavicle, her skull crushed in the mud-packed earth. She saw what happened to the black-toothed man's jaw and knew how easily it could be her. "Please don't kill me," she murmured, heeding the knight's advice.

The horse's big black eyes fixed on her face and it snorted but didn't back away. He was beautiful. His long lashes. His gleaming coat and silky mane. Like something out of a fairytale or dream. She knew little about horses, had only ridden twice in her life. Both times on holiday. Both times miserable.

She offered her palms to the great horse, trying not to think about what people always said, that animals can smell fear. Her nerves were shredded, the hours past a nightmare of impossibilities. She was freezing, in pain, and in throat-closing terror once again; that the black-toothed man would wake up, that Sir Benjamin Brandt would rise and pounce, that the knight would die, and that she was out here on her own, lost from the world she knew.

"I'm sorry I'm shaking," she murmured. "You can probably hear my heart racing. I wish I could tell you that I'm not afraid, but I think you know I'm scared. Look … I'm sorry about before." She nodded at the tree where she'd been bound. "I'm not a witch. I'm a good guy and the dude on the ground with the muscles and the blood, I think he's probably a good guy, too, despite the shitty things he says."

She glanced back; the knight's glazed eyes were fixed on her, his mouth pressed in a grim line. "At least, I don't think he's as bad as the guy with the black teeth or your guy." She raised her hands closer, to the beast's twitching nostrils.

The horse blinked, extending its neck to sniff at her fingers. Muzzle rumpling, it smacked its lips and Ana did her best not to flinch. It touched its nose to her fingers and snorted warm air into her palms.

"Hey, big guy," she whispered, tears springing in her eyes. She dared stroke her thumb over the soft skin of its nose, like warm velvet. He took a step toward her, lowering his enormous head, and she stroked the long bridge of his nose. "Hey, you're so beautiful. How did you get to be such a beautiful boy? You don't even know. You're just a horse. But you're so handsome, aren't you? Yes, you are."

Carefully, she ran her hand down his neck and untied the lead from the tree. Keeping up a flow of soft chatter, she guided the horse the long way around several trees, staying as far from the black-toothed man and Brandt as possible, until she reached the knight. He stared up at her, his ragged breath rasping in his chest.

"Do you think you can get on?"

He gestured to the black-toothed man. "Take my sword. Run him through."

"Excuse me?"

"If he survives … if his companions find him, if he relays what he knows about you, about my injuries, the horse … it will give them a grave advantage."

"You think I could kill him?"

"What do you think Oleg will do to you?"

"*I don't know.* I don't know what his deal is or what he wants. I don't know anything about anything that has happened to me since I stepped foot outside that cave. But I am telling you, for sure, I will not be killing anyone, anywhere, at any time. Are we clear?"

Not trusting him, she released the reins to grab the sword from where it had fallen. Again, it took both hands and the tip dragged, drawing a line in the dirt. "How do you even lift this bloody thing?" She paused. "How do you spell, *Had to borrow horse. Will return asap*, in old-timey German?"

CHAPTER ELEVEN

I t was an ordeal, getting on the horse. He did not have the strength to haul himself into the saddle and the girl was not strong enough to boost him from the ground. In the end, with Leon half collapsed over her shoulder, they staggered back to the stream, where she helped him onto a boulder to use as a step like he was a helpless little lord with his first pony.

Too weak for chagrin, he focused all his energy on not falling off the horse while she raced back to where their few belongings had been left on the ground beneath the cliff. She returned with Leon's gear and stowed it as best she could, emitting a whimper of relief when she found a spare woolen cloak in one of the saddlebags.

Bundling his ruined shirt, she instructed him to tuck it against the weeping wound. The arms of her shirt she tied together into a sling to carry the weight of his arm. Finally, with curses and prayers mixed together, she clambered onto the saddle before him.

"Put your arm around me," she said curtly. He briefly considered arguing against the suggestion for the sake of propriety but he was keenly aware of how perilous the circumstances were.

Despite the shock of proximity, he complied and leaned against her ice-cold back. He did not know what to do with his hand, so he gripped the pommel as it seemed neutral, safe. With a lot of awkward fumbling, she cast the cloak around them, creating a cocoon for their numb bodies.

He peered at the gray sky. "We want to ride northeast."

"I have no clue where that is." She tilted her head back, searching for the sun, her hair tickling his chin. He caught the scent of apple blossom and breathed again. She smelled impossibly good for someone who'd been scrambling in the dirt and fighting for her life.

It occurred to him that he must reek, having not bathed since he left the palace two days ago, his skin itchy with blood, sweat, and mud. She turned pleading eyes up at him, the pale green flecked with gold, and he told himself it was pain and exhaustion that addled his brain.

"It's this way," he finally said, waving toward the slope where they fell. "If we follow the base of the hill, it should bring us out into the valley. We passed a village on our journey to the caves. If we keep a good pace, we might reach it by nightfall. Then Eadin Palace, a half-day's ride beyond that."

As the horse nosed its way through the trees, Leon wrestled with the riddle of the girl. Nothing about her made sense. She seemed practical and quick-witted about using their resources, staunching his wound, making a sling, knowledge of causes of sickness. She'd frightened Brandt, fought Oleg's scout, knocked him down with a branch.

She clearly had some courage; the way she spoke was strange, defiant. That she would look a man in the eye struck him as bold and unsettling. If the display she'd put on for Oleg's scout truly was artifice, it was bravely done.

Yet, it seemed impossible that a girl her age would know of such darkness. Perhaps he was a fool to make assumptions. Pagan practices still haunted the remote regions. She could have seen the possessed in her village.

"You speak the Northern tongue," he said, keeping his tone neutral.

"Apparently." She offered no further explanation and Leon found it irksome but doubted he had the clarity of mind to perform an interrogation.

She sighed. "You think I'm a witch."

He hesitated. "I never said that."

"Your pause did."

She was not wrong. She and her friends may have been the targets of Oleg's vile plans but he could not unthinkingly trust her claims. More importantly, he could not trust himself to judge her claims soundly. He was a soldier, not a scholar or seer.

Still, as a soldier, he had a responsibility to protect the inno-cent as well as the interests of Eadin Palace. He had done a terrible job so far, letting his men down and getting himself into a ruinous predicament. If they could make it to a village, if there was a constable or priest, he could make arrangements to get the girl to Eadin efficiently.

The horse kept a brisk pace but every step jarred through Leon's side. He had lost too much blood; it was a struggle to keep his eyes open and it was getting harder to bear his own weight. If he leaned any lower on the girl, he would flatten her against the horse's neck. Thankfully, a pocket of warmth was growing where their bodies pressed together and he noticed he was shivering again. A good thing.

Thunder rolled behind them. A slate sky boiling to black beyond the hills. It was cold enough for snow. Patches lingered on the open ground. The cloak was a blessing, no doubt—thick, good-quality wool with a fur trim fit for a nobleman—but it would not keep out the wet if rain and sleet were in the offing.

He wondered again about the fate of his men and the girl's companions. Only great danger would have kept them from returning to search for him.

Scanning the shifting shadows of the tree line to his right, his vision kept sliding in and out of focus. Oleg's scouts were out there somewhere. How many others beyond the man they'd left unconscious in the woods with his shattered jaw, he dreaded to guess. They would track their quarry all the way to the palace doors before they gave up.

"What's your name?" the girl asked, her soft voice breaking the silence.

He cleared his throat. "Leon Alvaro."

"Is that … Spanish?"

"My mother was born on the Iberian Peninsula, Catalonia. Her family were traders who settled in Luft."

"Is that where you were born?"

"I was born in Eadin."

She paused as though surprised. "And your father?"

He stiffened and squared his jaw. "He was a Northman who raided her village. But she was brave and fought her way free."

"God," she whispered. "I'm so sorry."

"My mother was one of the few who survived the purge of Luft."

"Wait. Not the Great Northern Purge?"

He could not understand her tone, but it grated him nonetheless, and he did not have the wherewithal to keep the aggravation from his voice. "I suppose it could be called as such. She was there, the night Saint Ansel spoke to the waters and the earth opened, swallowing their enemies."

"Not Saint Ansel." The girl bowed over the horse's neck to groan more loudly. "God, I can't be here. This can't be real."

"I do not understand you."

"What year is this?"

Goose bumps prickled his neck. The question was too strange. Was she about to manifest the demon once more? He gripped his crucifix. "It is the year of our Lord, 1303."

She did not speak.

He waited. Surely, an explanation must follow. Yet, the

horse strode on and while she rocked slightly in her seat, drawing shaky breaths, she offered nothing more.

Finally, to at least fight his oppressive fatigue, he asked, "And your name?"

She shook her head, as though parting with the information struck her as pointless. "Ana. Ana Taylor-Hall."

He wanted to keep her talking to help him stay alert. "This is your father's profession?"

"What?"

"Tailor?" It would explain her access to unusual fabrics but not the nature of their design.

She sighed. "My father is a pilot."

Pilot. The role was not unusual but it struck him then how very far from home the girl might be. Small merchant vessels might traverse the Namen but only so far as Hame. Perhaps he was part of the Hanseatic League. What could bring her so deep into the continent? Unless her father owned a river skiff or barge. "Merchant vessel?"

She gave a mirthless laugh. "You mean boats?"

"What else would I mean?"

"Right, let's say … merchant."

He gritted his teeth. "You find the subject taxing?"

"*Taxing?*"

Despite the strain in his side, he pulled back from her an inch, just to separate their bodies, and she shivered at the rush of cold air that flooded the gap. "Why do you repeat my words in such a fashion? *Taxing.* You think me a fool?"

"You think *me* a witch or a whore or God knows—" She hung her head and rubbed her face as though fighting to keep a grip on her displeasure.

"You do not wish to convey your secrets."

"I *do not wish* to be here. I do not wish to have this conversation. I do not wish to explain my clothes or my hair or my *hurdy-gurdy* or my foul mouth or how I came to be in this place because I *cannot* explain it because I do not know how. In any way. Or by any means that will satisfy *you* or anyone else in this godforsaken hellhole. Because none of it makes any sense."

He opened his mouth to retort but she cut him off.

"The only explanation I can hope for is that none of this is real. That I slipped in the caves and banged my head and that this whole fucking thing is a hallucination. A dream. A nightmare. Perhaps I'm in a coma in a hospital and my mother has flown in and is sitting beside my bed right now, stroking my brow, calling my name. Wake up, Ana. Wake up."

Was she babbling to provoke him? "What about this seems ... unreal?"

"Where do I start?"

"Is not the pain in your body proof enough? The frigid chill in the air? The reek of blood?"

She drew another shuddering breath. "That's what I'm afraid of."

Pain drew him inward, the piercing demand. He could not rally his good sense to reason with the girl. He wanted sleep.

To give in to the dragging weight of his limbs and lie down on the snow-patched earth and not be aware of the world a moment longer.

"*Macbeth*," she said.

He stalled.

"The lines from the play. It was *Macbeth*. Three witches mess with this guy. It's a tragedy."

"I am not familiar with the work. Is it a morality play?"

"Ah ... I guess you could call it that."

She fell silent again and they rode on. Before he realized he was leaning, the warmth of her skin touched his chest. He let himself sink a little closer. She did not shake him off or push him back. She exhaled and there was relief in the sound and slight pressure as she let her weight sag into his, as though she too found comfort and some respite, at least from the cold.

"Snow is coming," he murmured.

She gave a small nod, the back of her head rubbing softly in the hollow where his shoulder met his neck. Apple blossom.

CHAPTER TWELVE

Her backside was sore, numb. She was losing feeling in her feet. The cloak reached to her knees but her calves were raw in the frigid air. The only true warmth in her body was her back, pressed hard against the knight's chest.

A grudging silence had settled on them. Ana kept her gaze ahead, as though she could will a sign of civilization into the landscape. A smoking chimney. Something. There was nothing but trees. The great slope wended onwards beyond sight. The thick forest crept once more up its banks and soon they followed the deer path into the trees.

The size of the horse still frightened her. They were so far off the ground. If either of them fell, it would be bad.

Leon's rough breaths grew longer and she suspected he was close to sleep or unconsciousness. She didn't know what to do. Let him sleep? He needed rest, surely. But what if it was blood loss that was drawing him under? What if his life was slipping away even as they plodded on.

The horse's steps had not faltered but they had been riding for several hours. It too must need rest. Water. Food. How did you feed a horse? There were rough grasses growing in meager clumps here and there but the horse hadn't seemed inclined to stop and eat.

A step over a fallen log jostled the knight in his seat. His heavy head rocked forward, his face sliding onto her shoulder. His hand slipped off the pommel and his weight doubled against her back. He was out. She realized now how much he had been holding himself up.

A mixture of pity and panic gripped her. Whatever he thought of her, the guy was in bad shape and whether or not she wanted to fully admit it, her only hope in horrible circumstances was now passed out.

She turned her head, catching a face full of loose curls. His hair smelled like the forest, like morning frost, which made sense, she supposed, given their situation. His body smelled of dried sweat and blood. Smelled like pain. At least he did not appear to be feverish. That was something. "Leon," she murmured, jiggling her shoulder, but he didn't stir. "Leon?"

Nothing.

She tried to lift his fallen arm but he was a big guy and leaning from the saddle felt dangerous. "Please don't bolt," she begged the horse, releasing the reins. She needed both hands to lift the knight's arm, like lifting his ridiculous sword, and wrapped it around her body. His big hand brushed her opposite hip, his fingers icy.

Without a scrap of shame, she hugged that huge heavy arm—clung to it, to him. She looped the reins around the pommel and let the horse lead the way through the trees, barely giving him an occasional nudge with her heels. She just hugged that arm like her life depended on it. It did depend on it. "Please don't die," she whispered.

She rubbed his skin with her cold hands, willing heat into his bones. Over and over, she stroked his arm, turning it into a mantra of touch, falling into the rhythm of his breathing.

Slowly, slowly, time passed and he seemed to warm, fraction by fraction, or was it some trick of her mind? His breathing grew deeper, less ragged. But the weight of his body was beginning to take its toll on her lower back. She pushed into him, trying to straighten up, but he was so heavy and the shift in weight made her afraid of losing balance.

She tried to ignore the growing ache and kept stroking his arm. It was not lost on her, the weirdness of being so physically close with a stranger. It forced her to think of Will, of Stefan—to notice the contrasts. Stefan was tall and toned, his body kept in careful shape by the gym. Will was taller than Stefan. He was a basketballer. He had shoulders. Fifteen minutes with those shoulders, that molded chest, those soft lips, before hell. She pictured the arrow buried in his eye and jerked in the saddle, shaking herself.

Pain lanced through her back, the muscles cramping. Leon was bigger than Will. She doubted he played sport—doubted he knew what sport was or even the point of such a frivolous pastime. He was built for battle—for war.

He couldn't be much older than her and yet he had the bearing of a grown man. She wondered how many men Leon had killed. How many of Oleg's men. How many battles he had survived. He had scars. Some fine ones on his arm. A deep, jagged one on his shoulder. She hadn't looked long at his naked torso but there had been marks there too among the hard ridges and valleys of muscle.

Perhaps he had a wife. Children. Didn't they marry young back … now? His wife might be fourteen and on to her fifth child. Ana screwed her nose up at the thought. She really hoped he didn't have a child bride and five children because that would be so gross and sad and, *ugh, damn,* her back hurt.

"Horse," she croaked, patting the beast's neck. "We need somewhere to rest."

The glossy black ears flicked back and forth and it snorted with a loud huff that felt strangely reassuring as it picked up its pace. Then, as though her words had tempted it, snow wafted past her face.

"And shelter," she said, her lips trembling. "We need shelter."

The sky darkened quickly as the horse marched on. Snow fell more thickly and her body flagged as Leon's weight pushed her down until she was hunched over the pommel. Even the horse had lowered its head, letting her rest, stoically bearing the burden of the two of them. She lost track of time in her fatigue and wondered if she might have fallen asleep. It was the rumbling of her stomach that roused her and then the sound of water babbling over rocks that made her look up.

"Clever boy," she murmured, stroking the horse's neck, and he huffed a soft snort.

There was a cabin nestled in a small clearing. A cabin built of stone and mud-colored mortar. The wooden shutters of its single window hung precariously from their hinges, a half-tumbled chimney perched crookedly above a moldering thatched roof. The door had fallen inward or had been pushed. There was no smoke. The grass grew long before the threshold. The leavings of a weed-choked garden patch suggested the place had been long abandoned.

The question of what to do next and the burden of how to do it pinned her again to the neck of the horse. She heaved herself up in the saddle, her back straining. "Leon," she said, struggling to clear her dry throat. "Leon," she tried again, louder.

His breath shortened but his head stayed leaden on her shoulder. She pinched his arm and kept calling his name. When that didn't work, she fumbled to untether the water skin on his hip. She took a sip and splashed the rest over Leon's face, jiggling her shoulders roughly. "Leon! Wake up!"

With a watery gasp, Leon's head shot up, his arm around her squeezing tight in a reflex that left her half winded. She smacked at his arm. "You're crushing me."

With a grunt, he let her go and sat back, groaning with pain. "How long have I been asleep?"

"God knows. It's getting dark."

"Hell's teeth," he muttered.

"There you go," she said. "You *can* swear."

Ana almost buckled beneath Leon's weight as she brought him to a tree after his strained plea to relieve himself. The poor guy must have been busting. She looked determinedly in the other direction and pretended not to hear the lengthy, hissing stream. It reminded her of her own humiliating nature wee the night before and that she would need to tend to her own pressing needs once they were settled.

Mercifully and enviably, Leon managed *his* situation one-handed and without fuss. When he had finished, she did not meet his eye and made no comment before helping him stagger to the cabin doorway.

It took a moment for her eyes to adjust to the gloom. Like a miracle, a bed sat against one wall, dingy blankets jumbled on top. The only other furniture was a stool and a small wooden chest. The hearth was caved in by fallen chimney stones, a cobwebbed pile of kindling abandoned beside it. Light glimmered through a ragged hole in the thatched roof, a small pile of snow collecting on the mud-packed floor. Despite the dilapidation, she could almost weep with relief.

She guided Leon to the stool, which groaned as he sat down and slumped against the wall. "Let me check the bed. There could be mice."

He didn't respond, as though the effort of making words might tip him back into unconsciousness. His lips were cracked and his skin chalky. She'd insisted he keep the cloak but it wasn't enough. She needed to get him warm and hydrated and to check the wound.

With the tips of her fingers she pulled the edge of the quilt off the bed, bracing for the skittering of vermin. Nothing. Just cakey dust. She dragged the fabric outside and slung it over a low-hanging branch. It had dark brown stains. Dried blood? She guessed from gruesome childbirth or murder. The thought of letting it touch Leon's wound made her skin crawl.

Next, she went back for the mattress. Canvas stuffed with straw, by the feel of it. Too heavy for her to drag outside to beat. She swiped her arm across it but it just raised clouds of rank-smelling dust. "Shit," she said, coughing into her arm.

Defeated, she sat on the bed to test its structural soundness. It was lumpy and hard and groaned beneath her weight.

"It will do," he said, his voice low and dry.

"It's so dirty. Your wound—"

"It will do." He leaned forward to stand and nearly toppled face first. Ana skidded to her knees to catch him, his face mashing against her neck. He was cold as winter.

"Leon?" she pleaded.

He groaned, and together they hauled him to his feet. She guided him to the bed, tucking the cloak under his backside, levering his weight as he sat.

"Wait." She peeled the cloak from his shoulders and smoothed it over the bed. It was much cleaner than the mattress. Back spasming, she helped him lie down and hefted up his legs. The bed was too short, or he was too big, leaving his feet dangling off the end. The jostling left him drawn and shaking.

She panted, kneading her lower back, and arched, her verte-brae popping like muffled firecrackers. Leon cracked open an eye and grimaced at the noise.

She stared at his broad frame, swamping the bed, and prayed the distribution of weight would keep the wooden slats from breaking. His shirt, tucked beneath his arm, was soaked red. She didn't know how he'd survived hours in the saddle. He was suffering, growing weaker by the minute. Dread pooled in her stomach; she'd have to check the wound. Her brain turned slowly, like a rusted wheel. What was needed first?

Water. Heat. Shelter for the horse.

She laid a hand on Leon's, where her shirt sling kept it braced on his chest. "I'll get water and see to the horse. Are you going to be okay?"

"What is 'okay'?"

"I mean, will you be all right without me?"

"I think it is too late for okay." His lips twitched in a brief wry smile and Ana's eyes welled, grateful for the small sign of courage.

She hesitated, then pulled her phone from her pocket and opened the screen. The battery was at 38 percent. She brought up her photos. The first was a selfie she'd taken with Gwen on the bus ride to Luft. It made her heart squeeze. She cupped it in his palm and showed him how to use his thumb to swipe through the images. "You can check out the pictures on my *hurdy-gurdy*."

His brows bunched together, his bleary eyes growing wide. He slid his thumb across the screen, back and forth, tentative over the first and second image.

"Yeah," she said with an embarrassed huff. "There's a lot of me and Gwen and some less than flattering images in there, but it might help you understand that I'm not from here. I'm not from ... now. Your now, I mean. Or at least it might explain a little why ... I'm different—why my friends are different—from you and the people here."

She paused at the threshold of the cabin, fiddling with the cork of the water skin, and took a moment to watch his face. Lit by the screen, he stared at the photos, lips parted, as he swiped slowly from photo to photo. She chewed the inside of her cheek and hurried to the horse, feeling like she'd just told him she was from outer space, wondering if she was cosmically screwing up history by letting him look.

There were rules, weren't there, with time travel? In movies, there were rules like not telling people what will happen in the future. Her stomach curdled as she considered what Leon had said about the date. 1303. In a few decades the Black Plague would ravage Europe and millions of people would die.

If she mentioned that, they'd definitely burn her at the stake.

The horse grazed on a patch of rough grass at the base of a tree, ripping tufts and munching, a black eye watching her as she crossed the ground. "Hey, big fella," she murmured, stroking his massive jaw. "Look what you found us. You did so good.

What a beautiful, clever boy." He brought his nose up to huff hot breath against her shoulder and his lips bubbled over her skin, making her smile. "Aren't you the sweetest thing?"

She took a moment to figure out how to unbuckle the saddlebags, the bedroll, and the knight's breastplate. A full water skin tumbled out from the bundle and she raced it back into the cabin. "Look what I found," she cried, popping the cork and testing the quality. It was clean and cold but not icy. "This will be better for you than water straight from the stream. It won't freeze you."

Transfixed, he swiped the screen, blinked twice, and dropped the phone. It slipped to the floor and she peered down to find a photo of herself in a bikini. Her long brown hair fell in loose waves down her back. She was standing at the rail of Gwen's parents' beach house in Portugal, half turned, looking back at Gwen with a pouty faux smolder.

There was side boob, ass cheeks—the works. It had been funny at the time. Gwen had been hyping her up, telling her to work it—*work that arse, girl.* She flushed with heat and grabbed the phone, stuffing it in her back pocket. "It was a joke."

He pressed his lips together and failed to meet her eyes.

How could she make a medieval knight understand why it would be acceptable for a young woman to dress like that, act like that, allow herself to be photographed like that without explaining the last 700 years of patriarchal oppression, women's liberation, social change, sexual freedom, body positivity, photography, and, well … comedy?

If he was unsure about her being a witch, he probably now thought she was a whore—and she doubted he was in any state to cope with a diatribe on the stigma of that sort of language or the politics of sex work.

"It's not what you think," she muttered, jamming the water skin into his hands and lifting his head to help him drink. "It was just a joke and you don't understand the context and frankly, I don't need to explain because: a, I have nothing to be ashamed of; b, it's my body; c, it's none of your business what I do with it; and d, you have no right to judge me, especially when I am busting my arse trying to save your life."

"Trying to save *your* life."

She dropped his head so it thudded on the mattress. "Yes," she snapped, jamming the cork back in the water skin and working hard not to cross her arms across her stupid bikini. "My life, too—"

"Ana," he said, breath rasping as he wiped his chin and neck where the water had spilled. His dark eyes flickered with regret as he fixed his gaze on her face. "Forgive me. Please. I *am* grateful for your help. I was not—I am not judging you. I am no judge. None. I was simply surprised. I felt that I had breached your privacy and I was ashamed. That is all." He drew a long breath and winced with the pain of filling his lungs.

She lowered her head and shrugged. "Whatever."

CHAPTER THIRTEEN

Fire crackled in the belly of Leon's breastplate. An ingenious use of the device, to help radiate heat. The girl had set it up among the hearthstones, adding rocks to keep it steady. After struggling with the flint, Ana, muttering curses, had been rewarded with an impressive blaze, cobbled together with the half-desiccated kindling. She'd added some rough logs, found in a stack behind the cabin, where a lean-to offered shelter for the horse and a trough of fresh rainwater.

They were rich in small mercies: food in the saddlebags—hard cheese, stale bread, and a half dozen russet apples, even a small sack of oats for the horse. Ana had gasped over a clean shirt, doublet, and thick woolen pants, yanking them on to find everything far too large. She had rolled up the pants and the sleeves and laced the doublet tight.

Another great boon had been finding two blankets in the wooden chest, far cleaner than the quilt. Fussing once more about cleanliness, she laid it over Leon, leaving the wound exposed.

Had pain and exhaustion not eroded his sense of humor, he would have chuckled at the sounds of her wrestling the horse's saddle from its back. The poor beast had the long-suffering of a saint; truly, the girl knew nothing about horses.

She had fretted about it getting too cold and had asked him what the horse might need. While he thought it would be fine under the lean-to, even in the snow, he knew *their* survival depended upon *its* survival and agreed that Ana should cover it with the stained quilt.

The examination of his wound had proven harrowing for them both, though she had been somewhat mollified by the discovery a small tin of lye flakes in a side pocket of the saddlebags. When he had explained to her it was soap, her eyes had brightened and she rushed to the stream to scrub her hands.

With swift efficiency, she had used his dagger to slice off the bottom portion of the shirt, tearing it into squares and strips to replace the sodden shirt beneath his arm. She managed the close inspection of his injury with a long narrative of expletives, apologies, and pleas to God.

He cried out when she cleaned the wound with a soapy wet cloth. He could not help himself; the stinging almost caused him to expel the raw bile of his empty stomach. Strangely, his loss of control seemed to steel her resolve, her expression turning to flint as she completed the repackaging of his wound. She readjusted his sling then folded a damp cloth to soothe his brow and patted his hand before leaving him to rest.

It was now fully dark and he watched the girl through bleary eyes, the firelight gilding her face, chasing exhaustion into sudden pockets of shadow when she turned her head. He had not forgotten the image from her musical box. It pressed at the corners of his mind. The shock of it. The demand. Fascinating and deeply unsettling.

In truth, he was too pain-addled for lust. Her defiant rebuke had rippled over him like thunder. His regret had come, delayed only by the great blanket of his pain. Shame had settled in his heart. For looking. He felt he had taken something with that look. Something that was not his to take.

He'd seen enough in the images to know she was indeed from another … place, an impossible place, filled with such buildings, carriages, machines, and materials that exceeded his comprehension. Questions piled up in his mind but he did not know how to voice them. One image seemed to depict a scene through a small window, high above the clouds, mountains and valleys far, far below. It had made his stomach drop. A perspective he had only come close to on campaigns where he trekked into the mountains.

"Who is this guy?" Ana said, interrupting his contemplation, as she looked up from the contents of the saddlebags. "This is an impressive kit, right? Like, he was ready for anything." She held up a leather roll, unwound to reveal a kit of fine blades, quills, ink, parchment, and sealing wax. Then she picked up the small tins of salve, herbs, and salt. There was an assortment of daggers, a small pot, a mug. "What do you think?"

He went to shrug but halted the movement, already wincing

at even the slight pull on his muscles. "Sir Benjamin Brandt is a black-hearted wretch. He owns a lot of land and he is in the pocket of Bishop Angeber. Neither of them are friends to Eadin Palace. I heard he killed an entire family and took their holdfast, near Reinwald."

"Children too?" She shook her head, examining the stamp in the leather. It was the same symbol as the one on the saddle blanket. A turret and tree. "And he hates Eadin?"

"I do not know the particulars," Leon said with a sigh. "Something to do with boundaries and water rights. He is not known to be a reasonable man."

"So, we're in a lot of trouble having taken his horse, then?"

"I believe so."

"I left a note and I took a photo of it with my phone in case he tries to make out like we're thieves."

"I doubt it will matter."

"What else could we do?"

Leon shook his head. A heavy cloud of worry rolled over his thoughts. Surely his men had made it back to the palace. He suppressed the gnawing in the back of his mind; they were in a remote forest, in a cabin he could not defend. Ana had done her best to refit the broken shutter over the window and had leaned the door across the entrance, but they were leaking light in the darkness—a beacon to any prowling bandits or scouts. Oleg's warriors were not the only concern in these hills.

"You say you're not a knight," she said, cocking her head. "Where I'm from, you could have been an extra in a fantasy show. Knights and castles … the whole bit."

He pursed his lips and turned his attention to the thatched roof. He did not know what she meant by 'extra'. But his discomfort sat with the issue of knighthood. "A knight is made so by the edict of a sovereign. Or a lord may serve his sovereign in the capacity of a knight. It involves tracts of land, managing tenants, and serving the district — the seat of one's responsibility."

"Which isn't you."

"It is not," he said tightly. He had no intention of explaining the torturous dynamics of his family, his status as bastard born, or the scorn of his stepfather and brothers. "I am a soldier. A palace guard."

She curled the corner of her lip. "Eadin Palace has no lord or lady?"

He sighed. "There are some nobles but their seats serve Eadin."

"Isn't your saint like a sovereign?"

For the first time since he woke up beneath her that morning, he noted a more tentative tone in her voice. "There are many at Eadin who bear the title of saint. Of course, none acknowledged by the church."

"I don't understand."

"Saints are made so after death, prayers answered in their name, miracles confirmed by church authorities."

"But your people use the title?"

"The saints themselves do not, but the smallfolk and those

who have witnessed their works call them so."

She widened her eyes. "Actual miracles?"

"Wonders."

She nodded, a mixture of awe and wariness in her pale eyes. Leon studied the girl, his vision smudging at the edges. He was used to that look of cautious amazement among people who lived outside the palace, beyond the town at its gates, when they heard whom he served.

It stirred his own wariness. Outsiders could be jealous, suspicious, fanatical, and dangerous. He wasn't sure which of those Ana might be. It wasn't simple curiosity in the girl's eyes. "Ansel holds a seat on Eadin's high council."

"Do you think she could help me ... my friends? Go home?"

It disconcerted him but he did not look away. He felt she took his measure and if he were not shivering, he might have begun to sweat. "I do not know."

Finally, she looked down, a quiver in her lips before she pressed them tight. There was something about the line of her jaw, the light painting the planes of her face, and the fire reflected in her eyes that arrested him. If she were really from another time and place, how truly frightened she must be. Lost. Hunted. Confused. Terrified for her companions and burdened with him.

"I am sorry," he said, surprising himself with the admission. "You must be ... overwhelmed."

"I could use less whelm."

He gave a soft snort. "You have been ... brave."

A rough whinny broke behind the back wall. Leon shot up in the bed, sending a slice of pain through his side. Ana dropped the leather holdall and drew one of Brandt's daggers, her eyes round as she backed away from the door. His long sword was in the opposite corner by the hearth. What on earth had he been thinking to let her leave it so far from his reach?

The horse whinnied again. A sharp bleat of outrage, hooves stamping in the dirt. Leon struggled to his feet, the cabin spinning perilously about his head. He willed himself to stay upright and lunged for his sword.

CHAPTER FOURTEEN

I t was an unhinged terror that gripped her—Ana couldn't think. She wanted to howl, knock the door aside, and run screaming into the night. Her body had no filter for the bolts of adrenaline that made her shake. She could barely hold the dagger.

Leon lurched past her like a drunk, pulling his sword from its scabbard. Teeth gritted with the strain, he raised the blade and pressed his back to the stones beside the door.

She fixed her eyes on Leon's grim face. He was sweating, his eyes glazed with pain. A thin line of blood trickled from beneath the elbow clamped to his side. It dribbled into the groove forming the vee of muscle that plunged below the waist of his pants. In the firelight, shadows accented the sculpted detail of his body, but she saw the tremble in his arms and knew it was taking every ounce of his will to stay upright and bear the weight of his sword.

He flicked his chin to the side, silently instructing her to move toward the bed. It took her a moment to comprehend his intention. Then she realized. He wanted her to stand in the open, drawing the eye of whoever might barge through the door. It would be their chance and Leon could attack from behind. Bait. She was bait.

The big horse pounded the ground, bugling in short blasts that made Ana jolt. She knocked aside the objects she'd arranged from the saddlebags. Several apples scattered across the floor.

The horse fell silent. The night beyond the shutters held its breath. No crunch of boots on snow. No snapping twigs or branches. Ana's imagination flooded the quiet with bloodshot eyes, blackened teeth, and cruel steel.

They could see her—through the gaps in the shutters, the wonky planks in the crookedly propped-up door. They could see her right now. Where she stood. Gripping the dagger. Frozen.

Did they know she wasn't alone? Had they seen Leon— lying on the cot before he launched himself across the room? They probably knew he was injured, knew she was vulnerable.

"Oh, God," she whispered.

"Hulloo the house!" a gruff voice called from outside.

Ana jerked against the wall, smacking her head, sending sparks across her vision. Leon's head whipped to the side, the tendons in his knuckles white as wicks on the hilt of his sword. The blade wobbled but he kept the tip pointing at the roof.

"We are brothers from the order of Saint Benedict," the voice called. "We mean you no harm."

His tone sounded weary and a little pissed off.

"We were delayed by the snow and have need of shelter."

A light flickered beyond the shutters. Lanterns? Torches?

"Your names?" Leon barked, and Ana pressed herself back against the stone at the sound of his voice. Was he going to just let them in?

"Brothers Ambrose, Balor, and Granward. We have food. We would be glad to share," the brusque voice said. He sounded like asking for help was supremely aggravating.

"Ambrose ... Ibrahim?" Leon called, his expression shifting to the edge of hope, and he squeezed his eyes shut.

"The same. What of it?" the voice snapped back, garnering terse, whispered responses from his companions, presumably Balor and Granward.

Leon exhaled in a rush, lowering his sword with a clang as the tip hit the dirt. He looked to her for help and Ana came to his side and whispered, "You know this guy? We're just letting them in?"

"I know him," Leon said, his eyes almost crossing.

"There are three of them and less than one and a half of us."

"They are men of God."

"That's not reassuring."

He gestured to the door and, with a resigned sigh, she hefted the boards to the side.

"Praise God Almighty," the voice cried in the clearing, a flaming torch flashing. "Is that you, Alvaro?"

"It is." Leon took a staggering step forward and crumpled against the doorframe. Ana grabbed him, her arms around his waist, as his weight forced her to her knees. His sword clattered to the ground.

"Um ... little help?" she called, her face mashed between Leon's shoulder blades.

CHAPTER FIFTEEN

The brothers crowded the room, their rough brown garments swallowing the firelight, their unwashed bodies adding to the musty reek of the cabin. Leon could not see Ana at all as the men bustled before the bed, peering at Leon's wound. She'd been shunted into the corner by the hearth, the saddlebags and their contents with her.

True to his word, Brother Ambrose and his companions had travel packs of their own and two mules now housed with the great black warhorse beneath the lean-to. Their wagon had fallen afoul of a broken axle and been left in a ditch on the road. A road, apparently, less than a mile east from their path.

Leon was ashamed he had been so incapacitated that he had not recognized where they were. Yet he could not decide if it was better or worse that they had not found the road. Better for avoiding Oleg's scouts. Worse for missing the opportunity of finding help from passers-by.

Ambrose was a large man, almost as tall as Leon, just as broad in the shoulder, but barrel-chested. He had dark skin and a short bristling beard, peppered with gray. His head was completely bald, missing the tonsure of his colleagues. He had fought alongside Leon's stepfather in his youth before the loss of his wife and children in his forties had sent him into the arms of God and a life of service.

Leon's memories of the man were pieced together from brief childhood encounters and later in a season of enforced contemplation when he was sent from Eadin Palace to the Benedictine monastery a year earlier. Ambrose had been his confessor, counsellor, warden, and trainer. He distantly recognized Brothers Balor and Granward from the monastery, both dark-skinned, middle-aged, and solemn, but had had no meaningful interactions with the men beyond silent meals.

"You should wash your hands," Ana's voice piped up from the corner. "If you're planning to touch his bandages."

Balor and Granward glanced back at the girl, but Ambrose cocked his head at Leon. "Handwashing? She is from the palace, then?"

Leon hesitated and decided on half the truth. "We were on our way there when an ... incident separated us from the group."

Ambrose narrowed his eyes. "Not an *Adeline* incident?"

Leon gave the big man a baleful glare.

"What's an Adeline?" Ana asked.

"It is *nothing*," Leon said sharply, unwilling to entertain tales of his past folly. "Brother Ambrose is jesting."

"I certainly am not," Ambrose grumbled, but let the matter go. "Your men left you?"

Leon closed his eyes. "There is urgency to our mission."

"The girl?"

"And her companions."

"And dangers on the road," Brother Ambrose muttered. "The girl is right. We will not touch the wound. Not here. It is filthy." He placed a calloused hand on Leon's forehead. "Fever is upon you, my boy."

"He needs to stay hydrated," Ana said. This time, her head appeared in the gap.

Ambrose turned to face her, his broad back blocking Leon's view. "What is your business in these parts, girl?"

"I … um, have no business," she said. "I was … lost. My friends. We were lost and then Leon's people … found us."

"There is more to tell," he pressed.

"I … um—"

"It is Palace business, brother," Leon interrupted.

Ambrose swung sideways, his head shifting back and forth between them. "And yet it is Sir Benjamin Brandt's warhorse tied behind your cabin and his saddlebags strewn on the ground and his clothes the girl is wearing."

Brandt. Leon shuddered and he doubted it had anything to do with fever. God help them. He felt Ambrose's eyes on his face, reading more than he wished to tell.

"It's not his fault," Ana said, sitting against the wall, as though the strength had drained from her limbs. "I took the horse. We needed it."

Leon shook his head. The last thing he wanted was to have the girl accused of horse theft. "We *found* it," he said, lifting his head to see past Ambrose's bulk, giving Ana a warning look to go along with his lie. "We found it, unmanned. There was no sign of Brandt or anyone else. And we were in dire need."

"Strange indeed." Ambrose lowered himself onto the stool. Granward turned to add logs to the fire, smiling at the breast-plate propped among the stones, while Balor knelt and opened his pack, pulling out a leg of ham wrapped in muslin cloth. Leon's stomach clenched. He was weak but he knew food would turn his stomach. Ambrose studied him and drew a long breath through his nostrils. "That such a man would abandon such a horse."

"Perhaps he fell," Leon said, grasping at the idea. "As we did." And he briefly described their tumble down the great slope in the dark and the wonder that neither of them broke their necks.

"You best hope he fell, boy." Ambrose patted his robe for a pipe. He drew a vial from his pocket and tapped herbs into the pipe's bowl before tamping it down. Balor touched a lit taper to the bowl. Ana screwed up her nose and looked at Leon as though she expected him to stop the man from lighting it. "You best hope he fell," Ambrose continued, "and broke his neck and that wolves dragged his body into a den and picked clean the bones."

A crawling sensation crept over Leon's chest and he began to shiver more violently.

Ana's worried eyes grew rounder. "What's his deal?"

Leon frowned, wishing the girl would speak plainly and not draw attention to her strangeness.

"His *deal*?" Ambrose drew a brief puff on his pipe, only taking the smoke into his mouth, not his lungs, releasing a pungent cloud toward the hole in the thatching.

"This Brandt," Ana said, hugging her knees to her chest. "Is he really bad?"

Balor and Granward exchanged a pursed-lipped look but Ambrose chugged a mirthless laugh, his barrel chest vibrating. "Bad?" Ambrose said. "Bad is perhaps too simple. Let us say, dangerous."

Leon was revolted by the thought of Brandt anywhere near the girl. The thought of how he could use the taking of his horse against Eadin Palace. The thought of how Bishop Angeber would use the taking of the horse as further evidence of Eadin's corruption.

The church had been building its case against Eadin Leon's whole life. His failure would add to it. He would be hauled before the council to explain this mischief. The captain would be expected to discipline him. He might lose his place in the company of soldiers who served Eadin. Find himself exiled and faced with crawling back to his stepfather's estate or whoring himself as a sell-sword to whichever noble would take him.

They would have to leave the horse here, beg the brothers to take them on the mules. Leave no evidence connecting them with Brandt's possessions—

"Calm your thoughts, boy," Ambrose said, peering into the bowl of his pipe and adding another layer of herbs. "We will deal with Brandt."

"Will he try to hurt us?" Ana said, and Leon blinked.

"There is no *us*," he croaked, and she gave him a wounded look before her expression shuttered. Regret speared through him, surprising and sharp, but he shoved it down. He could not afford to have this girl form a bond with him. She would be at the mercy of Eadin's council and he'd likely never see her again once they had returned her and her companions to their home. Besides, she had only stayed with him out of necessity, her own fear keeping her at his side.

"Charming as ever, Leon," Ambrose said.

He could feel Ambrose boring into his skull with those watchful eyes, likely discerning all that he found wanting during Leon's season at the monastery, still wanting in him now.

"Forgive me." He dropped his head back, the moldering thatch blurring in and out of focus above him. "I misspoke. I simply meant you will bear no blame for the horse. It is *my* responsibility. Should Brandt bring a complaint, it will not touch you."

"Leon," she said, the sound of his name making his stomach tighten. He pictured her wide pale eyes glowing in the hearth light. "You can't take that on. I was right there—"

"It matters not—" he began, but Ambrose patted Leon's foot, cutting him off.

"This is not the time or place for such debate," Ambrose said. "Let us take our rest. Tomorrow we make for home. You will sojourn with us at the monastery and when the lad is recovered, you can travel to Eadin Palace."

"We cannot wait that long," Leon said. "She must be taken to the palace without delay."

Ambrose patted his foot again. "What is life, but delay upon delay? Things are rarely as urgent as they seem." He leaned forward and pressed the pipe to Leon's lips. "Draw, boy."

"What *is* that?" Ana demanded.

"All the way down," Ambrose prompted.

Leon drew the smoke into his lungs, even as his thoughts struggled to rally. The potency hit within moments, curling through his limbs, a blissful, leaden weight, drawing him down into the mattress, folding his senses in a heavy blanket. The reins of his consciousness melted in his grip. Only pale-green eyes drifted before him, and the echo of his name like a sigh.

CHAPTER SIXTEEN

A na wasn't aware of falling asleep, curled on the bedroll, back throbbing and too exhausted to process her gnawing fear. She had stared for a long while across the snoring mounds of the brothers at Leon, slumbering fitfully on the bed, his face turned toward the firelight, the echo of pain still pinching his brow. The strong planes of his face had struck her as achingly beautiful—which probably meant she was a horrible person.

Will was dead. That lovely, sweet boy she'd barely gotten to know. She still wasn't over Stefan and this was a life-or-death situation—not an admiring the sculpted features of a medieval palace guard situation.

After a solid bout of self-loathing, she settled on hoping and praying that Leon would live—that Stefan was safe and Will was in a place of peace—in as much as she knew how to pray, before fatigue must have dragged her into unconsciousness.

A crash and flare of light jolted her from sleep. Disorientation made her nauseous and her head spun. She wasn't at home or the hostel. She was thrust, once more, into the waking

nightmare of the wrong place and time. Worse. Brother Balor
was on fire. So was the hole in the thatched roof.

She scrambled back, coughing into her elbow against the
clouds of smoke. Ambrose and Granward flapped through
the cramped space, batting at the hem of Balor's robe, while
a flaming bundle burned on the man's abandoned bedroll.
High-pitched squeals echoed from the lean-to where the
horse and mules had picked up on the clamor.

Instinct kicked in; she rushed forward, smothering the
bundle with her blanket, sending rancid smoke billowing into
the air. Ambrose and Granward crashed out the broken door,
dragging Balor into the night, coughing and hacking. The rush
of freezing air failed to clear the smoke, swirling it higher,
making it almost impossible to see.

"Leon!" she choked, falling on top of him. "Wake up. We
have to—"

A scream from beyond the cabin made her shrink against
Leon's chest. The soldier bucked beneath her, his hand grip-
ping her shoulder, and his gasp filled his lungs with smoke.
"Ana!" he choked.

She coughed and pulled at his arm. "There's someone out
there."

With more strength than she could have anticipated, Leon
surged upright. A rough bark of pain burst from his lips but he
didn't falter, letting her help him to his feet. They shuffled past
the smoking bundle as Brother Ambrose's voice boomed
through the night.

Leon almost tipped into the wall, lunging for his sword, but all he found was the empty scabbard. He swore darkly as she dragged him to the door, her lungs screaming for air. They made it all of three paces across the threshold before she shoved Leon to the frozen ground, behind her.

She didn't have words for the spectacle in the dooryard. Balor and Granward had fallen. Smoke still rose from Balor's robe but Ambrose stood before his brothers with Leon's sword raised in the moonlight, his bulk stretched in a warrior's pose, ready to strike. Two wild-looking Northmen crouched before him, one with a flaming torch and dagger, the other with a bow and arrow poised to fire. He'd already fired. Granward was gasping and clutching his shoulder where an arrow had pierced, right through.

"Give us the girl," the Northman demanded in the common tongue, gesturing toward Ana with his dagger.

Animal panic broke free inside her, helter-skelter through her bones. She tried to scramble backwards, her heels slipping in the snow as though she were about to slide off a precipice. The hard wall of Leon's body thumped into her back but she had to get away. She had to run.

"Be still," Leon hissed against her ear, clamping his arm around her, pulling her tight against his chest.

"Please, I can't—"

"Brother Ambrose will not let them take you," he growled. "*I* will not let them take you."

She didn't argue that Leon likely didn't have a chance of

stopping them but she clung to his arm, like she had clung to it on the horse.

"Give us the girl," the wild man demanded again, his eyes like glimmering pits. The other drew back his bowstring, the arrow aimed at Ambrose's chest.

"Why should we?" Ambrose cried, projecting his voice and brandishing the sword with a flourish as though baiting them. Ana shuddered; did he want them to attack?

"The rest of you will live," the Northman said, rising slowly from his crouch.

"We give you the girl," Ambrose echoed, his taunting voice booming again as though he wanted the entire forest to hear. "And the rest of us live?"

The Northmen exchanged looks, their eyes flitting to the trees and back to the monk.

Ambrose produced a great cracking laugh, then filled his lungs, his shoulders expanding as he tipped back his head and cried out in Latin, as though bellowing to the armies of heaven.

Ana recognized the *Spiritus Sancti*, a prayer—the monk was praying?

Set before the flaming torch, his silhouette loomed above her, his shadow concealing her. The wild men seemed frozen by the display, cowered by the thundering of his voice. Even in her terror, Ana twigged, the monk was putting on a fine show, distracting their attackers from his other hand, which fished in a pouch on the back of his hip.

He pulled out his fist and fine grit spilled between his fingers as he swung his arm around, his prayer building to a crescendo. Then something sparked in his grip and he swept his hand along the flat edge of Leon's blade, setting the whole length alight on "Amen!"

The Northmen jerked back, the bow twanged and Ana screamed as Ambrose slashed the flaming sword down, smashing the arrow from its trajectory. The other lunged with his dagger but Ambrose was too quick for him, slashing in a wide arc that cleaved the man's head from his neck. The skull's thud made Ana flinch and her throat burned with screaming. Leon squeezed her, dragging her back toward the cabin, where plumes of smoke still billowed from the open door.

The remaining wild man took one look at his fallen comrade and sprinted into the darkness. Ambrose charged after him, bursting into another stream of ominous Latin, as he crashed through the undergrowth.

Heartrending squeals rose from behind the cabin and Ana thrashed out of Leon's hold, leaping to her feet. The thatched roof was spitting flames, and the horse and mules were tied beneath the lean-to.

Leon's cry of warning was cut off by rough coughing, but she didn't wait, tearing around the back of the cabin to find the animals yanking at their tethers, braying, and bugling as the thatch rained sparks on their heads.

The warhorse had torn the wooden railing away from one of the support posts but the tether was still tied and his black eyes rolled as he bucked, the quilt trampled beneath his hooves. The mules stamped and hawed and tossed their heads. She ducked under the creaking structure and raced to untie the leads.

"It's okay," she cried, her voice rasping. "I've got you. I've got you."

She cursed herself for the firm knot and fought the leather tie until it came free. "There you go. There you go." The horse tossed his head and leaped backwards, disappearing into the shadows between the trees. "Wait!" she cried, but he pounded away, and she coughed and swore, seeing the black horse go.

A terrible crash signaled the collapse of the cabin roof, sending a hail of sparks into the sky that sprinkled down over the lean-to. The mules thrashed and brayed and tossed their heads. Ana lunged for their ropes but the knots were too tight, scraping her fingertips on the rough fibers. She couldn't get them free.

With a bellow of frustration, she lifted the fallen rail, splinters digging into her forearms. Only one nail held it against the support post and she pulled, throwing all her weight into a backwards-leaning lunge. The nail screeched in the wood and snapped free, sending her sprawling. The mules' hooves stamped by her head and she scrambled again to find her feet. The lean-to swayed, the thatch lighting up. She hauled the rail, pulling the mules clear just as the support posts gave way, triggering an avalanche of fiery thatch.

She came around the side of the cabin as Ambrose strode into the clearing. The flaming sword was sputtering in one hand and a severed head swung from its beard in the other. The picture of some avenging god, his eyes lit with glee. He stopped short at the sight of Ana, leading his mules by the broken rail.

"Nicely done, lass," Ambrose said, tossing the head to the ground beside the other decapitated corpse. "Mind your hair."

Ana dropped the rail and patted her hair, hot embers stinging her raw palms as she brushed them away. Meanwhile, Ambrose wrapped the sword in the folds of the corpse's tunic and slowly drew the blade clean, extinguishing the flames. He looked up at her with a knotted brow. "They were after you."

She hesitated, blinking at the bodies of the Northmen, then nodded.

He gave her a long assessing look, then crossed to Granward, who was sitting up, still clutching his shoulder. Ambrose stabbed the tip of the long sword into the dirt before kneeling to help his friend. Balor came tumbling from the smoking cabin with an armful of their belongings, looking singed about the eyebrows, his cassock blackened and smoldering from extinguished flames. Ambrose shook his head. "You had best tell all, girl."

Her ears rang and her head spun and she turned slowly toward Leon, who was sitting in the snow staring at her; then his eyes rolled back into his head and he passed out.

CHAPTER SEVENTEEN

Ana could have wept for the loss of the black horse as she trudged across the icy drift, focusing hard on not slipping and falling on her arse. They'd been walking since dawn and the day dragged on like a miserable gray dirge. She couldn't relax. Every snapping branch made her jump, every cawing bird or darting shadow.

She led the mule carrying Leon, who slumped, barely conscious, against the poor beast's neck, his boots nearly scraping the ground. Brother Ambrose walked beside her, smoking his pipe, while Balor led the other mule, likewise burdened with the hunched form of Brother Granward, who hugged his arm in a sling. The monks had taken the news of the Northmen's prophecy with restrained alarm and had kept their blades at hand ever since.

They had made slow progress on foot, staying away from the road, with frequent stops to give the mules and their injured companions relief. By the afternoon, Brother Ambrose felt it might be prudent to aim for a nearby village. A little hamlet by the name of Ulmenholz. There, he hoped they might find room at an inn or barn, a dry place to sleep, and the prospect of sending a message for aid to the monastery or perhaps Eadin Palace itself.

While Leon's wound had stopped bleeding, his skin was clammy with fever and he hadn't been able to keep down any food. Sips of the brothers' beer was the best Ana could coax him to take. It frightened her, the retreat in his eyes.

"Have you been to Eadin Palace?" Ana asked the monk as he puffed on his pipe—a different tobacco than the potent sedative he'd given Leon, judging by the smell.

Ambrose arched a bushy brow. "Naturally."

She studied his mischievous eyes and found a door cracked open. "Leon says Saint Ansel lives there."

"Among others."

She shook her head. "Living saints?"

"The church would not use such a term, but it is commonly used by the smallfolk. The correct term is thaumaturge." When she returned a blank stare, he explained, "A wonder worker."

"Miracles," she whispered.

"Sometimes."

"There are others? Like Ansel?"

"Seers, scholars, healers, artisans, warriors, poets, peasants, and princes."

"Princes?" Her lips parted in wonder.

"Well." He weighed the air with his palm. "Fellows with land and sacks of gold."

Ana felt like she was trying to hold a slippery fish, flapping between her hands, struggling to reconcile the monk's testimony against her limited knowledge of medieval Europe. Her history classes painted a far grimmer picture of ignorance, superstition, the chokehold of the church, the suffering of peasants and serfs oppressed by feudal lords. And what about imminent plague?

She shuddered.

The Eadin Forest field trip guides had failed to convince her of the palace as a bright burning oasis of enlightenment. "Where I come from," she began, "we've heard of Ansel."

Ambrose nodded. "Do tell."

She fixed her eyes on the path between the trees, wide enough for them to travel abreast. She felt suddenly in the spotlight, as though the brothers, Leon, the mules, and the forest itself were listening. "About the Northern Purge and the Namen River."

The monk drew deep upon his pipe and blew smoke toward the bowed gray belly of the sky. "Leon's mother witnessed the deed herself."

Ana darted a look at the young man on the mule, his eyes shut tight and brow knotted as though he was using all his strength to concentrate on staying alive. She met the brother's eyes. "He mentioned it."

Tingling swept up her neck, behind her ears, as a sharp wind funneled between the trees. She put her hand out to the mule, resting her fingers on the coarse hair, as though needing the reassurance of solid things.

"What else have you heard?"

"The Caulder Mill fire, the maiden and the cinderwyrm, the barley harvest."

He smiled and nodded. "Fine tales all."

Thick tree roots broke up the ground and they moved into single file. Ana let Ambrose go ahead, grateful for the break from the big man's searching gaze. She led the mule, and Leon cracked open a warning eye. She needed to be careful.

"How is Eadin Palace allowed to exist?" she asked Ambrose's back.

The big man shook his head. "It isn't."

A long pause followed and she glimpsed Balor looking back at Ambrose with sad eyes and pressed lips. "Is the palace in danger?"

"From the Holy Roman Church, from the Teutonic Knights and raiding Northmen, from Sir Benjamin Brandt and a collection of lords whose greed and envy are set against the walls of Eadin Palace."

"Why haven't they tried to destroy it?"

Ambrose shrugged. "Eadin has many loyalists, none so passionate as the surrounding town and villages, farms, crofters, our own monastery, and a half dozen local lords who would rally significant numbers and resources to its defense. Even if the church authorities were to press its advantage, they would find compelling resistance."

"And if the Pope snapped his fingers?"

"The sultan would likely send an army to defend Ansel and

then there would be a holy war." Ambrose hefted his shoulders. "Crusades have fallen out of fashion."

"There's a sultan?"

He paused in his path and gave her an odd look. "The Sultan of Sörgüt, who built the palace for Ansel."

She was utterly lost now. She didn't know anything about a sultan's involvement. Though, they hadn't gotten far in their field trip.

"You are not familiar with the history?"

"My education is a bit … patchy, where Eadin is concerned."

"It is a fine tale," Ambrose said, with a surprisingly dreamy sigh.

She was about to press him further when Balor called back to them. "The palisade!"

"Praise God," Ambrose said, lengthening his stride, the tale forgotten.

Ana considered asking what a palisade was, when she spotted the high fence posts through the gap in the trees. Sharpened to points, the posts were lashed together, braced, and planted firmly in the earth, forming a great wall at the head of Ulmenholz village. A medieval village. Like a movie set.

She followed close behind Ambrose as they left the trees and crossed the snow-patched grass to join the road to the open gates. A wagon trundled out of the village, driven by a man in a plain belted tunic and pants, his cap tied beneath his jowls, a coarse cloak around his shoulders. He turned to look at them as they approached and tugged on the reins to stop his sturdy ponies. "God be with you," he called. "Brothers, you are sorely needed."

He clambered down and waved at the gate, jogging toward the monks with a drawn expression. His weathered skin was pocked and pale, making his age hard to guess. He crossed himself and crumpled to his knees before Balor, clutching at the singed hem of the monk's robes. Balor sketched the sign of the cross above the man and helped him to his feet. "What troubles you, my son?"

"I was about to make for Eadin Palace. We have need of a saint, for there is devilry in the village and the people are in uproar. My wife was injured in the troubles."

"What happened?" Ambrose asked, his ear cocked toward the village, listening for the sounds of strife.

"It happened two nights ago when the earth shook. Our holy fool, young Felix. Madness overthrew him. It had been growing in him all sennight since the devil's lash tainted the sky."

Ana frowned and looked to Brother Ambrose. "Devil's lash?"

"The red star," he said, pointing at the gray sky.

Ana stopped breathing and looked up.

The Eldi Comet. Here. Now.

The sky had been heavily overcast since she stepped out of the caves. Not a glimpse of sun, moon, or stars. Not even a wink of blue. Was it all connected? The comet, the solstice, the earthquake? Is that what pulled them through time? That and the Northmen's prophecy? Goose bumps flashed over her skin and a watery feeling took strength from her knees.

The villager nodded, as though Ana's reaction was shock at news of the fool. "He took to the roofs, bawling and muttering and carrying on, like the star was talking to him. A voice only he could hear. No one could get him down. Rampaging from cottage to cottage. And the devil quickened him with frightening strength and a foul tongue. He caved a roof beam in our croft and it struck my poor wife." His lower lip quivered and tears welled in his eyes. "She breathes still but she has not woken from the blow. I am taking her to the healers at Eadin."

"God, have mercy," Balor murmured, and the other two monks repeated the phrase.

Leon heaved himself upright on the mule and almost lost his balance. Ana snapped out of her stupor and grabbed his good arm. "Steady."

"I am a soldier from Eadin Palace," Leon said, his voice slurring and husky with pain. "My name is Leon Alvaro. The brothers will see to the needs of the village but if you could carry a message to my men, they would reward you with silver to hear from me."

"Would you be willing to take Brother Granward, also?" Ambrose gestured to the monk, who looked gray-faced, hunched over his arm in its sling.

"What dark troubles have you faced in the forest?" the man asked, his expression growing wary, as though sniffing the danger they brought with them. "The village could not stomach more than has already been served."

Leon gave Ana a meaningful look. He thought her arrival was connected to their difficulties too?

She squirmed inside, hating the thought that he might be right. She didn't know how to process any of this. The Eldi Comet was here now too ... it was too much.

"Bandits," Leon said.

The man looked back at his wagon.

"We dispatched them," Ambrose said, broadening his stance, as though he might renew the man's courage.

The villager drew a resigned breath. "We would count it a blessing if the brother would travel with us. Though we have few—"

"We could go with him," Ana said. She didn't fancy getting involved with whatever "devilry" was afoot with the village or their "holy fool." Besides, the village looked small and flammable and the fence struck her as little deterrent if Oleg's scouts were on her trail. She said to Leon, "*Your* wound needs proper cleaning. Proper treatment."

Leon's bloodshot gaze flickered over her face. "Brother Balor, would you help Brother Granward onto the wagon while we confer?"

Ana bristled. He was going to shut her down. She looked to Brother Ambrose for support, but the grizzled monk folded his arms and rolled his lips into a tight line.

Out of earshot, Leon whispered, "Ana, I will not risk

parting you from Ambrose and Balor. They are warriors and men of the cloth. They can protect you better than I can."

"Leon is right," Ambrose said, lifting his chin. "The roads are not safe for you and Leon is not strong enough to protect you or this villager and two more injured passengers. If Oleg's scouts came, your presence would place this man and his wife in grave peril."

"And what if they come to the village?" she snapped. "They didn't hesitate to burn the cabin and this place is built of bloody matchsticks."

Leon winced at her swearing and gave the monk an apologetic look, but Ambrose simply raised his eyebrows.

Ana refused to feel guilty, shivering at the thought of the men hunting her and the prospect of more delay. While she wasn't in a hurry to face interrogation at Eadin Palace, the chance of being reunited with Gwen and people from her own time and place— she longed for it. Most of all, there was the impossible hope of Saint Ansel that had taken root in her imagination. A reckless and desperate hope for a miraculous solution to her problem.

"You could go without me," she said to Leon, surprised at how difficult it was to make the suggestion. She'd known the guy less than forty-eight hours and yet, despite everything, Leon made her feel … safe.

Safe was a ridiculous word. She clearly wasn't safe. Not here. Not in this time. But he was formative in her experience beyond the cave and she found comfort in being near him. While she liked Ambrose and Balor, and she was fairly sure they would protect her, parting from Leon frightened her more than she could articulate.

"She is right," Ambrose said. "We would see her safely to the palace. We might be able to loan a horse."

"I have no doubt." Leon hung his head. "But it would be a dereliction of duty for me to leave her—she is my responsibility."

Responsibility. The word clanged inside her head. She was his responsibility. Not his friend. Not his traveling companion. This wasn't a road trip. This was a disaster. And he was simply a soldier who had found himself saddled with her. She shut her mouth and said nothing more.

The villager called from the wagon, "What message would you have me convey, sir?"

They made their way over and Leon managed to stay upright long enough to give his instructions. He kept it simple: he was injured and he needed a soldier called Micah to send a unit of men to Ulmenholz to accompany him and *his charge* back to Eadin as quickly as possible.

The man repeated it back to him and nodded earnestly. Balor and Ambrose prayed for a safe journey. Ana tried not to stare at the poor man's wife, bundled in pelts, looking as though she was simply asleep in the wagon bed. Granward waved as the ponies ambled away, with a "God save you."

She hoped he would.

CHAPTER EIGHTEEN

S haken by news of the comet, Ana stayed close to Leon and she quickly discovered the benefits of traveling with monks. The guards at the gates welcomed the brothers with the same desperate relief as the man in the wagon.

They explained the "holy fool" was usually little trouble, sleeping in haylofts or wandering about muttering to himself harmlessly. The constable liked to keep him as it stirred faith he might be uttering the mysteries of heaven. Now his behaviour had taken a dark and violent turn and none could restrain him.

Ambrose listened and nodded, assuring the brothers would help and deftly introduced Leon and Ana as their happen-chances companions, saving her from having to speak at all. A young knight and his *squire* beset by bandits in the woods.

Close enough. She guessed squire meant boy servant, or some such, and Leon must have been suffering enough that he didn't balk at the title of knight. The guards didn't question it, agreeing that times were dark and it was a crime that honest Christians couldn't travel the roads in peace.

Apparently, monks and a knight ensured lodging. A brief parade of the main road under the watchful stare of harried townsfolk led them to a small cobbled square with a charming stone well, surrounded by several buildings more sturdy and stately looking than the stout thatched cottages that lined the road from the gate.

Ana struggled not to gawp. She wished she could snap some photos but her phone was almost flat and she didn't fancy being burned as a witch.

Her hungry eyes devoured the details, while her sense of smell was assaulted left and right. The reek of moldering hay, animal excrement, the fetid pall of a tanner's yard and butchered meat had her working hard not to retch. She pressed the back of her hand to her nose and breathed through her mouth, but oily smoke, billowing from braziers and chimneys alike, coated her tongue with the taste of charcoal and rancid fat.

There were no women in the road or square. A few men and grubby-cheeked boys. She supposed wives and daughters might be tending hearths, but there was something else in the atmosphere that kept Ana vigilant, her eyes darting to rooftops as though the holy fool might leap screaming onto their necks if they weren't on alert.

Every man she spotted carried a pitchfork, short sword, or some sort of implement for brandishing, and she wasn't the only one scanning the rooftops.

In the square, there was a little stone church, beset with arches, a steeple, and even a small rosette window of stained glass. Opposite squatted a building with a stack of ironbound barrels that suggested a tavern—a short walk to find penance for those who might overdo it on the ale. There was a large barn or stable where several of the pitchfork men gathered disheveled beneath the eaves like half-mauled chicks awaiting the return of a greedy fox. They peered at the monks with weary relief dawning on their faces.

Ana kept close to the mule, almost pressed against Leon's leg. The soldier was doing his best not to slump on the animal's neck and the effort made his lips pale. The guards brought them before a tall stone building they called the constable's house, with broad steps rising to an arched door.

One of the guards leaped up the steps as though he were about to proclaim salvation and rapped his knuckles on the ironbound wood. The men with their pitchforks took it as a cue to gather also, expectation lighting their tired eyes.

"What news, brothers?" a lanky fellow called. "Have you come to bring aid?"

Brother Ambrose turned, his expression careful. "God keep you, my sons. We are as much in need of your help as you appear to be of ours."

The door cracked open. "Piss off!" a voice griped from within the house before the door shut again with a resounding *clack*. The guard shot an apologetic look at the monks, while the men who'd gathered behind Ana, Leon, and the brothers muttered in disgust.

"Constable Hueber!" the guard called, rapping his knuckles on the door again. "Help has come! Two servants of the Lord and their companions."

A protracted pause embarrassed the assembled men but the

door cracked open again and a thick head thrust through the gap. Rheumy eyes made quick calculations and the pinched mouth opened and closed like a disgruntled goldfish. This guy was in charge?

"You brothers are welcome, I suppose," Hueber said, though his expression made the greeting doubtful. He jabbed a finger at Leon and Ana. "Those two can find a croft."

Balor and Ambrose exchanged a look. "*Those two*," Ambrose began, "are our charges. Sir Leon serves Eadin Palace. He is badly injured and his wound requires attention."

Affronted, Hueber stepped into the doorway, his pouchy face quivering about the jowls. "There are no knights at Eadin Palace."

"Sir Ransome Wade is my mother's husband," Leon croaked, reluctant but clearly in enough of a bad way to play a "do you know who I am?" card.

Impressed murmurs from the pitchfork guys suggested to Ana that Sir Ransome was indeed an impressive card to play.

Hueber thrust his chin forward. "*Your mother's husband? And you're the bastard get of God knows who.*"

Ambrose took a step up, bringing his hand to rest on the hilt of the sword strapped to his hip. Leon's sword. "You will be compensated for your trouble when Leon's men arrive from Eadin Palace to escort him home."

"What faith can I place in a lying monk?" Hueber spat. "*Sir* Leon, you called him."

Ana braced for Ambrose to draw the sword and fillet the stroppy bastard on the threshold. Astonishingly, the monk placed his hand on his heart and lowered his head a fraction. "I meant only to honor my injured companion for his faithful service to the Lord, giving up rank and title for Eadin Palace."

"Let them in!" a man called from behind Ana.

"God Almighty, Hueber," another called. "You've an answer to all our prayers on your very doorstep!"

A general clamor of agreement swept up behind them and it felt good to Ana to have the favor of the crowd, if not the man in charge.

Hueber snarled but jerked his head around to yap into the hall, "Sarah, you useless wench. We have guests."

The guard looked faint with relief and ushered them toward the step, while several men relinquished their pitchforks to help Leon down from the mule. Ana collected the saddlebags and kept her head down, following the procession up the steps, when a crash and cry from across the square stalled them. They turned as one as a commotion rose from the stables.

Shutters high in the stable loft slammed open, wrenching one from its hinges. A naked young man stood in the gap, gripping the window frame one-handed, the broken shutter clutched beneath his other arm. His filthy body bore the marks of injury, bloody welts rising on his arms, thighs, and abdomen, suggesting the cruel strokes of pitchforks. His flesh clung tight to prominent ribs and hollow cheeks. Shadows haunted the deep sockets of his blazing eyes.

"Spirit!" the man cried, spittle flying. "She said you would come!"

The pitchfork men who were not helping Leon jogged across the square, their eyes lifted to the naked man. One called, "Felix, come down from there. You'll do yourself an injury!"

The fool didn't look at them, his gaze fixed instead on the group gathered on the constable's steps. He flapped the broken shutter and Ana had a horrible feeling he was gesturing at her.

"I told them! I told them, she said you would come!" He tossed the shutter with such force it somersaulted through the air and crashed against the pitched roof of the well.

Ana flinched and the men around her muttered, "God save us," and crossed themselves.

The naked man cupped himself between his legs and shook his balls at the pitchforks below. "One of seven! One of seven!" He pointed at the sky. "She knows your name! Little thief! Little witch! She means to stuff herself! Grow fat on your marrow, and bones!"

Ana flushed and gripped the saddlebags tightly, peering over the bundle like she might use it as a shield.

"She knows your name, Ana!"

Ana swayed and the tingling that swept up the back of her neck, behind her ears, turned to a ringing drum.

"One of seven! One of seven!" he cried. "She sent her dogs to sniff you out." He tipped his head back and howled, long and high, before flinging himself back inside the loft.

"Well." Hueber smacked his lips together. "I suppose that gives you a taste of things."

CHAPTER NINETEEN

L eon collapsed on the bed, dizzy and nauseous. His stomach turned and he lurched up again. Ana barely found a receptacle in time, an empty piss pot, pulled from underneath the bed. The villagers who had supported him up the stairs exited at the first sound of his heaving, though his empty stomach produced nothing but yellow bile.

Ana knelt before him, combing back his lank curls with trembling fingers. He sat up, panting, and studied her haunted face, but she wouldn't meet his eye, setting the pot aside.

She had looked like *she* might have thrown up on the front steps, at the sound of her name ringing out over Ulmenholz's little square. *She knows your name, Ana!* The impossibility of the girl's name on the fool's lips, coupled with his reference to the number seven and the black heat of his eyes, the wild foaming of his mouth, was chilling.

She had the look of cornered prey, her gaze skittering from the door to the window as though ready to toss herself from the third story at any moment.

The uncanny words rattled inside Leon's throbbing skull. *Little thief. Little witch. One of seven.* He thought of the prophecy. *Seven to appease. Seven to mend. Seven to sow. Seven to rend.* Is that what the fool meant?

Leon felt as far from Eadin as he had ever been. Separated from his men. Separated from the saints. Locked in the fever of his body. Weak as water and utterly pathetic. He was helpless to do *anything*.

Wordlessly, Ana began peeling his sweat-damp clothes away and he did not resist, even when the serving girl came into the narrow room with a heavy bucket of steaming water. Sarah, Constable Hueber had called her. A sturdy, round-faced girl who covered her mouth to hide crooked teeth. Pale curls wisped from beneath a crisp clean kerchief and her cheeks flushed at Leon's naked chest.

"I'll need another," Ana said, her voice a husky croak. "If you have it. And drinking water."

The maid nodded, gesturing to the flaming hearth opposite the bed. "I will bring a pot for your fire." Her eyes slipped over Leon, equal parts scandalized and eager, as Ana helped him lie back on the bed. "Is there anything else I can fetch your lordship?" she asked him.

"I am not a lord," he said, his voice rough with pain.

"He's not been able to keep anything down," Ana put in.

"Broth?" Sarah suggested brightly, touching her curls, biting her lip. "I have some honey and ginger tea for fever."

"And any clean linen you could spare," Ana said, her voice suddenly hopeful. "I need to clean the wound and rebandage his side."

"Right you are, I will be back in a wink." Her eyes took another greedy gulp of Leon's torso as she backed out the door. He didn't have the strength to care.

"She's keen," Ana said, not looking at him, a weak attempt at deflection. She unlaced his boots, tugged them free, and reached for the belt of his pants. He grabbed her wrist.

"Is that necessary?"

She blushed fully and if he wasn't sick with pain and fever, he might find the sudden bloom in her cheeks charming and her proximity to his crotch distracting in the extreme. He let the notion slip past. A demon-possessed man, a man bereft of reason, had predicted Ana's arrival in Ulmenholz. It was in no way reassuring.

"The brothers can get you undressed and under the covers." She rose to her feet and turned to the window, gripping the frame. The gray afternoon outlined her silhouette, yet she seemed frail beneath the bulky clothes. Shame smote his heart for pushing her away. She was all alone and far from familiar shores, lost in dark, open water. The young fiend's words, moving like the shadow of huge, unspeakable things just beneath the surface.

Hadn't she worked to keep him alive the last two days? He owed her more gratitude than suspicion, but shame or no, suspicion burned in his throat and her otherness seemed even more pronounced in the wake of the holy fool's declaration. *Little thief. Little witch.*

The door opened again and Ambrose entered, closing it behind him.

Ana turned, her eyes huge with fear and uncertainty. Ambrose stared at her. Leon stared at her. When the monk said nothing, Leon stared at him, staring at her. Finally, Ana broke the silence.

"He needs to get out of those damp clothes."

Ambrose did not reply but he crossed the wooden floor slowly and Leon clutched the coarse blankets covering the bed. Surely he wouldn't strike her? Ana shrank against the windowsill.

Ambrose drew a small vial from his sleeve. "Ana, would you drink this for me?"

"What is it?"

"Holy water."

She gave a small brittle laugh. "I'm not a witch."

"I believe you, lass, but it will set your mind at ease and the lad here, fretting on the bed."

Her brow crumpled and she shook her head and took the vial, uncorking it carefully and emptying the contents into her mouth. She gave Leon a defiant look, tipped her head back, gargled ostentatiously, and swallowed. The monk snorted. "Will that do, lad?"

Leon ground his jaw, ashamed anew to find himself flushing with relief.

"Shall I make her recite the Lord's Prayer?" Ambrose asked.

"Our Father, who art in heaven…" Ana began.

"No burning or smoke pouring from your throat, then?" Ambrose cocked his head.

"It won't be necessary," Leon ground out, staring hot-cheeked at the ceiling.

"Here, lass, best put this on for safety's sake." He pulled a thin leather cord from his pocket with a small silver crucifix. "Holy silver, blessed by the Pope himself."

She shook her head, sniffing and teary-eyed. She didn't argue but pulled the necklace over her head, cupping the icon in her fingers. "I went to Catholic primary school in New Zealand."

"Zeeland?" Ambrose nodded curiously, before turning to ruffle Leon's hair. "Cheer up, my boy. Your men will be here by morning. Your girl is no witch and we will manage poor Felix before the day's end."

CHAPTER TWENTY

I t was fully dark and creeping toward midnight. Ana sat helplessly on the rug before the hearth, watching Leon wrestle with sleep. Earlier, the brothers had stripped, washed, and rebandaged the open wound. It had not traveled well, swollen and seeping with worrying streaks of red signaling infection, yet the brothers settled him beneath the sheets without fuss. Sarah had returned with a pot of water, a bowl of broth seasoned with healing herbs, and the honey-ginger tea.

The girl had lingered at the threshold, mooning over Leon, deep in some imagined romance, before leaving with a sigh.

Ana had managed to get him to take about half the broth before exhaustion sucked him under and she was ashamed to admit she was relieved when he fell asleep. The awkwardness between them had only been amplified by Ambrose's pronouncement that she wasn't a witch. Guilt on his part and resentment on hers.

After dinner, Brother Ambrose had reported that Felix was missing from the stables and the villagers couldn't find him. The village priest was abroad, visiting holdfasts further afield, and the constable was grudgingly grateful for divine assistance.

The report unsettled Ana, who hadn't left Leon's room since they arrived, terrified Hueber, or anyone else, might get a solid look at her. Sarah had brought her food, a thick slab of fluffy pastry stuffed with fatty meat, egg, onion, and spinach, which she devoured. Now it sat heavily in her stomach and her gnawing thoughts were a torment.

Stiff from sitting so long, she rose and crossed to the window, opening the shutters to look out upon the night. She scanned the rooftops for signs of movement. A crescent moon sliced through a break in the clouds, carving the rough outline of buildings in silver. Before they went into the caves it had been a full moon. It made no sense.

At least she could see some stars and sure enough—there. A red flare caught her eye and her stomach dropped. Scudding clouds obscured it. Then it winked again. A red smudge, so bright in the night sky, just as she'd seen it above the ruins of Eadin Palace. The Eldi Comet.

Her throat ached with trying not to sob. She remembered Stefan rattling off facts from his stargazer's app. Once every 700 years. It seemed impossible that mere days ago her only concerns were a broken heart and the humiliation of academic failure. Now she was lost in time and running for her life? Fallen into some magical trap.

Had they really tapped into something … supernatural? In a way, she thought of time travel as something that science might be able to explain eventually. Weren't there theories about the space–time continuum? Wormholes? But prophecies and demon priestesses ... The very idea of being one of seven, foretold by God knows what—where was the science for that?

She tried to imagine how Stefan was reacting to all this. The way he'd roll his eyes. But the facts were piling up. They were already experiencing the impossible; they'd passed through time. The comet was right there. The devil's lash. A gibbering stranger knew her name. Knew she was a thief. Thought she was a witch. Her breathing grew shallow and she gripped the windowsill to steady herself.

Then a shadow shifted in the square, drawing her eye.

A huge black horse stood by the well and set her heart racing. "Leon," she whispered. "I think Brandt's horse is in the square." But Leon lay twitching in the firelight, lips muttering wordlessly.

She stared at the horse. How was it here? Did the guards admit it through the gate? How had no one seen it? Then again, it was late and even the tavern had remained closed, entertaining no patrons, she assumed because of fear of the holy fool. She leaned out the window for a better look. The horse's black coat shimmered in the moonlight, mane and tail catching in a sudden gust of wind. She needed to know it was him.

The wind grew insistent and tingling bloomed behind her ears. Dizziness struck her anew and she stumbled back, catching the top of her head on the window frame. Dazed, she fumbled to close the shutters but the wood stuck. Icy gusts whipped the heavy curtains, stirring the hearth into an uproar of flames, and she yelped and ducked beside the bed.

There had been an unnatural wind in the caves, right before chaos and death. The sense memory shook her. Was it more than wind? Some power or malice behind it? Her scalp prickled and she shrank against Leon's shoulder.

Heat radiated from his skin. "Shit, Leon, you're burning up."

His eyelids flickered and his head rocked from side to side but he was lost in fever. Tentatively, she touched his face, palming his brow with a trembling hand; the other she pressed to his chest, where his pulse beat fast beneath her fingers. "Leon, please."

A fresh surge of wind shoved into the room, billowing the curtains halfway to the ceiling, blasting her face, taking her breath, filling her lungs with ice and fire. A sob tightened her throat and she whispered, terrified some *thing* ... some power might be listening in. "For the love of God, Leon, get better," she begged. "I can't be here. Do you hear me? You need to get better. Now. *Please.*"

An image coalesced in her mind's eye, as though the fever were taking form, like a gargantuan leech made of pulsing shadow, its obscene maw sunk in Leon's chest, sucking at his life force.

She groaned and shook her head. Was she so strung out she was losing it? Heat rose suddenly in her chest, reminding her of the blue spark from her vision in the caves, and with it came an inexplicable rush of fury. She *was* losing it. Tears sprang in her eyes and she hissed Tears sprang in her eyes and she hissed at the vision, *"Piss off!"*

Leon bucked beneath her hands and she stifled a squeal, nearly tumbling to the floor. The hearth flames leaped in unison, warping her shadow on the wall behind the bed, forming a squirming mass that lunged toward the ceiling, winking out of existence, before the shape became her own once more. Instantly, the wind died.

She gaped, ears ringing in the silence, the burning easing in her chest.

What the hell just happened? None of this was normal. The wind. Seeing things. What was she supposed to think ... to believe? That magic was real? Miracles and spirits and prophecies? Every rational synapse in her brain revolted against the idea—even as her heart thudded in her chest and her skin prickled in the aftermath of ... whatever that was.

One thing she couldn't deny was her mounting desperation. She had to get out of there and find Ansel. Was desperation a kind of faith?

"Leon?" she murmured, her voice shaky, but he lay still and unresponsive. Tenderness squeezed her heart and she gave into the impulse to stroke his brow, relieved to see the knot of pain had lifted. God, she was so tired. With a sigh, she pressed her forehead to his temple and whispered, 'Get better, Leon. I need you.' She touched her lips to his cheek, sparking a fluttering in her stomach that made her feel silly and embarrassed.

She was as bad as the maid. 'I have to go check if that's our horse,' she muttered. 'I'll be back. She tucked the blankets up to his chin. "I have to check if that's our horse. I'll be back."

Teary-eyed, she dug the remaining bundle of grain from the saddlebags, grabbed the cloak, and tiptoed into the hall. The stairs were steep and narrow and every creaky floorboard made her cringe. The front door was held with a greased iron bolt and she slid it free, peering back into the thick gloom of the hall, waiting for Hueber or the monks to jump out and demand to know what she was doing.

The air was frigid on the front steps. While the strange wind had died, the abrupt stillness frightened her more. Mist pearled close to the cobbles and ink-dark shadows throbbed, watchful beneath the eaves of the surrounding buildings. It felt … unreal, as though she were suspended in a liminal space … a dream. This was a dream. Or she was a dream. Something that didn't exist. That couldn't exist. Not here.

Her gaze flittered to the broken shutters in the stable loft and the rooftops above. She was going to spook herself into going back inside if she didn't hurry up.

She forced her feet to move, toe to heel, to keep her steps silent on the cobbles. She clicked her tongue. "Horse," she whispered. "Here, horsie."

The big black beast turned its head, nostrils flaring as it scented the air. It gave a soft whinny and turned with a small skip that made her stop in her tracks. The horse trotted across the short distance, erasing any doubt. This was their horse.

She was struck anew by how huge he was as he eclipsed the space before her and pushed his nose into her face. He lipped her cheek and huffed hot breath on her skin. She gave a soft teary-eyed laugh and schooled herself not to step away or fear his teeth.

Stroking the velvet softness of his muzzle and the mighty stretch of his jaw, she murmured nonsense. "You found us, didn't you? You found us, you brilliant, clever boy. Aren't you precious? Yes, you are. You are so precious. That should be your name. Precious."

In answer, he hooked his chin over her head and tucked her in against his shoulder. Her tears slipped free and she wrapped her arms around his neck. She couldn't explain the feeling inside her, the sense of joy in the animal's unwarranted affection. While it couldn't cancel out the dreamlike strangeness of the misty square or the backlog of nearly three nights of dislocation from time and place, it was unexpected, soul-deep comfort. "You found me."

Finally, he huffed and lifted his head, nosing for the bag of grain hooked in her belt. "Are you hungry? Huh?" She opened the bag and held it for him while he set to it.

She closed her eyes, letting the sound of his crunching and his steady, warm presence calm her. In the morning, Leon's men would come and, whatever else, she would soon be with Gwen and the others. Ansel would be there, a whole castle full of saints, and they would figure something out—a way home.

She opened her eyes and the holy fool was there, standing by the well. A patched and threadbare blanket wrapped around his shoulders, the flaps failing to cover his nakedness. Ana froze and the horse lifted his head, his ears flattening. Precious snorted and stamped his hoof, turning side on to the fool, as though to keep him in plain sight.

She couldn't think what to do. What to say. Should she scream for help? Run back to the constable's house? Bolt the door behind her?

She braced for him to start shouting or denouncing her but he simply stood there, staring. Her pulse thumped in her ears and her earlobes felt hot, while the chill air set her body shivering. He was young and emaciated and the wounds on his exposed skin looked raw and angry. She couldn't tell the color of his eyes, but they were set deep with hunger and ... loneliness.

How could she know that?

Yet she did ... somehow ... in her bones. He was lonely. The knowing of it tempered her fear and she wondered about his family. Who cared for him, here in the village? Perhaps the man who called him Felix and warned him to come down from the loft before he hurt himself.

"I think you've got everyone a bit worried," she said, her voice barely one notch above a whisper, but out in the freezing square it still sounded too loud.

He blinked at her and his knuckles whitened where he gripped the blanket.

"You must be cold." She nodded at his bare feet. "And hungry?"

A line formed in his brow and his eyebrows bunched together. Had she said the wrong thing? He blinked again but made no motion to speak or move.

A tendril of wind wound around her ears, catching her loose curls, and she hunched her shoulders. "How did you know my name?"

His eyes welled and she swallowed, terrified he might start bawling. She twined her fingers in the black horse's mane, wondering if she had the strength or athleticism to vault onto the animal's back and gallop into the night if the young man started shrieking.

"Ana," he said, with a croak, spittle stretching between his lips. He shook his head and gave a little shudder, a tear slipping loose from the rim of his eye. "I found your horse."

"You did?" she said. "How…"

"You kissed the boy with the arrow in his eye."

She swallowed. "Will?"

"I saw you falling in the dark."

Ana blinked and her shivering wasn't just from the cold.

"You killed the man with the black teeth."

A horrible liquid sensation drained the strength from her bones. She wasn't sure she could stay upright. "I didn't— I didn't do that."

His eyes flicked to the horse.

She shrank inwardly. "He's just a horse. We found him in

the woods and the man—the man with the black teeth was frightening him." She was babbling. "He put a rope around my neck. He tried to hurt me."

His lips turned down, like a frightened child, his fingers digging into the blanket. A faint keening rose in the back of his throat and his shoulders shook. The air around him shifted and mist swirled at his feet. He dropped into a crouch and blinked, his eyes opening to shine like an animal's in the darkness. Goose bumps flashed across Ana's skin. She felt that something else was looking at her through the holy fool, eyes glowing silver.

Precious snorted and stomped his hooves. Ana took a step back.

"Double, double, toil and trouble…" Felix whispered.

Ana's ears roared like she was in a wind tunnel. How did he know those words? The lines from *Macbeth* she'd used to frighten the man with the black teeth.

"Little thief. Little witch."

"Don't you call me that," Ana said, her voice spiraling up.

Felix ducked and hissed, and at the same time a gasp rose on Ana's left. In the shadows of the constable's house, a figure huddled, pale face beneath a bright white kerchief, a cloak around her shoulders. Sarah? The housemaid.

"I'm not a witch," she said louder, for the eavesdropping maid. "And I don't want anything from you. I just want to go home. That's all."

He shook his head and his tears fell and the keening grew louder.

"Sarah," Ana called, working to keep her voice calm. "Get help, if you wouldn't mind."

Felix did not register the girl, but bared his teeth at Ana, his feet, hands, and private parts cloaked in mist, the blanket hanging from his shoulders. "The Kjálka is waiting for you. She claims you for her plate."

She shivered, opting for brusque authority. "That's enough nonsense, thank you very much. It's cold and dark and you need to go home." She clapped her hands at him, like she was trying to shoo a stray dog.

He recoiled and snarled.

"Don't you bloody well snarl at me," she snapped, and Precious stamped his hoof on the cobbles.

Felix covered his ears and wailed. "She seized you from beyond the veil! She plundered you as chattel from time!"

Ana and the horse took another skittering step back. "*Be quiet,*" she hissed.

He clamped both hands across his mouth and lost his balance, rolling onto his side. His back arched and he thrashed to and fro, and Ana was at a total loss as to what she should do. Sarah still stood gaping in the shadows of the house. "Sarah!" she hissed. "Go get Brother Ambrose, *please.*"

Footsteps scuffled behind her and Ana whirled around to find three people rushing up the main road from the cottages. She cringed and looped her fingers in the horse's lead.

"What unholy noise is here?" A stocky man in his bed-clothes pulled a cloak about his shoulders, accompanied by a young boy holding a flaming torch. Both carried blunt bits of wood like miniature baseball bats, likely for clubbing things.

Shit. Ana shrugged at the men and said, "I saw my horse from the window. When I came out to check on him, your guy came out and started yelling and carrying on."

The man and his son gaped at the horse. More men approached behind them, and seemed appalled by the horse also; a couple even crossed themselves. Ana frowned and shook her head. "We lost him in the woods." Then she seized on their backstory. "The bandits that attacked us, we thought they'd stolen him, but he's managed to find his way back, which is pretty good luck, right?"

One of the men made a sign with his hand, warding off evil. This was officially a nightmare. She hoped and prayed that she was still unconscious at the bottom of the cliff and perhaps she would wake up with a blinding headache, away from all of this.

"Seven to appease!" Felix shrieked. "Seven to mend! Seven to sow! Seven to rend!"

The words hit Ana and her stomach shrivelled. *One of seven.* Leon had told her the Northmen's prophecy. It was too much.

The stocky man edged around the horse into the square but Precious was nervous and stamped his back hooves in warning. The men all produced soft cries and Ana counted more pitchforks than there were before. She wished with all her heart the horse had stayed outside the palisade where he would have at least been safe from the superstitious panic of medieval villagers.

The stocky man crossed himself. "He's got that devil glow in his eyes again." All the assembled men crossed themselves.

"This is the girl!" Felix wailed, rising to his knees. "She killed the man with the black teeth! Double, double, toil and trouble!"

"Oh, shut up," she snapped. Again, he clamped his hands over his mouth, rolled his eyes into his head and slumped.

"Holy Mother."

"God Almighty."

"Angels save us."

"Is that a girl?" The stocky man's son pointed his cudgel at Ana and the round eyes of the villagers fixed on her with new horror, taking in her baggy pants, overlarge shirt, and doublet.

"In such immodest clothes," one muttered. "To trick us."

"What?" Ana yelped. "That's not true. I haven't tricked anyone. I never said I was a boy."

The collective gasp and recoil was farcical. She shook her head, losing all patience. "Would somebody please wake the constable and fetch the monks instead of standing here gawping like—" She didn't know what to compare them to, but she was more than a little afraid the cudgels and pitchforks were about to be turned on her.

Thankfully, the stocky man's son saw sense and jogged up the front steps of the constable's house and banged his cudgel on the ironbound door. To Ana's dismay, yet more men and some brave women were coming up the main road with more torches and implements for self-defense.

"This is a disaster," she whispered to Precious.

"She talks to the horse," a man said, loud enough to carry across the group now forming a large semicircle behind her.

"You're making him nervous," she said. "I'm just trying to reassure him."

"She controls the horse," another whispered.

"He's *my* bloody horse," she said, though it wasn't technically true.

The constable's door banged open and several things happened at once. Felix rose to his feet and threw off his blanket. Precious skittered to the side, his rear hooves clattering near a knot of villagers, who shouted and brandished their pitchforks. Felix roared, "Little thief! Little witch! The Kjálka claims you!"

Women shrieked at the words and men's voices rose in fear, and the constable almost fell down the steps as Brothers Ambrose and Balor came barreling out behind him.

"Peace!" Ambrose cried, in his great carrying baritone, and Ana could have wept with relief to see the big, sensible man, kind and fierce and—

"Seven to appease! Seven to mend! Seven to sow! Seven to—" Felix charged at Ana. She yelped and Precious squealed, swinging around wildly and knocking the holy fool to the cobbles with his rump. The crowd of villagers cried out. The constable yelled for order but Felix screamed again, jerking upright, blood on his temple, and hissed.

Precious reared and brought his hoof down on the young

man's head with a horrible cracking sound. More screams rose as Felix fell, blood spilling down his face.

"Witch!" cried the stocky man. "You turned your devil beast on our holy fool!"

"Peace!" Ambrose called, scrambling down the steps. He came up beside Ana and it was all she could do not to cling to the man. "This is a misunderstanding."

"She controls the horse!"

"She wears men's clothes!"

"She spoke curses over us."

"She cursed the lad!"

"This is devilry!"

"She is a deceiver!"

Several men dragged Felix's collapsed body back toward the constable's steps. "There, lad, can you hear us?"

But the light had gone from Felix's eyes and he lay immobile. One man laid his ear to the boy's chest. "God save him," he begged. "He's dead."

A wail rang out; a woman fainted and another begged, "The witch slew him!"

"It was an accident!" Ambrose cried. "He frightened the horse, that is all!"

"What doom have you brought to my door?" Constable Hueber demanded of the monk. "A witch dressed as a boy? Deception. Corruption!"

"No!" Ana shook her head. "That's not true."

"Let us calm down." Brother Balor was there, also standing

as a barrier to keep the villagers at bay. "Return to your homes, return to your beds. We will see to the lad. Bless him and—"

"Why should we trust any of you?" the stocky man demanded. "Look what trouble has come from your interference!"

"Kill the beast!" a man shouted. "Burn the witch! Drive the devils from our door!"

The men surged forward. Ana's ears rang with the clamor as she ducked behind Precious. Then a shout rang out. Leon stood atop the steps before the constable's door. "Stop this foolishness at once!"

CHAPTER TWENTY-ONE

I t was a nightmarish scene in the square. Leon deeply regretted not risking the road with the man they had met at the
village gates. Perhaps Oleg's scouts would have shown more
mercy than was currently on display before him. Thankfully,
the brothers were there, standing between Ana, the horse—*the
black warhorse*—and a host of agitated villagers.

He spotted the fallen fool and his caved-in skull and heard
the bellowed accusations, comprehending full well the inrush-
ing tide of hysteria when he saw it. Experience had taught him
too well how quickly these situations might spiral into rashness,
the flames of an angry mob too easily kindled, fed whether by
fear and ignorance or lies and outrage. This had the look of
some combination of all four.

"Cease this wild talk!" he cried, catching Ana's terrified gaze
as she pressed herself into the side of the great horse. The horse's
eyes rolled and he pawed the cobbles with his hoof, a warning
to any who might attempt violence on the maiden.

He had neither the time nor comprehension to consider how
the beast came to be in the square. He had woken to the raised
voices through the open window, his fever gone and strength

returned. Perhaps not full battle strength but vigor enough to rise, stuff his feet into his boots, haul a shirt over his head, and make it down the stairs without tumbling.

He could find only a short sword among the saddlebags and eyed his long sword, yet undrawn, at the monk's hip. He had little memory beyond entering Ulmenholz's palisade. After that, a blur of heat, utter darkness, pressure on his chest, and Ana's voice urging him. Here now, he could only thank the good Lord he was awake and able to act before Ana found herself strapped to a post atop a pyre.

"This girl is under the protection of Eadin Palace, claimed by Saint Ansel! If anyone dare lay a hand on her in violence, there will be consequences!" He pointed his short sword at the crowd and kept a slow steady tread down the steps. The people looked askance, some glaring, as though weighing the merits of defiance against obedience to an unknown man's claim. He knew only the name of Eadin Palace carried any weight in his threat. He also knew he was taking great liberties in promising any such retribution and if it came to it, he would be hauled before the council for making such claims, but extreme circumstances required the risk. He could see the question in Brother Ambrose's raised brow behind the wonder and shock in beholding Leon risen from his sickbed.

The big man shrugged and turned to the crowd. "You have heard the decree! This girl has been claimed by Eadin Palace. The saint has claimed her. Let sense return, my friends! No harm was intended."

"But harm has been done!" Hueber swelled in his bedclothes, hands clamped on his hips. "She has slain our holy fool! What compensation will Eadin offer for such a loss?"

"As I understand it," Ambrose countered, not lowering his booming voice, "your fool has been crashing about the rooftops and sent a beam down on the head of one of your own villagers. Likely killed her! That is the damage we know of. Heaven knows what other mischief he has done. And his body clearly shows that your people have attacked him and marred him with implements of their own before we came among you."

Muttering rippled around the assembled villagers and Leon scanned the crowd for signs of anyone who might break the peace and lunge at the girl.

"Nonetheless," Hueber pressed on, "he was *our* fool, to do with as *we* saw fit. Not a target for your witch or her foul beast."

"Spit that word from your mouth, one more time," Leon said, stalking toward the man. "You should be very careful about making false accusations. Eadin Palace will not look kindly upon such talk."

"You threaten us with the censure of Eadin Palace. Have your so-called saints established themselves as our judge and jury now?" Hueber said. "There is but one law in the land and even Eadin Palace must kneel before the Holy Roman Church."

"No *law* has been broken," Leon declared.

Hueber scowled, his face darkening. "Murder by witchcraft!"

The villagers rumbled with agreement and Leon's heart sank. Ana looked moon pale, her huge eyes swallowed by panic.

Brothers Ambrose and Balor shot him a warning look. He'd pushed the matter too far.

"You are under arrest." Constable Hueber took a step toward Ana but monks and horse alike joined Leon in blocking the man's path. The constable swelled again. "For the practice of witchcraft, the ensorcellment of an innocent beast, and the murder of a holy fool."

"Don't be ridiculous!" Leon cried.

"Take her to the holding cell at once." Hueber gestured at two men with pitchforks, who, in turn, eyed the monks, the knight, and the horse with resigned determination, relinquishing their forks to produce short swords of their own. The villagers stepped back, huddling together, eyes wide and hungry. They wanted action and Hueber was giving it to them.

A startled cry broke from the group and their gaze rose above Leon's head. He turned to find Ana standing on the edge of the well, using it to lever herself onto the warhorse's back. "Don't come near me!" she cried.

She pulled the small rectangular box from her inside pocket and Leon, filled with dread, mouthed "no." But there were men coming in around the well and she touched the surface and it lit up with bright images.

Gasps rose around the crowd. "Heaven help us!" a man pleaded, and several others repeated the sentiment and more.

"This is my phone," Ana said, strength filling her voice. "I'm not a witch and I'm really sick of having to say that. I just come from another time and place and you probably wouldn't understand. And this horse ... he's just a horse. A really nice horse, who seems to like me for no reason. He was frightened when Felix rushed at me and was only trying to protect me, I think. But I'm very sorry Felix got hurt." Her voice broke and she flashed the phone around, swiping more images onto the screen. The crowd were spellbound, many with their hands clamped over their mouths, watching in awe or dismay.

"He seemed quite sad and lonely," she said. "And I'm not trying to sound judgy, but I think he probably had some mental health issues not helped by everyone calling him a holy fool. So, I'm going to go now."

"You will do no such thing!" Hueber bellowed, but Ana tapped her screen twice and a sound erupted from the tiny musical box. She pumped the edge of the box with her thumb and the sound spiraled high and shrill, making the villagers shrink back in horror. Ambrose and Balor looked at Leon.

"Go," Ambrose muttered. "We will meet you at the palace."

Leon didn't wait for another prompt; he dashed toward Ana and copied her instinct to use the edge of the well for a foot up, landing squarely behind her. He grabbed the reins and nudged the warhorse with his heels, sending it bolting forward. Cries of outrage and screams rose. Ambrose and Balor jumped out of the way, barging into Hueber and his cronies, sending them tumbling to the cobbles.

The horse charged down the road toward the palisade, where the gate was indeed left open, and with Ana trembling before him, the strange, rhythmic music booming, they raced through the gate and into the night.

CHAPTER TWENTY-TWO

Ana must have fallen asleep at some point. It was the sound of rushing water that roused her, coupled with the dryness of her mouth. The light was bright beneath her lashes and she squinted, her eyes running. She became aware then of the horse beneath her and a firm warm body pressed at her back, her head lolling in the slope of a shoulder, her face bouncing against a neck. Leon's arms were wrapped around her, keeping her from slipping to the side without a saddle to hold her in place.

She lifted her head and Leon cleared his throat. "Good morning."

"I'm sorry. You should have poked me in the ribs," she croaked. "How long have I been out?"

"You needed the rest."

"Not very fair on you," she said.

The night was a blur. They hadn't bothered speaking, all their focus on staying on the horse's back. They rode fast and far from Ulmenholz, the holy fool's words chasing her through the dark: *She knows your name, Ana. Seven to appease. Seven to mend…* She let Leon guide the horse; he knew better than her. They risked the Roman road during the first few hours, for the sake of making good time, but as the darkness lifted deep in the hours before dawn, Leon had guided the horse off the path and back into the woods. She had been rocked to sleep by the steady motion of Precious's steps, warmed beneath the cocoon of their shared cloak.

"You must be thirsty."

She considered his wry tone. "Was I snoring?"

"In a delicate fashion."

She groaned and rubbed her face. He placed his hands on her hips and her eyes popped open at the easy intimacy of his touch. Her stomach fluttered like it had last night, this time with a rush of tingling up her body. *Bad Ana. You kissed him while he was unconscious. Very bad.*

"If you swing your leg over, I can lower you down."

She blushed and nodded, lifting her stiff leg over Precious's neck. Leon helped her slide down the horse's shoulder, her feet hitting the thin coat of snow on the riverbank. Her breath misted the air but the sun was a gift.

It was the first blue sky she had seen since she stepped out of the cave into *now*. Duller in daylight, the dusty red smudge of the Eldi Comet hung in the sky. She gave it a reproachful look, then glanced away.

Sunlight refracted on the water and spangled the snow-gilded trees like something from a fairytale. She knelt on the bank, wincing at the ache in her hips, her thighs, knees, and back. She felt old and broken. The water was frigid and she shivered as she drank, scooping it in her hands, gasping as it spilled down her chin and dribbled into the neck of her shirt.

Leon joined her and Precious turned toward a clump of thistles at the base of a silver birch. She sat back on her heels and watched Leon drink. He looked stiff and sore but there was no sign of fever and his copper skin had resumed a warm glow. She stared at the taut column of his throat, the size and breadth of his hands, then realized she was staring and looked away.

Nearly four days ago, she had been so deep in her grief about Stefan, and the ruin of her academic plans, she had tried to erase it with booze and force a situation with Will. Shame swept through her. Poor sweet Will. What kind of monster was she to be looking at another guy?

It wasn't right. It couldn't be real. She wasn't over Stefan. She was just … mixed up—whatever her fluttering and tingling was about—confusing. Leon was a good person. They'd been forced together. Intimacy forged by necessity. For survival.

The damp seeped into the knees of her pants and she got to her feet, groaning again with the effort. "How are you well?"

He splashed his face a couple of times and dragged his wet palm around the back of his neck. Bracing his hands on his thighs, he blinked up at her, water beading on his long dark lashes. "I don't know."

"Before I went outside last night"—she didn't mention the debacle in the village square—"you were burning up. Delirious. Writhing on the bed."

He frowned, then scooped more water for a final deep

drink. He rose to his feet, his hair dripping, rivulets of water slipping down his neck, dampening the vee of his unlaced collar. She tried not to stare at the sculpted groove between his pectorals. She could remember too well what his chest looked like and the thought was distracting in the extreme.

He shook his head, spraying water, then ran his hand up into his hair, drawing it back from his face. "I believe you."

"Can I check the wound?"

He wiped the back of his wrist and forearm across his chin and under his neck to catch the water, but his skin remained damp and goose-fleshed. His brown eyes studied her face with new intensity. She dropped her gaze and fumbled at the hem of his shirt. He turned and lifted his arm, letting her ruck the fabric high. She tried not to stare at the ridges of muscle and fumbled with the bandage. He studied her while she tugged the wrappings aside and her blush grew embarrassing.

"You're staring," she muttered.

His mouth curled up at the corner and he averted his gaze to an overhanging tree branch.

Ana's brain stalled when she beheld the closed wound and the raised red scar. No weeping blood, no pus, no streaks of infection. The skin around the scar was still a little swollen but this was nothing like the open mess she'd seen yesterday. "Leon," she breathed, shivering anew. "Have you seen this?"

He bent to look, peering awkwardly beneath his arm, his brow contracting with disbelief. He patted the tender flesh with his fingertips. "Impossible." He blinked rapidly and lowered and raised his arm again. "There is an ache but nothing like yesterday's pain. Holy Mother…"

"That's so … weird."

He eyed her with fresh wonder. "I felt your hand on my head—on my chest. I heard your voice. You told me to get better."

She released his shirt, letting it fall, and tugged at the hem. *Oh, God.* Had he beed aware of the kiss? "I was freaking out. I was terrified you might … not get better."

"I heard you." He took hold of her upper arms, gentle but urgent.

By reflex she brought her hands to his chest and gave a single airless laugh. "I thought you were in la-la land."

"La-la land?"

"It's a saying."

"Ana," he murmured, a rare smile transforming his handsome face into something dazzling.

Reckless, she swayed toward him, closing the gap to mere inches. Clearly, her body didn't care it had only been four days. It didn't care about what was real or what was right. Maybe she was a bad person. Maybe she could accept that. Be the monster. Because there was one thing she couldn't deny— Leon's pull was magnetic and all those dead receptors that refused to fire for poor Will were lighting up for him.

His gaze dropped to her mouth and his hands slid up over her shoulders to cup the back of her neck, his thumbs framing the sides of her face.

The tenderness of his touch, the anticipation in it, eclipsed her grief and shame, and she fanned her fingers over his shirt front, over his heart, letting him know she wanted whatever this was.

But then he blinked and pulled back an inch. "This is a miracle. Ana, you worked a miracle."

It was like being doused in river water. She pulled out of his hands. "Don't be ridiculous."

He swallowed and blinked again, like he had been doused too, taking a step away from her, as though realizing he'd been too close to crossing the line. "What else can it be?"

She shrugged. "It's weird but it's hardly a miracle."

"You laid your hands on me and commanded me to be well in the name of God."

"In the name of?" she spluttered. "I—I said 'for the love of God.' I'm pretty sure that's like a low-key swear not a—not a holy proclamation."

"I remember what you said."

Why was her pulse hammering? It had been a weird, disorientating night as Leon succumbed to fever. She'd banged her head on the window frame and lost her balance. Panic had skewed her perception. Her eyes had played tricks on her, making monsters of shadows in the firelight. That strange wind … she shivered at the memory and threw her hands up. "You're making a big deal out of nothing."

He squinted at her. "Why are you trying to diminish this?"

"I'm not. I'm trying to make it—the size that it *is*. Which is not…" She held her arms out wide. "It's more like…" She brought her hands in like she was holding a football and jiggled her palms.

"We must get you to Eadin Palace. They will know."

She shook her head and turned to Precious, the great black horse flicking a velvet ear toward her in acknowledgment. She felt like a fistful of firecrackers was going off in her chest and she ran trembling hands over his shoulder, checking his coat for signs of chafing. Precious was a real, practical concern, something … down to earth. They'd been on his back for hours with no saddle and it distressed her that they might be causing him pain. "We should walk for a bit."

"Ana."

"He needs a saddle. We could be hurting him."

"*Ana*," he said, "I am not trying to frighten you."

"Well, you are." She gave him a hard look over her shoulder. "Promise me you won't tell people I did that."

He caught his lower lip in his teeth and scanned the snow-coated bank, his hands on his hips. He looked outrageously handsome with Brandt's stolen cloak trailing behind him and the sun catching gold in his dark damp curls. "Ana…"

"I'm serious," she insisted. "We're not pulling up at a castle full of saints with wild stories that I'm one of them. *I am not.* I have not performed wonders. Just because we can't explain it doesn't mean there isn't a completely reasonable explanation for what has happened." She brightened suddenly, remembering the constable's maid. "Sarah gave you healing herbs. They were in the broth. Who's not to say she's the miracle worker or her herbal remedy was the secret?"

He rolled his lips into a thin line and raised his eyebrows. She was immediately annoyed—she'd seen that doubtful expression too many times on their journey. "Leon," she snapped, "I am asking you not to tell them about this. Will you respect my wishes?"

He folded his arms, the shirt Sarah had given him straining over his shoulders and biceps. "It is not that simple."

"It *is* that simple. Don't you care what I want? Aren't we..." She scrambled for the right word. "Friends?"

He hesitated.

The word was too loaded. Friends don't kiss. She definitely wanted to kiss him, and a moment ago she thought he had been about to kiss her. Suddenly, she wasn't sure and she blushed again, dismayed at the realization that he may not have wanted to kiss her at all.

The urgent touch, the way he'd cupped her head in his hands and breathed her name ... that whole thing might have been wonder, not desire.

Shit. He'd been excited about a *miracle*. He thought *she* was a miracle worker. And that was apparently not someone for kissing. *Shit. Shit.* It was humiliating. He hadn't wanted her at all. He wanted to marvel over her "works."

"We are..." he finally said, his jaw working, "friends ... of a sort. Traveling companions."

She shook her head and muttered, "Don't bloody strain yourself."

CHAPTER TWENTY-THREE

Leon bit into a crab apple, surprised to find some crunch left in the shriveled flesh. They had filled their pockets in silence, almost stripping the gnarled tree by the deer path. Ana had fed most of hers to the horse before leading him on through a narrow column of bald pines. They walked on foot and he guessed she sought a narrow path to force him to trail behind. Even the beast seemed to flick its tail in irritation, as though warning him to stay back.

He stared at the animal's rump, berating himself for cowardice. *Traveling companions.* That was the best he could offer? No wonder she had turned her back on him and stalked away.

While silence had been a relief at first, now it was a torment. His thoughts were in freefall. He stretched his arm out again, marveling at the freedom of movement, the decrease in pain. He pressed the scar beneath his shirt. It *was* a miracle.

She was in denial. This was not a normal healing. He should not be up and riding through the night and striding around a forest after a fever like that. He should be weak as water. He wanted her to admit it, but he did not know how to bridge the gap between them or break the prickling silence.

Friend.

Was it such a hard word to admit? She'd looked so hurt when he failed to affirm the title. He did not have *girl* friends. He knew girls. At Eadin Palace. In the town and surrounding villages. But they weren't *friends.* He'd had sweethearts and a couple of tumbles with a tavern barmaid. The whole disaster with Adeline ... but hardly friendship.

Micah was his friend. Tabor and his men from the barracks were friends. Ana was too strange, too beautiful, too...

The image of her naked body surged into the foreground of his thoughts. Those scandalous threads of fabric barely covering her curves. He wasn't suffering from fever and pain now. His body reacted with force and he exhaled through his nose. No. A man does not have thoughts like that about a *friend.*

Heaven help him, he'd been so close to kissing her. Another heady wave of desire rolled through his blood and he breathed out through his mouth. He would never be able to get the image out of his mind. It would plague him. Curse the girl's musical box.

"What was the sound that came from the ... phone?" He stared at the back of the girl's head, her shoulders stiff as she strode ahead. "Last night," he said, keeping his tone light. "When you were terrifying the villagers with your supposed witchcraft..."

She turned her head, letting him catch the profile of her scowl. "You've changed your tune, then? Was it the lack of smoke billowing from my throat after the holy water?"

"That and the cross not singeing the fine skin at your neck."

She didn't turn her head again but bit into a crab apple and heaved her shoulders with a sigh. She was not going to relent easily. "Maybe I am a witch and the devil cured your fever."

He gritted his teeth; she was mocking him.

She patted the horse's neck, feeding him the remainder of the core, and he produced a pleased wicker in the back of his throat. "They seemed to think Precious was the devil. Or that I had possessed him with the devil. Perhaps Precious worked his dark magic on you."

"Precious is a ridiculous name for a warhorse."

The horse lifted its tail and dropped several sizable turds in Leon's path.

"Good boy," Ana crooned, stroking the animal's jaw as they strode on. "You tell the bad man." The great beast turned his head and lipped the side of her face, making her smile sadly.

Leon dodged the horse shit, uncertain whether to be irritated, charmed, or deeply suspicious. The animal was taken with her. He had to bribe his mare with carrots to get her saddle on without being nipped. Ana knew nothing about horses and this great brute adored her. He shook his head. "What was the sound?"

She dug beneath her cloak and pulled out the cursed object and ran her thumb over the screen. She sighed. "I'm down to eighteen percent battery, so I'll only give you a snippet."

He did not know what 18 percent battery was but he would

not bother asking for an explanation; she would only roll her eyes.

She flicked through the screens and tapped the surface and sound rose from the device that made the hairs on the back of his neck rise. It had a fierce beat and layers of melody with some raucous scratching noise over the top.

"What is that?"

"Music."

"What instruments could make such an infernal racket?"

She turned her head again to show him half a frown. "Guitars, bass, drums, synths, vocals, mixing, sound production, sampling, and whatever else."

He knew drums but none of the other words meant anything to him. "I cannot understand the woman's words."

"She's singing about her ex."

"Ex?"

"Her ex-boyfriend."

Boy friend. He hesitated, not wanting to start another fight.

"Her ex-lover," she clarified primly.

"A man she loved?"

"Yes."

"But no longer loves?"

"I think she still loves him."

He considered the forceful delivery of the lines and the raw emotion carried by an instrument that sounded like the rusted gears of a portcullis. "But she sounds most angry."

She tapped the screen, the music stopped and she shoved the device back in her pocket. "She is."

They trudged on and he wondered if his men were passing in the opposite direction out on the Roman road. Perhaps they had already reached Ulmenholz and the constable was assaulting their ears with accusations of murder, witchcraft, and God knows what else.

Likely Micah would have come himself if he believed Leon on the brink of death. He would not swallow the constable's drivel whole, too level-headed to be swayed by the mention of devils. However, if Edwin was among them, he would be unsettled and he would voice his trepidation.

No. Micah would quash any foolish talk and if he brought a healer, they too would speak reason. Still, he could find little comfort in the thought of Eadin Palace being presented with new woe and Leon in the thick of it. As if there were not enough enemies prowling at the gates, looking for any excuse to drag the saints into disrepute.

"Will the brothers be in trouble?" Ana asked.

"I think not," Leon said with more confidence than he felt. "They answer to their chapter, not the lord of the district." He didn't voice the possibility of the bishop's displeasure. If the constable applied to Bishop Angeber for inquisitors, there could be trouble. But that would take many weeks of messengers, deliberations, and the sending of men of authority. He could only hope that Ana would be well gone by then—assuming Ansel and the council had some means by which to return her and her people to their correct ... place.

The thought sank his spirits. She was curious and strange and aggravating, but without pain and fever consuming him he had to admit there was pleasure in her company and the strange intimacy they had shared on the journey.

"I like Ambrose," she said, regret in her voice. "He doesn't seem like a priest."

He knew what she meant. Ambrose was devout but he had no interest in impressing or oppressing others with his piety. He was a practical man of faith who understood the world and in his gruff way cared for those within his reach.

"I hope he's okay," she said.

Leon knew what she feared was being the cause of the trouble and imagined she regretted her dramatic departure. "You did the right thing."

She stopped in her tracks and turned fully to face him. "Did I?"

He stopped beside the horse and considered her drawn expression. She was exhausted from days on the road and lack of sleep. She was far from her home, her family, and friends. Lost in time. He wished they were on the horse again, just so he could have the excuse to hold her. When she'd fallen asleep in the early hours of the morning, her back pressed against his chest, her head on his shoulder, her face against his neck ... he'd been able to forget all the reasons why getting too close was a bad idea.

She did not belong here. Oleg, the Butcher, was after her. It was not Leon's place to get involved. She might be a witch. Or a miracle worker. A saint. But she was also, simply, a girl. "They would have tied you to a post, built a pyre, and burned you."

Her face crumpled. She shook her head and lifted her palm in a gesture of utter helplessness. Tears sparkled on her lashes. "Do you know how unhinged that is?"

He couldn't bear to see the hope drain from her eyes and moved before he thought better of it. He clasped her shoulders. "Angry people, fearful people, do terrible things."

"That poor guy," she said, a catch in her throat.

"It was an accident," Leon said, assurances jumping from his lips without qualification. "The horse was only trying to protect you."

"Will they hurt Precious?" She looked up at him, her nose growing red at the tip.

"We will keep him safe." Why was he making promises? There was no chance he could ensure the beast's safety. If Brandt claimed him, if the constable sent men to claim him— what could he do? Eadin would not keep a stolen horse.

"I'm not what you think," she said. "I'm not a miracle worker."

He didn't argue, he wiped her tears with his thumbs, and cupped her neck again, his fingers sliding into her hair. Her eyes dropped to his mouth and her lips parted, swollen from crying. Her hands came to his chest and she pressed her forehead to his collarbone, and like a fool, he slid his arms around her and kissed her hair. "You are a miracle."

CHAPTER TWENTY-FOUR

"**D**on't say that," she groaned against him, but didn't push him away. When his lips touched the top of her head she could have bawled. Instead, she wrapped her arms around his waist and clung tight.

It was like she'd been disintegrating for days—from the moment she stepped out of the cave. On the road, Leon might have only been holding her to keep from falling off the horse, or to ward off hypothermia, and maybe it was nothing but forced proximity but, God, it had been a lifeline.

"You are impossible." He stroked her back and kept his cheek pressed to the top of her head. His warm breath stirred her hair and she dug her fingers into the muscled stretch of his back.

What she'd snuffed out on the riverbank, what had been building between them for days, sparked again. Whether it was right or wrong, she lifted her head. His eyes were dark and deep and he looked at her in a way that made her blood rush.

He leaned down, slowly, and she tipped her face to meet his kiss, a sweet and searing collision. She smiled against him and her eyes flickered open as he smiled back. Neither of them pulled away.

"Ana," he said, but it wasn't a question, just her name made somehow more with his breath.

Her pulse leaped and she lifted her mouth to his, grazing his lips, top then bottom, drawing him down to seal it. Then she found his tongue and the silky give and take unspooled heat low in her belly, shimmering with promise.

It was a sensory override, pulling her all the way into now. The night's terrors, faded. The uncertainty of what lay ahead, eclipsed. Grief ... shame ... neutralized. She was reduced to nerve endings and receptors, lost in the apple-sweet taste of him and the warmth of his arms. God, she wanted to sink into him—a full body immersion.

As though sensing her thoughts, he smoothed his hands down her back, pressing her more firmly against him. She answered, circling his neck, digging her fingers into his scalp. A soft moan hitched his breath and he broke the kiss to search her face. "Forgive me. I should ..."

"You should." She knotted her fingers in his curls. "You definitely should."

He caught his lower lip in his teeth and blinked at her, half dazed, then slid his hands down slowly, slowly, over her backside. She arched into his touch, a sigh rising in the back of her throat, and her eyes rolled shut.

He cupped her arse, like a meditation. She pulled him down and their foreheads pressed together, their breath coming short, mingling where their lips almost touched. She brushed a kiss over his cheek, his jaw, drawing a line of kisses, up to his ear. "Leon," she begged.

"Tell me." His lips grazed the underside of her jaw, his tongue flicking, teasing the tender skin. And she tipped her head, rising on her toes, inviting more … of everything.

"Ana," he whispered, brushing his fingers lower, catching her mouth again with his. He scooped her leg and caressed the swell of her hip in a slow thorough arc, finding her soft heat.

Precious reared and squealed and they broke apart as the sound of crashing erupted from the dense bushes. Three men with blades and bows and kohled eyes. Like the men who'd attacked the cabin in the night. Like the black-toothed man who'd dragged her from the creek with a rope around her neck.

Fear like a flash flood wiped out even the memory of desire, leaving Ana shaken to the core.

Leon unsheathed his short sword and pushed her behind him, hemming her against Precious, who pawed the ground with his hoof and snorted.

Ana looked about wildly. They had nothing to protect themselves.

"They will not kill you," Leon said. "They have not tracked you all this way to kill you, Ana."

She couldn't understand why he was saying this. To comfort her? They could kill *him*. She wouldn't let it happen. "Let them take me," she said. "They'll kill you if you try to stop them, Leon, and I couldn't stand it."

The men circled in a wide berth, two leering but one with fierce caution. This was the third attempt made by Oleg's men. They weren't going to stop. They would hunt her until they had her or she was dead.

"Leon," she began, about to plead again for him to listen to reason, but he grabbed her around the waist, swinging her legs up and landing her on Precious's back like she was nothing more than a sack of potatoes. He slapped the horse's rump and she barely managed to grasp its mane before the animal bolted.

Oleg's men shouted in outrage. She caught a harrowing glimpse of two leering Northmen as they surged toward Leon, but the other stood and drew his bow. He was going to shoot Precious.

"No," she rasped, but Precious was like an arrow himself, barreling through the trees, his tread hammering the earth. She squeezed her knees and leaned over the horse's neck trying to hold on. The clash of steel echoed behind her and the horrible whir and thud of an arrow hitting Precious in the rump.

He squealed and skidded and she almost tumbled onto the snow-patched dirt but he righted his step and ploughed on. Ana could barely lift her head with the tumult beneath her; Precious had slowed only a fraction. Tears blurred her vision, for the horse, for Leon, for the impossibility of what to do.

"Precious," she called, patting his shoulder. "Precious, slow down, boy. Whoa. Stop. Stop." Finally, the great stallion slowed enough that she could peer back at the arrow, sunk in the rounded muscle. "Precious, I'm sorry," she gasped. "I'm so sorry, sweet boy." She leaned down and stroked his neck. "I don't know what to do."

The horse limped on as though it knew where to go. What *was* she supposed to do? She couldn't leave Leon behind. But she had no weapon. She had no means of threatening the Northmen. No leverage to bargain.

It made her heart sick to think what they might do to him. He might be dead already. Like Will. "I need help," she said aloud. "*I need help.*"

She looked back, prompting Precious with her heels. There was no sign of pursuit but she had to consider they might have horses hidden in the trees. She couldn't waste time.

"Eadin Palace. They'll know what to do. They'll send help for Leon, and get that arrow out. They won't let Oleg take me."

Precious seemed to have a plan already, heading down a slope between the trees with a rough snort. He picked up his pace and she knotted her fingers in his mane and did her best to rise and fall with his steps, worried about the pain she might be causing him. Her thighs and lower back were aching. The trees thinned, suggesting a clearing, and then she realized—it was the road. The Roman road.

"Wait," she said, squeezing her knees, and Precious stopped, but there was no sign of travelers, no sound. She patted the horse's neck. "Okay, Precious. As fast as you can bear."

He took a few limping steps and then lengthened his stride. She clung to his mane, praying for Leon, a half-incoherent mantra. *Help us. Save him. Save us.*

Her eyes stung with tears, the cold wind freezing them to her skin. Somehow, Precious ran on, despite the arrow and the trickle of blood down the side of his leg. At least the road was broad and clear, knifing through the trees.

It wasn't long before his limp grew more pronounced and she couldn't stand it any longer. There was a slope rising before them and there was no way she would make him carry her up it; he must be in agony as it was. With a shuddering sob, she brought him to a stop and slid down his shoulder.

The winter sun was high overhead. It must be midday or close. There in the distance behind her came a wagon pulled by a pair of draft horses. Their steady pace suggested they were in no hurry, and not pursued by bandits or Northmen. She saw no glint of armor on the passengers. As they drew on, she made out the kerchiefed head of a woman holding the reins.

Precious's neck was damp and he was panting. He kept the weight off his back leg and she wanted to howl. "You did so great," she murmured. "You are so strong and brave; look how far you brought me." She scratched his ears and kissed his soft nose. Thankfully, the wound had stopped oozing but she hated to imagine how deep it was. Infection might be setting in. She decided to risk waiting for the wagon.

When the horses drew near, she raised her hand and the woman pulled the wagon to a stop. A man rode with her. The couple eyed Ana with curiosity and her horse with alarm. They appeared middle-aged, their tan skin weathered and heavy-lined from work in the outdoors. Their clothes were rough-spun but clean and well-hemmed. Ana couldn't begin to make assumptions about their station or occupation. The wagon appeared empty except for a smattering of hay. "God keep you," the man said, but it came out as a question. They were searching her face as though struggling to find the answer to a complex equation.

It occurred to Ana they could not tell if she was a boy or girl. "Hello," she said, trying to look as meek and non-threatening as she could. She swallowed and gestured at Precious's rump. "I'm sorry to trouble you but we were attacked." Her voice broke.

"We saw no trouble on the road," the man said, narrowing his eyes.

"We were in the forest," she said, feeling like she was not all in her body. Was she really explaining that she was attacked by Vikings? "My companion was ... he saved me but my horse is injured. I need to get to Eadin Palace but he's still out there…" She ground to a halt; they were looking at her like she was from another planet—she wondered if that was technically accurate.

The woman's face softened and she blinked at Ana in wonder, while the man cocked his head. "But Eadin Palace is just over the hill," the woman said. "You can ride in the wagon if you like." Ana burst into tears.

CHAPTER TWENTY-FIVE

Ana sat in the wagon, her back pressed to the side rail so she could face the man who sat swiveled in his seat, offering a profoundly comforting stream of mindless chatter that required little from Ana beyond occasional nods.

They were coming to Eadin for business, mister had need of a new reaping implement for the spring and mistress had a niece who kept bees and had a baby on the way and thank heavens she's but a stone's throw from the palace where the midwives were second to none. And, Lord, how appalling to have lost a companion to bandits and my, such a horse as he'd never seen, the poor beast to be fired upon, and God save them, that good Christians could not travel in peace these days but to suffer the horror of bandits was unspeakable, poor lad.

He called Ana lad, perhaps more from hope than in any certainty of the fact. The mistress said nothing, content to let her husband fill the silence.

The slope rose up and up and Precious trailed behind the cart, his lead looped through Ana's fingers. His limp made her heart ache but he still nuzzled her fingers when he came close. She had stopped crying but worry for Leon still made her chest tight as she listened to the man, tempering her awe as she took in the great beauty of the winter forest. There were evergreens sugared with settling snow, not yet bowed, crystal droplets melting from their tips. The air had changed and the whiff of civilization infused each breath.

The musty tang of rotting hay hung heavily about the cart but there were cooking smells wafting on the air now. Her stomach squeezed and grumbled and her mouth watered. Finally, they reached the top of the hill. The road swept to the right, giving her a view to the left, where a town spread beneath the foot of a great slope. On the mount rose Eadin Palace. Immense and impossible, it overlooked the sprawling township and the surrounding farmlands, where hedges formed natural paddocks for sheep and goats and pigs.

It was like the lid of a 5,000-piece puzzle. The cottages were steep-roofed, thatched, and patched with snow. Chimneys offered ribbons of smoke to the blue sky, and the fields rolled, velvet green. The scene was so welcoming, so peaceful, so ridiculously idyllic after the horrors of Ulmenholz, the trauma in the cabin, and the terror in the woods that she wanted to fold herself into the perfection of the landscape and sleep.

From here, the long southern wall of Eadin Palace stepped down the hill in three tiers. The sight of it gripped her with that inexplicable longing she had felt when she gazed upon the ruins before their ordeal in the caves. It was confronting in the extreme to see the structure whole and undamaged. The Sacred Grove at the heart of the palace peeped above the walls. The sound of rushing water called in the distance.

A palisade much taller than the one at Ulmenholz bordered the town and a great iron gate sat open for business between two stone towers built atop raised hillocks, protecting the entry. Guards at the gate wore chain mail and helmets; their spears gleamed in the sunlight. "Are these Eadin Palace soldiers?" Ana asked, sitting up straight. Should she go to them and beg help to find Leon?

"No, lad, these are town guards." The woman shook her head. "You've never been here before?"

Ana was saved from answering when they were stopped before the threshold on account of Precious, his size and magnificence, and the arrow in his rear. The mister did the speaking and Ana simply nodded and looked woeful.

Two guards came to inspect the wound but Precious flattened his ears and stamped his hoof and they backed off. "We are taking him to the horse master at the palace," the mister explained, gruff and to the point.

The main avenue through the township was broader and grander than Ulmenholz's, with balconied buildings of sand-colored stone, jewel-bright shutters, and red-tiled roofs. Cobbled streets wound left and right into busy lanes and leafy terraces. There was a sense of order and industry, with men and women at their labor and children busy with their own mischief. They attracted little attention, apart from a few double takes for Precious and occasional gasps of concern about the arrow—but no glancing suspicion or wary stares aimed at Ana. This was a place of commerce and trade, accustomed to out-of-towners.

Every now and then, Ana glimpsed a brown face and she found herself searching beneath kerchief and cap for Gwen or Stefan, Olly or Keira, but that was just giddy hope, squeezing past her panic for Leon. The busyness of the town ground their journey to a halt; there was a queue of carts, and men and women loading and unloading goods.

Ana thanked the mister and his wife for their great kindness in stopping to help her, explained her task was urgent, and clambered down to walk on with Precious. The cart driver and her husband wished her heaven's blessings and hoped her companion was recovered safely. She nodded and said nothing; she could barely swallow past the lump in her throat. She hurried away, weaving between wagons, murmuring to Precious and promising him that help was ahead.

The palace loomed large, the bustle of the town ending at a wide stone bridge over a dry moat before an enormous gatehouse and raised portcullis. Several guards and officials directed the approach and departure of people who had business with the palace.

She joined the queue and peered beyond the gate to a great arch through the outer palace building. Sunlight dappled the Sacred Grove, wherein a broad gravel path hemmed the trees. A bell clanged above the arch, chiming the hour, followed by raucous shouts, then a flurry of children racing along the path, disappearing beyond sight, with whoops of hilarity. She hadn't heard laughter since they went into the cave, not true, pure laughter like that. It made her want to bawl again and she bit the inside of her cheek.

Two women pushed wooden carts laden with piles of grainy loaves along the edge of the queue, offering them to those in line. If people were selling food, the wait might be a long one. Urgency propelled her to step out of the line and approach the gate, garnering complaints from those waiting to be let through. A tall blond guard with a close-cropped beard stepped out to stop her, his brown eyes sharp with impatience.

He laid his hand on the hilt of his long sword with lazy elegance, no doubt a practiced move to motivate compliance. He wore a brown leather bib over his chain mail, stamped with a crest. He looked to be in his mid-thirties, blandly handsome and sure of himself. "Back in line, boy."

"I need to speak to a Lieutenant Micah?" Ana replied loudly, her voice cracking with renewed panic. She wished it hadn't come out as a question, but the guard was unimpressed by the name and his eyes narrowed as he looked at her more closely. "I was traveling with Leon Alvaro. We were attacked by Northmen. He saved me and sent me ahead, but he's still out there. He could be hurt. You need to send help. Please."

The guard stepped closer, his brow furrowing. Ana held her ground, though Precious flattened his ears and shifted his bulk to ward off the soldier. The man halted, eyeing the warhorse.

"Your name?"

She didn't want to answer and give away her gender. "Our horse was shot. Leon told me to come here and get help. He *needs* help. He's still out there. I don't know—"

"*Your name.*"

"Andrew," she said, finding herself matching the man's impatience. "And you are?"

"That's enough cheek." He pointed to the right wall of the gate. "Stand there and don't move." The guard turned on his heel to stride away.

"My horse is injured!" she called after him, with such indignation the whole queue renewed their glares.

"Shut your mouth, boy." Another guard took a step toward her.

She ducked beneath Precious's jaw, letting the horse form a barrier between her and the stares of the people. The blond guard had reached the palace arch and spoke to two men dressed in the same uniform. They all turned to look back at Ana, eyes wary and expressions hard. One of the men slipped inside a set of double doors and the other two stood conferring.

Wooden wheels creaked behind her. It was a woman with loaves. "You look road weary," the woman said. "You must be hungry."

"I don't have any money," Ana said curtly, watching the guards.

"Loaves are free for pilgrims."

Ana kept her eyes on the serious conversation happening by the palace arch. "I'm not a pilgrim."

"You've come to Eadin Palace for help," the woman said with a wry snort. "That makes you a pilgrim."

Ana glanced back at her, distracted. The woman was middle-aged with light-brown skin, green and brown eyes, and bright streaks of silver in her long dark braid. She reminded Ana of the tour guide by the Namen River, the one with the muslin skirt and feather earrings. This woman wore a plain gray rough-spun gown and a brown woolen wrap with a sturdy apron, where she tucked her hands while she talked.

"Are there really saints? In there?"

The woman pursed her lips. "None that would accept such a title."

"But there are"— Ana could hear the desperation in her own voice—"people who can do things ... help?"

"If they're able."

Ana sighed, eyeing the long queue. "How long does it take to get in?"

"Depends upon the need." The woman rested a gentle hand on Precious's flank. "Your poor beast."

Precious didn't flinch but turned his head and blinked.

Just then the blond guard and his compatriot disappeared through the double doors. Ana groaned and rubbed her face.

"You might feel better with some food," the woman pressed.

Ana wanted to snap at her to go away, but the woman wasn't wrong; she hadn't eaten since the maid's pastry at the constable's house and her stomach was growling. "They're free?"

"For pilgrims," the woman nodded, passing her a loaf. She cocked her head. "You have a curious accent, child. You have traveled far."

She didn't phrase it as a question but Ana nodded. "You could say that."

"You're in trouble. You need help."

Again, an obvious statement of fact but for some reason Ana's eyes welled.

"And not just for your horse," the woman said.

Ana shook her head. "My friend is in trouble. He might be … I don't know if he's still alive."

The woman grew very still, listening, a crease knotting her brow. "You're … lost."

Ana stifled a sob but found herself blurting, "I am. I'm lost. I lost my friends. I don't even know if *they're* alive. I lost … my way. I can't really … explain. I just want to go home but it's impossible. It's … not—"

"He's alive," the woman said, her gaze fixed on the middle distance.

Ana shut her mouth, a flash of goose bumps prickling her skin. "What?"

"He's alive."

Ana stared at the woman gazing into space, watching her brow knot in concentration. Ana's voice seemed to dry in her throat and she had to swallow before she spoke. "Who are you?"

"Mistress Hollinsen," the woman said, distracted. "I serve in the palace. May I?" She reached for Ana's face, slowly, as though gentling a wild animal that was threatening to bolt. Overwhelmed, Ana froze and let the strange woman touch her face. She rested her hand over Ana's mouth, lightly. "Speak."

"Speak?" Ana mumbled through the woman's fingers; they

smelled of bread and honey. "I don't understand. Say what? You're scaring me."

"Holy Mother..." The woman grew pale and she crossed herself, her brown and green eyes fixed on Ana. "You're one of *them*. One of the seven from the caves. You're not supposed to be here."

Ana blinked, her tears spilling. "You know my friends?"

"They're here."

A small sob broke in Ana's throat. "They're alive?"

Mistress Hollinsen looked past her to the gate and back over her shoulder to the town. "We don't have much time."

Ana blinked at her. "What?"

"Listen carefully." The woman gestured to Ana's mouth. "I know this is not your given tongue."

Ana almost dropped the loaf. She brought her free hand to her mouth, blinking rapidly.

"I dreamed of snow. A dark cave," Mistress Hollinsen began, speaking in short sharp statements. "In the cave, a shadowy figure stood before a blazing hearth. People watched. They were frightened. Angry. The shadow thrummed with malice. It began to speak. Its teeth gleamed in the firelight. Terrible long teeth. A great maw. It was casting a spell. The only word I recognized was seven. It kept saying seven. I woke sweating and terrified."

Ana shook her head. "You saw this? In a dream?"

"The night the fire star appeared."

Ana felt like her head was being pumped full of air and pressed her hand to her brow. "What does it mean?"

"I think your gift of speech is ... my doing."

Ana opened her mouth but nothing came out.

Mistress Hollinsen looked frustrated and crumpled her apron pocket, shifting her weight from foot to foot. "Understand, miracles are rarely tidy."

"How has my speech got anything to do with you?"

"I prayed for understanding. I prayed to Saint Jerome for the gift of understanding."

"I don't know who that is."

"The patron saint of languages."

Again, Ana's mouth hung open.

"I prayed and understanding came. The shadow was summoning seven for an offering. *Seven to appease. Seven to mend. Seven to sow. Seven to rend.*"

Ana shuddered. The holy fool's words.

Mistress Hollinsen looked at her in dismay. "I did not know who or what the seven were. I did not know if what I had seen in my dream was happening now or if it was a vision of things to come. I just kept praying. Then I saw in my mind the entrance to the sacred caves and a new moon rising. I knew it was the solstice to come. I warned the council and our guards rode out."

"And you think..." Ana said slowly, struggling to wrap her mind around what she was hearing. "You think your prayer hit us too?"

"I asked heaven to lend my grace to those who needed it." She shook her head in wonder. "A bead of light flew from my lips ... like a blue spark."

Ana remembered the vivid dream from the hot pools and the blue spark searing her throat before she woke up choking on water. She tried to grapple with what she was hearing but had no framework to comprehend a fraction of it. She stood at an absolute loss while Mistress Hollinsen again peered beyond her to the gate and then back toward the town.

"You couldn't have prayed for a lightning bolt to *smite* the shadow?" she asked airlessly. "For heaven to spare us?"

Mistress Hollinsen winced. "I did not know if it was real."

"It's called the Kjálka," Ana said bitterly. "It's real enough that Northmen have been hunting me for days."

Mistress Hollinsen flinched but Ana was too broken to care. What was she supposed to do with all this information?

"I'll fetch the captain. Wait here."

The woman abandoned her cart and stepped past.

"Wait." Ana grabbed her wrist. "Can't you just take me with you?"

"No," Mistress Hollinsen said, suddenly stern, looking beyond Ana to the town. "You must wait here."

Ana dropped her hold, rebuffed.

The woman strode through the gate without hesitation. A young guard merely gave her a deferential nod. Ana's thoughts spiraled in freefall as she stared at the woman's retreating form. The urge to cry out, to beg for her not to go, made her throat tight.

Was that a saint? *The* saint? The thought made her shiver. No. She said her name was Mistress Hollinsen. Did saints have last names?

The woman disappeared through the door in the arched passage and Ana wished she had said more, asked more. The agony of wasted time ate her up. Leon needed help *now*.

Precious turned his head and nipped at the loaf hanging at her side. Her stomach growled and suddenly she felt very faint. She tore a piece and fed it to the horse before stuffing some in her mouth. It was oaty and dense, with a honey crust. Inexplicably, the sweetness made her eyes well.

Finally, a man emerged, accompanied by the blond guard. This man was tall and imposing. He was older, middle-aged, and carried an air of authority, reinforced by the deference of the blond guard. No sign of Mistress Hollinsen.

Ana did her best not to look frightened or guilty but she was both. When the men stopped before her she straightened her spine and forced herself to look directly in the older man's eyes.

He gave her a piercing once-over. "This is not my lieutenant's horse, *girl*."

Ana couldn't stop the heat from mounting in her cheeks. The blond guard glared at her for taking him for a fool. She felt as though she were about to leap from a precipice. "No," she agreed, stroking Precious's jaw. "He belongs to a guy called Benjamin Brandt."

Both men stiffened.

"*Sir* Benjamin Brandt?" the older man growled.

"You come to the gates with a stolen horse?" the blond man demanded.

"We didn't steal him," she said, suddenly more exhausted

than she could bear. "One of Oleg's men was trying to steal him and abduct me. I think my friends are here? We escaped the earthquake in the caves."

This garnered an even harder look and the older man cast a glance at the waiting crowd. "Keep your mouth shut." He gave the blond man a sharp nod. "Get her inside."

"What about Leon?" she demanded. "What about Precious?"

"*Precious?*" the captain said, enunciating his astonishment.

"He needs help."

The man exhaled through his nose and waved over yet another guard, tall and young and eager to please. "Take this beast to the horse master."

Precious stamped his hoof and the young guard hesitated. Ana cupped the stallion's muzzle, letting him lip her fingers. She gazed into his beautiful eyes. "Go with the man," she murmured against his nose. "It's safe. I'll come and find you as soon as I can."

They were interrupted by the clatter of many hooves mounting the bridge. Her first alarm came from the look on the captain's face and the matching hardness of the blond guard's jaw. She felt rather than knew that worse trouble was upon her.

Six men, mounted on horses, clad in leather armor and chain mail. A seventh in a russet cloak, with bulky furs about his shoulders, formed the arrowhead of their approach. She recognized his dark hair and the grim mouth that promised retribution.

The people queueing at the gate pressed back against the rails of the bridge and several people ducked their heads and would not look at the men. The other guards looked to the captain, their hands reaching for the hilts of their swords.

Precious whinnied in recognition and Ana felt absurdly betrayed. She turned her back on Brandt and made desperate eyes at the captain. "Arrest me," she whispered. "Quickly, please." The captain only frowned. "Don't let him take me," she begged the blond guard, who seemed irritable but torn. By the look on his face, he was no fan of Sir Benjamin Brandt. She threw her hope on this. "Please," she whispered. "He attacked me in the forest. He is not good."

"What has this thieving witch done to my horse?" Brandt demanded. "Anubis!"

"You claim this beast?" The captain gave away nothing in his stern tone.

"And the horse."

Ana trapped her trembling hands beneath her arms. "Please, don't let him take me."

"This is Eadin Palace business now," the captain said.

Brandt narrowed his eyes. "I require the return of my property, my soul, and justice for the assault on my person."

"He attacked me," she whispered, shaking all over now. Her eyes darted about, looking for an escape route, but there was none. Where was Mistress Hollinsen? Surely she had some authority here?

Ana was hemmed between the guards at the gate and Brandt's cronies. Leon was likely dead or dying in the woods.

Her friends were somewhere in the palace beyond reach. Will was dead in the snow. Schoolkids lay dead in the cave, trapped forever. Northmen wanted to kill her. She was in the wrong time and place. She couldn't be here. Her chest was so clenched she thought she might hyperventilate. *Please, God.*

The captain cocked his head. "Your soul?"

Several bystanders crossed themselves and muttered, *God save us.*

"Obviously, I don't have his soul. I only said it to scare him off—he was trying to hurt me." She reached for the captain but stopped short of gripping his arm. The man gave her a hard look, part confounded, part calculating.

"The witch is standing before you with my damaged horse, wearing *my* clothes," Brandt said with a cold laugh. "Stolen from *my* saddlebags, which I notice seem to be missing along with my saddle and the scabbard of my sword, and somewhere on her person she keeps my likeness in a box. She claimed it was *my soul* and I should like it back."

The word "witch" swept among the bystanders like wildfire.

"Bring your complaint to the magistrate," the captain said. "The girl will remain in our custody until a hearing is called. The horse's wounds will be tended and he will be returned to you, sir."

The young guard led Precious—Anubis—away and Brandt's expression blackened. He slid from his mount and drew his long sword. His men dismounted with him, echoing the movement. Ana considered vomiting right there on the bridge.

"Give me the girl," Brandt snarled. He nodded over his shoulder. Three of his men grabbed bystanders and held blades to their throats. Screams shrilled from the bridge, attracting attention from the town. Ana stumbled against the blond guard, who held her roughly by the arm.

"I shall keep her as pledge," Brandt said, "until my horse is returned and compensation is paid for my losses."

The half dozen other Eadin Palace guards drew their swords and on the fortifications above the gate, archers nocked arrows to their bows. "Don't be a fool, Brandt," the captain bellowed, not yet drawing his own sword. "You'll be dead in a heartbeat."

"The difference between us, you pious prick,"—Brandt's lips pulled back from his teeth—"is that I will actually slit throats. You on the other hand will not risk the lives of innocents for the sake of a witch."

"Give him the witch!" a woman screamed, whose shrieking daughter was held by a brute, his blade already pressed to her throat.

"Stop it!" Ana yelled, beside herself.

The blond guard tightened his grip, bruising her arm to the bone. "Be still," he hissed, slipping something into her hand. "The lady told me to give you these until you meet again. She says, you must remember, her grace is with you."

It felt like a few beads tied with string. She frowned, uncomprehending, but the soldier looked resolute.

"Give him the witch!" Others joined the cry.

Ana shook her head. "I'm not. I'm not."

More people rushed the bridge and soon all of Brandt's men had taken hostages and the air was fraught with panic. The captain looked at the melee and ground his jaw. He still hadn't drawn his sword, calculating the risk and the cost. "We will not let him keep you," the captain murmured to her, before gesturing to his guards to put their weapons away. While they complied, the blond guard looked at the captain, aghast.

"Please," Ana begged, gripping the beads. "Don't do this."

"There will be slaughter and rioting if I do not," the captain said. His mouth was hard but there was regret in his eyes. "We will come for you, when the time is right."

A roaring sound filled Ana's ears, like the pounding of ocean waves. She felt lightheaded and dislocated from her body. She looked beyond him to the arch of green trees, her chest aching with peculiar longing.

To have glimpsed the Sacred Grove, glimpsed the walls of Eadin Palace, and be dragged away was cosmically cruel. She wondered if Saint Ansel was in there somewhere—oblivious to the trouble at her gates. She wondered if Mistress Hollinsen would tell her Ana had been there. It was such a puncturing thought, all the energy generated by terror and desperation seemed to drain away, a quick, thorough evacuation, leaving her empty.

She looked up at the captain, recognizing a warrior who knew how to strategize and weigh the odds in the heat of battle. He was resigned. So must she be. "Tell Gwen I was here."

He regarded her, then nodded tightly. "I will."

"Find Leon. He saved my life."

The blond guard drew a deep breath and tugged her forward. "Don't fight him," he whispered from the side of his mouth. "We will come."

She didn't say anything, she didn't even really struggle after that.

"Put her on my horse and the rest of you back away," Brandt snapped.

The blond guard hoisted her up into the saddle and she felt something cold and hard slip inside the edge of her shoe. A blade. He winked at her bewildered glance. "Don't fight," he said. "Unless it's for your life. Ansel is with you."

"Ansel?"

"Mistress Hollinsen," he said, with a parting nod. "Remember what she said, her grace is with you."

Ana sat winded.

The departure was swift and mechanical, hostages shoved back at their companions and the mounting of horses in an efficient sweep. Brandt's men formed a shield behind them, and the bastard was up in the saddle, grasping her roughly and spurring them back down the bridge. "I will await the return of Anubis," he called over his shoulder.

CHAPTER TWENTY-SIX

Daylight fled like a frightened villager. Leon stumbled over tree roots, weak from hunger and half drunk with exhaustion, as the sun slipped below the horizon like a door snapped shut. The distant howling of wolves made the hair on the back of his neck prickle. He'd left a trail of blood. He could only hope they'd find the bodies of the Northmen first and fill their bellies, preferring an easy meal over one that still had strength to fight.

Did he though? Have strength?

One good knock and he'd be a second helping for the pack. He swallowed painfully, his throat parched. His boot caught on the sudden rise of the ground and he tumbled to his knees with a grunt. When he looked up, he realized the trees had thinned, revealing the Roman road.

He could make out the path up the hill and his heart seized hope. The village would be just over the rise and the torches lighting the ramparts of Eadin Palace would gleam across the valley. He staggered upright, wincing at the hot slice of pain in his thigh and bicep. He'd taken some cuts from Oleg's scouts before desperation and the grace of heaven guided his blade to the right marks at just the right moments.

He'd made quick work of binding his wounds before letting the gallop of his pulse propel him into a run, hoping to catch up with Ana and the warhorse, but he'd lost their tracks before long.

Surely she would have found the road. He told himself she was safe in Eadin Palace and the council would be helping her. Yet doubt was at the edge of his thoughts. Why had no one come to search for him?

An answer came with the approach of horses and he darted off the path to hide behind the trees. Even if he were uninjured he'd take the precaution, though the road this close to the palace was unlikely to attract bandits. He couldn't be sure how many of Oleg's men might still be out there.

It was a party of four riders and it didn't take long for relief to flood through him when he recognized the familiar figure of his friend. He stumbled onto the road and waved his arm. "Micah!"

"Saints be praised!" Micah cried, pulling his mount to a halt. Edwin, Tabor, and Oakin rode with him. They leaped from their horses with cries of joy and grasped him, clapping his shoulder, clasping his arm, patting his back.

Leon hissed at the sting of his wounds.

"He's hurt," Oakin warned the others. "I told you."

"He's alive!" Edwin declared.

"Thank Odin," Oakin agreed.

"Alhamdulillah," Tabor murmured, slinging Leon's arm around his shoulders and almost lifting him from the ground.

"Forgive us, brother," Micah said. "The night we lost you, Oleg's scouts came raiding for those who'd fled the caves. We barely escaped with our lives. We've been searching for you since. Then word came from Ulmenholz and we rode out at once, only to find the village in uproar and you were gone."

"It was all a misunderstanding, Ulmenholz. I will explain all, but Oleg's scouts have not given up." He gestured to his wounds and his friends hissed in sympathy. "I count it a small price if Ana made it to you. Tell me she is safe."

Micah hung his head.

Leon gripped his forearm, his thoughts leaping ahead to calamity. She was hurt. She was dying. She was dead. It was his fault. He'd let his desire rob him of sense, so lost in the taste of her mouth and the press of her body, he had failed her. A dereliction of duty. "Tell me."

"We have ridden day and night," Micah said. "To Ulmenholz and back. We were not there when she arrived."

Edwin supplied a grim nod. "With Brandt's injured horse."

"*I* took the horse," Leon declared. "It was not her doing."

"The horse is being tended to," Micah said, but there was reluctance in his voice that frightened Leon and he could not bear it.

"Speak."

"She came to the gates and…"

"*Where is she?*" Leon demanded.

"Brandt took her."

Leon stared at his friend and for a moment it was only Tabor that kept him upright. "Took her?"

"He must have been watching the gate. He arrived with a band of men, hard on her heels." Oakin said.

"Called her a witch and a horse thief," Edwin said.

"He took bystanders hostage," Tabor said. "Held blades to their throats."

"The captain was facing a riot," Micah explained.

"The captain was there?" Leon demanded. "And he *let* Brandt take her."

"Brandt threatened to cut throats," Edwin said.

Brandt's soul. The musical box. Leon let loose a roar of frustration, then hung his head, defeat swamping him, dragging at his limbs. He could feel his men staring. "Tell me the captain went after her."

The prolonged silence forced him to look up and the regret in Micah's eyes crushed him. "He would not leave her undefended," Leon insisted. "He would not do nothing."

Micah looked at his feet. "It was only by heaven's mercy that we returned to the palace, to stock up on provisions, and heard what had passed. The captain summoned us, he wanted us to go after her, promising to send others to search for you."

Leon balked. "Then what are you doing here? You should be making for Birkenholz!"

"Schreiber put a stop to it."

Edwin and Oakin spat in the dirt.

"Schreiber?" Leon wanted to punch something. It was

Schreiber's insufficient instructions from the council that had sent them ill-prepared to the caves in the first place. Schreiber, always at the crossroads of his misery.

His thoughts leaped to poor Adeline, who had paid with her ruin when Schreiber discovered her and Leon's affair, exposing them to the censure of the council. "This time, I will fucking kill him."

Micah shook his head. "Schreiber was right. Brandt is in the pocket of Bishop Angeber. He warned the council that reprisals may invoke the wrath of Rome."

"Is that not the bread and butter of our saints?" Leon cried. "Invoking the wrath of Rome?"

"Come, brother." Micah gripped his shoulder. "*We* have been ordered not to act. *You* have not received this order. We can return to the village without entering the palace, without being seen. We stop you bleeding, we find you a horse and feed you so you can stay upright in your saddle. A mere pause to gather your strength and together we ride for Birkenholz."

Leon straightened, only to deflate again. He groaned and rubbed his face. "If you are discovered, you risk your place in the guard. I cannot ask this of you. Any of you. I will go alone."

His men looked back at him, defiant and eager. Micah patted his arm. "We never found you. We've been searching the woods with no sign."

"It is foolhardy to risk it," he said, half choked.

Oakin snorted, while Tabor folded his arms.

Edwin bounced his eyebrows. "Love a lick of foolhardy."

Micah lifted his palms as though he was helpless to stop the inevitable.

Leon swallowed, fatigue and throat-closing gratitude leaving him unable to speak. He nodded and gripped Micah's forearm, blinking against the sting in his eyes. Tabor rumpled his hair. Edwin gripped the sides of his face and pulled his head down to kiss his forehead with a theatrical smack of his lips. Oakin laughed, patting Leon's shoulder, before Micah and Tabor boosted him onto Edwin's horse.

While the thought of Ana in the hands of such a man as Brandt made his guts recoil, he could only hope the evil prick's superstition would keep him from laying a finger on her. He willed the girl to play the witch's part, using all her powers of pretense. Let her roll her eyes in her head, foam the spittle on her lips, make her voice as rough as the pit, and curse the bastard's balls off.

CHAPTER TWENTY-SEVEN

Ana sat in the corner of a small cozy bedroom. Not a dungeon cell or cage. No chains or shackles or implements of torture. Her brain did not know what to do with this fact or the bowl of stew, clacked on a stool by a no-nonsense housekeeper with the unlikely name of Mrs Pimms. Steam curled from the gravy, bobbed with cuts of venison, carrots, peas, and potatoes, sprinkled with parsley. A plate of crusty bread and curls of butter sat next to it but no knife for spreading. Obviously, no knife.

The housekeeper's lean rump swung before Ana's face as she bent to stack logs on the fire. One of Brandt's guards stood in the doorway, presumably to ensure she made no attempt to assault Mrs Pimms or escape down the hall. The man looked somehow bored and wary at the same time. He'd heard what Brandt had called her. Witch.

"That will do," Mrs Pimms muttered, straightening up and arching her pained back. She wiped gnarly hands on a stained apron but her gown beneath was clean and well kept. She wore a white cap tied under her chin and a gray-blonde braid lay over her shoulder. She cast a shrewd eye across

Ana's head. "What have you been about, missy?"

Again with the hair.

Ana stared at the woman's lined face. Her cheeks, nose, and forehead gleamed a permanent sort of pink, likely from a life spent managing a hearth. "Mrs Pimms, is it?" Ana said, with as much dignity as she could muster. The woman's eyes widened in amusement. "Does it bother you to know that your master has abducted me? Against my will. An eighteen-year-old girl, far from home, lost and friendless in a foreign land."

"Abducted?" The woman snorted. "Nonsense."

Ana flicked her eyes at the guard in the doorway. "Is it a regular thing, abducting girls? Is that what your master's into?"

"Enough of that filthy talk." Mrs Pimms folded her arms. "If you are under arrest, there's no doubt good reason for it. Only harlots, gossips, and women of ill repute have their heads shorn—which are you?"

"Women of ill-repute?" Ana muttered. "I'm a high school senior from Hamburg on the shittiest holiday known to man. I would like to go home."

Mrs Pimms rolled her lips into a hard line.

Ana looked to the guard. "You could help me. Take me back to Eadin Palace. They would pay you for my freedom."

The guard snorted, recognizing the lie for what it was. The Eadin Palace guards had handed her over without a fight. The man turned aside, nodding for Mrs Pimms to exit.

"Eat up, girl, and get some sleep. Count yourself lucky the master has not thrown you in with the pigs." She paused on the threshold. "And if I come back and find you have damaged a single thing in this room, I will tan your cheeks myself. We have little furniture left as it is."

The door shut with a clap and the heavy iron clank of a key ramming a lock into place. Ana drew the blade from her shoe and gripped it for comfort. The blond guard had said they would come for her. When?

She stared at the closed door and waited for tears but none came. It occurred to her that she had also stopped shaking, primarily because exhaustion had sapped her core. A hot meal, a warm room, a bed and desk and bedpan had not been anywhere in her expectation, arriving at Brandt's estate in the dark.

Brandt had not spoken to her or touched her or addressed her existence in any way beyond keeping her in the saddle. And when the initial terror ebbed and weariness got the better of her, the rhythmic jostling of the ride had rocked her into sleep.

Still, it irked her to picture herself slumped against the vile man, her head nestled into his shoulder, his arm about her waist, as it had been with Leon. For the hundredth time, she wondered if Leon lived, if he was injured, if he'd made it to the palace, if they were helping him, if he thought of her.

Of course he thought of her. If he lived. He'd spent the last four days keeping her alive. Doing his duty but still showing her kindness and tenderness in their last moments together.

If he lived, was he regretting that tenderness? Regretting that kiss? It had cost him his awareness of the creeping threat of Oleg's men. It had cost him a fight. Three against one. She wondered if his wound was okay, if he'd suffered new injuries.

Her stomach gave a painful growl and with no one left to spite, she grabbed the wooden spoon and shoveled the stew down her throat. Rich, aromatic, delicious. If it was laced with poison, she wasn't sure she cared. The bread was heavenly, the butter too—spread with her little blade. She stretched her shrunken stomach until it hurt.

Finally, she climbed onto the bed—it was soft and comfortable. She couldn't bring herself to slip beneath the sheets but she did draw the comforter from the foot of the bed and tucked it up to her chin. She left her shoes on. In case. Of what? She didn't know—just in case. She felt in her pocket for the length of knotted beads and peered at the strange gift. It looked like it had been cut or ripped from a necklace.

Saint Ansel had given her the beads to keep until they would meet again. She considered throwing them in the fire. That woman had left her on the bridge like she'd known this would happen. *You must stay here.* And all that wild talk about her dream and her prayer to Saint Jerome. She had seen the Kjálka, heard the prophecy, knew she was one of the seven but *let* her be taken by Brandt and his men.

What was she supposed to think? She closed her eyes for a moment, to rest them; and despite the fitful sleep she'd managed on the journey, she slept again.

When she blinked, the room was bright with sunlight streaming through the unshuttered windows. Buckets of steaming water sat by the hearth, where a new fire burned. Last night's dinner had been cleared away and a fresh plate lay on the stool, a small loaf with a plate of butter, cheese, sliced pear, and ham. Another cup of something sat next to it.

She scowled at the thought of Mrs Pimms bustling about the room while she slept like a lamb. Perhaps the stew had been laced with a sedative. But her head didn't ache and there was none of the cotton-wool effect of sedation. She hated the idea they would read her sleep as compliance. Maybe she should smash the place up—crash the stool through the window, just so they knew where she stood on being held captive.

Half panicked that someone would walk in, she used the bedpan, then stripped naked, hid the blade in her shoe, and washed. The stacks of linen, she presumed, were drying cloths, smaller squares for washing and a hard block of soap that smelled of honey and vanilla. She kept one bucket for her face and hair. Clothes had been laid on a chair, stockings and fine embroidered slippers sat beside them. She eyed it all with suspicion but she couldn't help the small groan of pleasure in sluicing her skin in hot water.

While the worst of her scrapes from plummeting down the cliff were healing well, her body was a sea of bruising. Still, she washed until the water was murky and wrapped a drying sheet around her before tending to her hair. She lathered it into a frothing sop and squeegeed the foam with drying cloths before dunking her whole head in the bucket to rinse.

Of course, that's when one solid knock preceded the door opening. She leaped upright like a gymnast executing an Olympic landing, sending an arc of water through the air, splattering her captor.

Brandt scowled and wiped his face on the sleeve of his shirt. Ana gave thanks to all the powers of heaven that she was wrapped, at least, in a drying sheet that reached her ankles. There was none of the blatant staring she had endured beside the stream. She wasn't sure if the sudden drenching was the reason for his restraint but there was a look of guilt in his eyes.

Mrs Pimms bustled up behind him. "I said she was asleep!"

"It's near midday," he said, gruff and unforgiving. "Get dressed and join me in the library."

Ana glared at him, but too aware of her vulnerability to retort with anything rude or combative. He could simply cross the room, clobber her, and drag her naked down the stairs.

"Mrs Pimms, kindly collect my clothes for laundering," he said, turning on his heel and stalking out, his boots clomping down the hall. Mrs Pimms filled her wicker basket with the stolen clothes and paused over Ana's shoes.

"Not those!" Ana said, remembering the hidden blade. "They're mine!"

Mrs Pimms redirected her viper's strike to the green string

bikini and denim shorts, eyeing the fabric with open confusion. "Where did you get these?"

"Home," Ana said. "Please don't take them. They're all I
have."

Mrs Pimms pursed her lips. "You can have them back once
they have seen the laundry tub."

Ana swallowed. "Thank you."

"I would not keep him waiting." She closed the door behind
her but there was no lock turned. It occurred to her there had
been no sound of a key before Brandt had walked in. Could
she have escaped in the night? What game was this arsehole
playing? Did he believe he could trick her into thinking she
wasn't a prisoner? There must be a guard outside the door.
Down the hall. One of his cronies waiting to pounce at the
slightest misstep.

There was no underwear to speak of, just a fine linen
underdress thing with billowing sleeves and a roomy sack-
shaped overdress in duck-egg blue that fell to her ankles. She
figured the length of soft, braided leather was a belt to gather
the waist. She had to dig the billowy sleeves out of the cuffs of
the overdress and some distant part of her traumatized brain
recognized that if she were back home and not terrified that
she was about to be tortured, raped, or murdered, she would
totally be getting into the medieval dress-up vibe.

There were fine woolen stockings that tied above the knee,
scratchy but marvelously warm, and a dark-blue triangular
wrap thing of thick knobbly wool, which she hadn't a clue

how to wear. In the end, she draped it over her shoulders and crossed the long bits about her chest and back, tucking the tails under the braided belt, like a vest. She slipped the blade in the folds and hoped she wouldn't impale herself. She put on her own shoes. Better for running in.

There was no mirror. She'd scrubbed her face and even rubbed a soapy finger around her teeth—foul beyond description. There wasn't much she could do about her mop of damp hair, but she tucked tendrils behind her ears and tried the door.

It opened. She stuck her head into the hall. No visible guard. The building was a smallish castle but still a castle. Stonework and wood. If he hadn't confiscated her phone, she'd be taking snaps. She'd turned it off after Ulmenholz to save the last dregs of her battery. She hoped Brandt hadn't smashed the thing open to free his soul.

There were two more rooms that led off the hallway but both doors were locked. A light at the end of the passage drew her to a staircase with a high window illuminating the space. There was no one about.

Unsettled, she took the stairs slowly, clinging to the banister, craning to hear voices. No cries of tortured souls, no sounds of unfortunates pleading for mercy. She reached a landing and two young women came up with buckets and scrubbing brushes. They wore the same dresses as Mrs Pimms, braids and caps and aprons and all. They gawped at her bare head and exchanged a scandalized look.

"Excuse me," Ana said, lifting her chin. "Where can I find the library?"

One nudged the other and she said, "At the bottom of the stairs to your right, Miss."

They waited, letting her past. But when Ana took the next flight down she heard them giggling and muttering. They definitely mentioned her hair.

She was starting to take offense. Gwen had worked hard to fix the shambles of The Butchering and she had received nothing but compliments back home—aside from Stefan's double take. There was no accounting for medieval taste.

At the bottom of the stairs a wide hall led to several open chambers, sparsely furnished with rugs, animal pelts, trestle tables, benches; no paintings or tapestries, but darker squares suggesting they might have hung there once. A few sets of antlers and iron candelabras. The flagstone floor was sprinkled with rushes, and mullioned windows framed green lawns and gardens beyond. It was cold but that was to be expected in a stone building with no central heating. She was grateful for the woolen clothes left by Mrs Pimms.

A hulking frame stepped into the hall, one of Brandt's goons, and she skidded to a halt, bracing to run. "She's here, Benjin," he said, presumably to his master, before stepping out of the way and gesturing for her to enter.

"See if Gunther needs help, Bryn." It was Brandt. "That shiftless pillock of a son cannot tell his head from his arse, and his father is too old to manage the thatch by himself."

"Yes, sir," the goon replied, suddenly formal in her presence, nodding as he went off.

Ana stepped into the library and worked hard not to stare about in awe. There was only a single wall of books behind his desk but still, she could imagine that was quite something given the times. There were two large trestle tables with maps laid out and pinned by curious weights. There was a chair and a hard-backed bench with cushions that formed a sofa of sorts before a giant hearth. A fire crackled in the grate, offering a blast of heat into the high-ceilinged room. Nothing decorated the stone walls, though again square patches remained where once there might have been hangings.

Brandt sat at a desk with a plate of half-eaten food next to a pile of papers. He was shaving the end of a quill. An actual quill. Like this was a movie. And he looked aggravated. Her mobile phone sat in a pewter dish to his left.

She swallowed. "Got your soul, then?"

He looked up sharply. "No."

When he didn't say anything else she wandered past the closest table, letting her eyes trail surreptitiously across the map. A significant chunk of the left-hand side of the map was torn away in a jagged curve and a two-inch gap separated the parts. She was too wrong-footed by the man's hospitality to risk prying, so she averted her eyes and took a seat by the hearth. The heat was marvelous. She leaned toward the blaze, hugging her arms, and waited.

The cutting instrument made a satisfying scraping sound

on the tip of the quill and he gave himself to the task with considerable focus. She wondered if this was part of the ploy to unsettle her before he did something properly awful. Didn't he murder a family once?

The silence stirred her fear. She couldn't trust the food, clothes, or hospitality. He would have let his men slit the throats of innocent bystanders to get his way. "I left you a note," she said, "that we would return your horse."

He didn't lift his head but swiveled his piercing gaze toward her and glowered through the disheveled fall of his hair. He was intimidating. Even without his billowing cloak or the traveling furs on his shoulders—even seated, he was imposing. Though his shirt was unlaced at his throat and his cuffs rolled back mid forearm, there was nothing casual about the situation. He wore a fitted tunic over his shirt and an amulet with a silver turret and tree, just in case it wasn't clear who the master of the house was.

She looked away and muttered, "Technically, it wasn't theft."

He dipped the end of the quill in an inkwell and spread his hand over a piece of parchment. He scratched a few words and dipped again before deigning to speak. "You left me bleeding on the icy ground next to a half-dead wild man."

She thought for a moment. "To be fair, I had just been attacked by both of you."

He paused over the paper. "I did not *attack* you; I *apprehended* you. A stranger, roaming my lands without leave, indecently disrobed, openly disrespectful, wielding foreign objects, and clearly not to be trusted. It was my duty to investigate."

"Grabbing a girl by the hair?"

He pursed his lips, the muscle in his jaw shifting. "Perhaps I was overzealous."

"You saw me." She sat up, stiff-shouldered. "I was clearly injured. Defenseless. Freezing. Lost. Afraid. Literally no threat to you—at all."

He inhaled and exhaled through his nose but turned his scowl to the top of his desk. "For all I knew, you were injured because you had murdered a family of peasants."

"And took off my clothes to run through the forest in triumph?"

"Playing the witch?"

She slapped her hands on her knees. "I was trying to frighten you."

"I saw you casting your spell on the Northman."

"And you heard me explain that to Leon."

"You speak the Northern tongue."

"So?" She resisted the urge to point out that the language detail was more alarming than reciting *Macbeth*.

"What decent girl could pretend such evil?"

"A good actor, fighting for her life," she said, humiliated to feel the tightening in her throat and the welling in her eyes. "You could not begin to comprehend what I've gone through since I stepped foot in this place."

He sat up and leaned his elbows on his desk, an invitation to elaborate.

"Believe me when I say that if I could leave here, this whole godforsaken time, and go back ... go home, I would."

"What is stopping you?"

"What's stopping me?" Her breath hitched. "Let's see. First it was an earthquake that killed half my class. Escaping that, only to stumble onto a battlefield, where most of the other half were killed." Her voice broke and tears pricked her eyes but she forged on. "Then there was a patch of running for our lives and trying not to die of hypothermia. I was chased off a cliff, lost all my friends, then I was physically assaulted by a handsy nobleman and almost abducted by a feral Northman. Followed by a couple more attacks, a fire, a mob of angry villagers, and then just when I'm about to reach safety"—she clapped her hands together and pointed them toward Brandt—"You again."

"You could have ridden home the moment you stole my horse."

She sniffed and swallowed hard. "I wish that were true."

He looked at her, narrowly. "What does *Eadin Palace* have to do with it?"

She raised her shoulders. "Leon thought the saints might know a way to get me home."

"Calling them saints is heresy," he said flatly.

She blinked. "Right."

A scuffle of rushing footsteps had her jerking to her feet,

when a girl ran into the room with a grubby round face and a tiny, half-strangled rabbit, eyes bulging, in her clutches. "Look what Pimms gave me!"

"Blast it, Maudwyn," Brandt glowered at the child. "Get it outside before it shits everywhere."

"Pimms says shits is foul talk, Uncle Benjin." She crossed herself and performed a dainty turn toward Ana. "Are you the witch?"

"No. My name is Ana. I think your rabbit is choking."

Maudwyn adjusted her hold, supporting the poor wee thing beneath the rump and placing it gently in the pocket of her apron. "Are you going to fix me?"

Ana blinked at the girl. "Fix you?"

"Christ, Maudwyn," Brandt muttered.

"That's my mama's dress," the little girl said, coming to stand uncomfortably close to Ana, leaning her elbow on the armrest of the chair. Feeling awkward, Ana sat down, uncertain what to say.

"Is it?" Ana looked at Brandt but he seemed resigned to letting her flounder. "Mrs Pimms let me borrow it."

"Like Uncle Benjin's horse?"

Ana bit her lip. "That's right."

"But you did not ask," Maudwyn said, with a pious tilt to her chin. With Ana seated, the girl was taller than her. "Uncle Benjin was very cross about that, as he loves Anubis very much, even though Bryn says he is the devil's own spawn."

"Is that why he's called Anubis?"

"'Tis a heathen name." Maudwyn crossed her hands on the rest and spoke solemnly. "The Egyptian god of the dead."

"I didn't know his name when I borrowed him," Ana explained. "I gave him another name."

Maudwyn's eyes and mouth grew round, and she checked to see if there was outrage on her uncle's face, but he kept a flinty stare. "What did you call him?" the girl whispered.

"Precious."

"Precious?" Maudwyn let loose a great hooting laugh and Brandt clapped his quill on the desk and rose to his feet with an indignant scraping of chair legs.

"Ridiculous name for a warhorse," he muttered.

"That's what Leon said."

Maudwyn could not stop laughing. "Did he try to bite your head off?"

"No," Ana said, warming to the girl. "Of course not. He's far too sweet."

"Did you hear that, Uncle Benjin?" Maudwyn almost hopped from foot to foot. "Anubis is far too sweet!" Her delight was unfettered and as her uncle came around the desk to chivvy her out of the library, she suddenly stopped and stared above Ana's head, her eyes glazing. "Oh dear. The angel has come."

"Lie down, Maudy," Brandt commanded, darting forward, his expression stark. But before he could reach her, the girl went stiff, her whole body clenching, her face contracting into a pained wince, and she crumpled to the rug.

Ana lunged to catch her but was too slow. Maudwyn hit

the ground, the back of her head banging on the floor. "Fuck," Brandt muttered, skidding to his knees and scooping the little girl onto his lap. The rabbit squirmed in Maudwyn's apron pocket. He pulled it out and shoved it at Ana. He then searched the girl's hands, examining her fingers, which triggered another round of expletives. He poked around the collar of her dress and found nothing there.

"Can I do anything?" Ana asked, half perched on the edge of her seat. "Is there someone I can fetch?"

"She should be wearing her cramp ring," he said to himself, before drawing a steadying breath. He scanned the room. "She'll come around. It usually only takes a minute or two, though she'll be cold and tired when she wakes."

"I could find a blanket?"

He lifted her gently from the floor. "Help me."

Ana dithered but left the rabbit on her seat and followed him, clearing the books and papers from the sofa bench. He lifted the girl onto the cushions and plucked a blanket from the armrest. Ana watched the incongruously tender ministrations of the man before she rescued the rabbit, which seemed too stunned to contemplate leaping to freedom. She knew how it felt.

Brandt sat on the end of the sofa bench, elbows on his knees, hands clasped loosely between the spread of his legs. Calloused hands, flecked with scars and rings of dirt beneath his nails. He was no pampered lord. Silence crammed the air between them but he didn't meet Ana's eye and she had no clue what to say, though she was fairly certain she wasn't scared anymore.

"She's supposed to lie down when it's coming on—otherwise she wallops the back of her head, or smashes a tooth."

Ana wanted to ask if it was epilepsy but had no clue what it might be called back ... now. Her cousin used to have seizures— she recognized the body clench before Maudwyn fell slack. "She can tell when it's coming on?"

He nodded and seemed as though he wouldn't say anything else but then felt compelled to explain. "It started when her mother died. Sometimes she can avert them; she'll have you recite the Lord's Prayer or a psalm of protection until the queerness passes."

Ana frowned. It couldn't be epilepsy. A person with epilepsy might feel the seizure coming on but could do nothing to forestall it, as far as she knew. "I'm sorry about your sister," she murmured.

He offered a grudging nod.

"How old was your niece when her mother passed?"

"It was almost a year ago. Maudwyn was nine."

"She seems very sweet."

"She's a hellion, a snoop, and a thief," Brandt muttered.

Ana wasn't entirely sure what a hellion was but she nodded. "My kind of girl."

CHAPTER TWENTY-EIGHT

Leon rode at the head of the company, his eyes on the overcast sky. It was getting late and soon the hidden sun would dip below the hills and darkness would flood the forest. He knew they would not reach Birkenholz until late in the night but still, the urge to race along the Roman road boiled in his joints and marrow.

He was desperate to make up for lost time, horrified at the hours wasted in sleep, but his men had been days on the road, searching for him, equally ragged and weary. Micah had urged him to rest, arguing that exhaustion would put them at risk in battle. For their sake and Ana's, he'd conceded.

They had taken shelter in a farmer's barn on the outskirts of Eadin, paid for food, bandages for his wounds, and laid out silver for the loan of a horse. To his shame, sleep had come sooner than he expected. His dreams had been plagued with horrors, Ana broken, abused, dead, as he battled faceless enemies to reach her. Too late.

"Leon," Micah called. He looked back to find the stern-faced lieutenant reining in his mount. Leon was riding too fast. The shake of Micah's head warned him he would overtax his horse. He nodded and though it ate him up inside, he slowed his pace. They still had the return trip to consider and he would likely bear Ana before him.

The thought of holding her again thrilled through him and he was glad his friends could not see his face. What a shame that his time with Ana had been so overshadowed by his injuries. Yet pain and fever had glazed the memory in high color; he could picture her by the fire in the abandoned cabin, her face cast in gold, her pale eyes made molten. Her body in the musical box, those curves and the searing look she cast over her shoulder. He shifted his weight in the saddle and shook his head.

If Micah could search his thoughts in this moment, he would say his time with Ana had compromised his judgment. Yet, he told himself, whether he desired the girl or not, honor alone would compel him to action ... wouldn't it? She was his responsibility.

If he had been with her on the bridge, none of this would have happened. Ana would be safe in the palace, reunited with her friends and working with Saint Ansel to find a way home. It was his *duty* to right the wrong.

There were few travelers on the roads. He wondered if word of the Northmen had spread. Crows cackled in the treetops and the pounding of hooves rumbled ominously in his ears, like war drums. His friends were too quiet. Edwin wasn't singing. Oakin wasn't spinning bawdy yarns. Tabor wasn't telling Oakin to shut his filthy mouth, and Micah wasn't agreeing with him.

If he glanced back, he'd see grim expressions. Like him,

they must be contemplating what lay ahead and considering the prospect of close-quarters fighting once they forced their way inside the keep at Birkenholz. None of them relished this sort of clandestine scheme. Open battle was honorable. This felt like skulking.

Were they regretting their decision to help? The risk to their lives, their place in the palace guard? He shoved the thought down. No. His friends were brave and loyal. If censure came, he would take the punishment, not them. Besides, once the council met Ana, they would understand. Once they heard of the miracle she had performed in healing him—he would convince her of the crucial relevance of telling the council—surely, they could not fault his choice to intervene.

CHAPTER TWENTY-NINE

Ana sat before the library hearth, balancing a plate of cold meat and bread on her knees. It must be late; it felt late, but she was disorientated by the long afternoon of waiting and hours spent alone. Maudwyn was still sleeping. Brandt had carried her to her room and sent for a doctor, then left Ana with a guard at the door for the rest of the day.

When he returned, the courage she'd found in their first confrontation dissipated. His taciturn silence, as he sat at his desk back at his paperwork, was extremely unsettling. Surely he would make his intentions clear. He hadn't abducted her from the bridge with no purpose.

She tore off a corner of thick, grainy bread and nibbled the edge, eyeing him. Mrs Pimms had brought them dinner, with a frown of disapproval. *It wasn't civilized. Guests should eat in the great hall. The master should have let her prepare them a proper meal.* Brandt had dismissed her. Ana resisted pointing out she was a prisoner, not a guest.

"They won't do anything weird to her, will they?" she said.

Brandt didn't look up, but his lips soured. "What?"

"This doctor you've sent for." She set her plate aside. "It's not like, gargle this toad and stand in a barrel, or tape this ferret to your chest and bay at the moon type of deal ... is it?"

"Are you a healer?" he asked flatly.

She folded her hands and stared at her scraped knuckles. Leon's scar swam before her eyes. "Where I come from, we're big on science."

"Where you come from." He enunciated each word.

She bit her lips. "Yes."

He sat back in his chair and linked his fingers across his stomach. "You find us backward?"

"I find you ... as you cannot help but be ... in this time." She cringed inwardly; she sounded like a pompous, condescending prat. "I mean. It's different. We have ... stuff ... it's just ... different. And that's not anyone's fault."

He picked up her phone. "This different stuff?"

"Technology."

He cocked his head dubiously. "What is it for?"

"Communication, primarily."

He narrowed his eyes.

"I mean, if I'm in one place and you're in another, I could call you on my phone ... if you had one. If you had coverage—look, I can't, this isn't a useful conversation. It doesn't matter." She got to her feet and tried her hands on her hips but that didn't feel right. She crossed her arms and lifted her chin. "What's happening here? You arrested me. Are you going to kill me?"

He made no effort to reply. He simply stared at her for an uncomfortably long time.

"Well?" she said, her voice going high.

"If I were going to kill you," he said slowly, not shifting from his relaxed pose. "You would be dead."

"So … what? I'm your prisoner?"

"I am deciding."

She huffed and stalked toward a trestle table where the large map lay pinned flat with rocks. The western third of the map had been ripped away and lay beside it pinned like an island. "I don't belong here. I shouldn't be here. It's not safe."

"It is not."

She looked back at him and he sighed, rising to his feet. He made his way around the desk. Ana remembered the blade hidden in her vest but when he joined her at the table she didn't feel inclined to reach for it. Yet. He was a head taller than her and she was forced to tilt her head back to look right at him. "I want to go home."

He ran his lower lip through his teeth and contemplated the layout of his map. "Point to home."

She sighed. "It's not on the map."

"The wild man, the Northman with the black teeth. What did he want?"

"Me, apparently. My friends."

"Did he hurt you?"

"Enough." She pulled at the collar of her gown, showing the rope burn on her neck.

"You fought him."

"You saw what I did."

"Played the witch."

She nodded, a little shocked that he seemed to accept she was pretending far more easily than Leon. "I was afraid."

"What did he want from you?" he pressed again, leaning on the table, supporting himself on the pads of his fingers. "My land is protected, there are Danes well settled here and in surrounding districts. Oleg took a great risk."

She swallowed and briefly summarized what Leon had gleaned about Oleg's demon priestess foreseeing the arrival of the students. It sounded ludicrous, yet saying it aloud sent an icy wash creeping up her scalp. She thought of Ulmenholz's holy fool and his unnatural knowledge of her name. She thought of Mistress Hollinsen's dream and Saint Jerome. There was no way she'd tell Brandt about any of that; it would only taint his view of her even more.

"A sacrifice?" Brandt repeated, repulsed. "Oleg the Butcher means to feed you all to his beast?"

She shrugged and stared at the map, a feeling of profound dislocation pulling her up through the top of her head. It was like watching herself in a movie. A strange laugh escaped her throat. "You have no idea how weird this is."

He looked at her sidelong. "And you believe Ansel might save you?"

"I don't know. It was Leon's idea." And her desperate hope.

"Your companion?" He watched for her nod. "You doubt him?"

She looked up and found his eyes drilling into her again. Bright hazel. "I don't know what to believe. I'm here. Which is impossible. I've seen things that are impossible. I thought Ansel was a story. She is—where I'm from—a story, an idea. I suppose if you want an impossible solution to an impossible situation, she might be a good place to start?"

He worked his jaw, seeming lost in his thoughts, strands of dark hair having slipped the knot to hang loose around his face. He looked … unhappy.

"You don't like Eadin."

Again, his expression soured. "I do not."

She regarded his stern face. He seemed much older than he looked, burdened, tired. "Leon says they do a lot of good."

"Does he?" He clicked his teeth and pointed at the ripped portion of the map, running his finger along the frayed edge of the canvas. "This is where the Namen River flows. Now."

Ana was slow to grasp the meaning, as she stared at the ripped-off third. "This was … your land?"

He gave a brusque nod. "My family's. I was two years old when the earthquake struck and the river turned. Hame claimed the land and livestock across the western bank of the Namen. We lost half our holdings. Several crofts were swept away in the night, farmers, their families. Bodies never found."

Ana's hand drifted to her mouth. There had been no

mention of lives lost by the tour guides, other than the purge lords who tumbled into the chasm. She touched the murky lower half of the map. "What happened here?"

"Fertile farmland, flooded and turned to bog."

"What are these markers?" She pointed to a selection of round tokens with Roman numerals.

He exhaled through his nose. "Places where we have tried to grow wheat and marsh roots. Watercress is best but it's been a slow and hellish rebuild with tenants who have lost their means. Mastering a new way has not been … uncomplicated. Building homes on marsh, developing channels for boats to trade…" He sighed. "My father did his best for our people. He even petitioned Eadin for compensation."

She watched his face grow hard, bitterness glittering in his eyes. "They wouldn't help?" she murmured, strangely wounded at the idea that Eadin would fail to respond, as though she bore some responsibility for their lack of action.

"They felt they had more pressing matters to attend to, such as building a palace. Meanwhile, Bishop Angeber still requires taxes as though no land were lost."

New questions piled up in her throat but the least relevant spilled out. "How old are you?"

His brow wrinkled at her impertinence. "Two-and-twenty. How old are you?"

"I'll be nineteen in May." Why did she say it like that? She looked away. "And you've been dealing with this by yourself? Where are your folks?"

"My parents?" A dark curtain seemed to close behind his eyes and he straightened. "My father passed when I was twelve, my mother a year later. My eldest brother when I was sixteen."

And his sister last year. She thought of wee Maudwyn, upstairs. He must be lonely. "That's awful. I'm so sorry."

"It is hardly any concern of yours," he snapped, and stalked away to the fireplace to stab at the embers with an iron poker.

Stung, Ana stayed with her back to him. Did she think they were having a moment? Building a rapport? He was right. Why should she care? She didn't care. Maudwyn seemed sweet but he was still the prick who roughed her up by the river. Scared the living shit out of her on the bridge. Took her prisoner. She'd had enough.

It was time to make plans. She'd go to bed and think of a way to escape. No sitting on her ass. She had the knife in her vest. She'd put it to use if she had to. Tomorrow. Right now, she felt as heavy as stone and longed for oblivion.

Not flouncing, not marching, nothing petulant—she crossed to the double doors, not giving the sullen lord another look.

"Ana," he said, staring into the fire, "I have crofters who cannot pay their taxes and I will not demand a cent more from the poor wretches. However, I find I am running out of things to sell." He gestured at the mostly empty room and bare walls. "The money Eadin pays in compensation for *your crimes* will clear their debts and satisfy Angeber's coffers. You stand as pledge until the return of my horse and Eadin Palace pays. Then you will be free to go."

CHAPTER THIRTY

Ana hurried up the first flight of stairs, relief coursing through her. Hope made her lightheaded. She could club Brandt with his poker for keeping her in fear when he knew what he was doing all along, but she couldn't bring herself to hate him. Not after the revelations over the map or the needs of his people. She rounded the switchback for the next climb and stopped short on the landing with a gasp.

Maudwyn sat on the top step, a ghostly blot in her nightdress, the bunny in the hollow of her crossed legs. Ana almost fell down the stairs with fright and clutched her chest. "You gave me a heart attack."

"Nibbs woke me," the child said, scratching the bunny's ears.

"Nibbs?"

"It is a good name," the girl said, peering at her with hollow eyes.

"You should be asleep," Ana said, her heart still pumping hard in her chest.

Maudwyn cocked her head. "Was Uncle Benjin cross with you? Sometimes he sounds angry but really he's just sad."

Ana sank down on the drafty stairs beneath the girl. "That's a grown-up thing to say."

"Pimms says it, when Uncle Benjin gets ropable."

Ana smiled. "Is he often cross?"

Maudwyn frowned, considering. "He says I am oft times bedeviled."

She chuckled and patted the girl's bunny. "I think he loves you very much."

The girl smiled, her lower lip wobbling. "I'm hungry."

"You missed dinner." Still giddy with the update on her prisoner status, Ana remembered her abandoned plate and regarded the little girl. "Shall we raid the kitchen?"

Maudwyn grinned. "Are you oft times bedeviled?"

"I think I might be."

The kitchen was located on the ground floor, along the corridor from the library. Maudwyn led the way, signposting landmarks with happy chatter. A receiving room. The great hall, a chapel, the door to a small barracks, servants' quarters, and the washroom. Ana was glad to have the girl as company, less intimidated by the shadowy depths of the castle.

Hot coals still glowed in the great kitchen fireplace. A sturdy trestle table dominated the center of the room, its polished planks worn and smooth. The ceiling was low and bowed with thick beams, baked black by heat and smoke and torchlight. Mullioned windows winked on a velvet night in the grounds of Birkenholz. Ana's reflection warped in the buckled panes, their candle flames bending and stretching.

Ana lit a candle and Maudwyn foraged in the larder. She let Maudwyn forage in the larder, hauling out a loaf of bread, a clay jar of butter and another of honey, and a thick wedge of hard cheese. Ana dug out knives and plates and Maudwyn stood on a stool. She couldn't help but wonder if it had been designed just for the little girl, to hack fat slices from the loaf. The baby rabbit sat on the table between them, whiskers vibrating, as it nibbled through a leaf of stolen silver beet.

"Will Mrs Pimms be upset to find a rabbit on her kitchen table?"

"She prefers them strangled and skinned."

Ana winced. "I suppose she would." The bread and honey tasted more delicious than anything she had eaten since she escaped the caves, likely also because she felt hope in her heart for the first time since then. "Where I come from, we call this a midnight feast."

The girl grinned, cheese gumming her teeth. "I like that."

Ana poured them apple cider from a flagon covered with a muslin cloth and Maudwyn swigged hers like a man downing a pint.

"I am always starved after a turn," the girl said, releasing a man-sized burp that made them both laugh. "Pimms says no one will ever marry me, with that sort of carry on."

"You've a few years before you need to worry about that," Ana said with a grimace. She watched the little girl tear another chunk of bread between her teeth. "Does it happen a lot? These fainting spells."

The girl shrugged. "What is a lot?"

"Every day? Every other day? Once a week?"

She shrugged again. "Sometimes it is two or three times in a day. I suppose that is a lot. Then there will be a patch of days where nothing happens. Then there might be a bit where it happens daily."

Ana chewed her lip, thinking again of her cousin's epilepsy. "Your uncle says there are times where you can stop it from coming on."

Maudwyn nodded. "I say the Lord's Prayer or have someone say it for me."

"It helps?"

"A queer, dizzy feeling makes my head feel hot and the candle lights go a bit funny. Sometimes, I see the angel — when he comes, I know I cannot stop it and lie down before I fall. I was a bit slow today. Caught short."

A crawling feeling crept up the back of Ana's neck. "Tell me about the angel."

Maudwyn shook her head. "Talking about him makes him come. I don't want to faint again."

She nodded but her heart made a quick step in her chest. It wasn't epilepsy. Not from what she understood from her cousin's experience. Still, she hated the idea of the girl having to live her life in fear of being overcome.

"I am not allowed to go riding by myself," Maudwyn said, screening her mouth with her hand as she talked and chewed at the same time. "Only if I ride with Bryn or Uncle Benjin."

It was hard for Ana to picture Brandt's goon with the little girl. She'd watched the man hold a dagger to a peasant trader's throat. "Is he nice, Bryn? Your uncle's men?"

"Most of them. Bryn is best. He buys me honey-roasted nuts from the market on Saturday mornings."

"Yum," Ana murmured, struggling to fit it all together.

"I am not allowed to swim, neither. Not by myself." She screwed up her little nose. "That is the worst bit. In summer."

Ana sipped from her cup, leaning her elbows on the trestle table. "Are there children to play with?"

Maudwyn's face brightened. "Plenty. Beattie, Mabel, Aleswyth, Paulie, Nicholas, though he's an awful prig some-times. Mattias, Willem, Rita…" She rattled through the names of the village children. Some were tenant farmers' children.

Ana was a little bit surprised and pleased to hear that Brandt wasn't a snob nor insisted on his niece associating with the children of aristocracy. Maudwyn talked about playing knights in the castle grounds, foraging for truffles with the pig farmer's best sow, building huts in the woods. It all sounded … normal.

A clanging down the hall interrupted Maudwyn's story and they both froze, bread in hand, and stared at the closed kitchen door. Heavy boots pounded the hall and a rough voice rasped, "Fetch the master—riders at the gate."

Brandt's voice rose. "Malcolm?"

"We couldn't hold them off, sir. They will be on the steps in minutes."

"Find the girl. Make sure she stays in her room. Lock the door if you must."

Ana and Maudwyn looked at each other and raised their eyebrows in alarm. Maudwyn scooped the rabbit into her pocket and nodded toward the larder. Ana blew out the candles and they felt their way in the dark glow of the hearth coals.

The larder was chilly and the smell of cheese and smoked meat thickened the air. Maudwyn led them to the far corner, to a gap between sacks and barrels. They hunkered down and Maudwyn burrowed her way into Ana's arms. The little girl's solid warmth offered a welcome buffer to her rising anxiety.

Men at the gates? Could it be the soldiers of Eadin Palace? The blond guard said they would come. A mad hope seized Ana. Leon might have reached his men and come for her. Would they fight to free her? A flood of adrenaline made her joints seize. She wanted to escape but she didn't want anyone to get hurt. Not because of her.

The larder backed onto the main hall and she could make out the muffled sound of voices.

"...this time of night?"

"Have Bryn gather the watch ... grounds with ... swords ready."

"...numbers, Benjin ... not like him..."

"That scheming, self-righteous bastard..."

Self-righteous bastard.

Brandt thought Eadin was full of self-righteous bastards.

He'd called the guard at the palace gate a self-righteous prick. It *must* be Eadin. Come for her. But Precious couldn't be fully healed—unless their wonder workers had performed a miracle. If he was, Eadin wouldn't come in the night to trade ... hostages. Would they?

Is that what she was as a pledge? A hostage?

Whatever the case, she couldn't let them fight.

Though ... Brandt had ordered her locked away. A dark realization settled in her mind. He wanted to use her as leverage in his feud with the palace. God, she truly had been naive, letting herself believe he was some misunderstood, tragic figure in all this.

"Maudwyn," she whispered. "I can't let your uncle fight with these men."

Maudwyn wriggled in Ana's lap and she could feel rather than see the little girl looking up at her. "No," she begged. "Do not go out there. It feels ... wrong. It is not safe."

"It's not safe to do nothing."

"Uncle Benjin can fend them off. He is a great warrior."

"I don't want him to hurt these men. I think they're my friends. Come to rescue me."

"Rescue you?" Maudwyn shook her head. "From what?"

Ana sighed. "I think ... *they* think your uncle is a bad man who might hurt me."

"A bad man? Uncle Benjin kills bad men. *He* isn't bad. Sometimes he has to do bad things. To keep us safe. To keep our people safe."

Ana's mind boggled at the child's spin-doctoring. "Still. These are *my* friends. I don't want them killed and I don't want your uncle to get hurt. Do you understand?"

A clatter of hooves and heavy wheels rumbled on the gravel path and Ana froze, straining to hear. A wagon? That didn't make sense. Hardly sneak-attack mode. She couldn't get her head around it, but she knew she had to act. She shuffled out from under the girl, who clung to her sleeve. "Maudwyn, please. Just stay here. Don't come out."

"Ana," the little girl begged.

Ana peeled herself free and ran out into the kitchen just as the bolt on the great arched door to the keep slid back with a reverberating *thunk*. She yanked the kitchen door open and ran into the hall. "Wait!"

She skidded to a standstill at the group of men gathered in the entrance way. There were no swords drawn. No raised voices. Brandt looked at her like he'd been run through with a lance. Two of his men stood with him, gawping at her in bald horror.

The new arrivals regarded her coolly, two armored guards with weapons sheathed at their hips, flanking a tall slender man in a long black cloak. He was white, middle-aged with silver in his short-cropped hair, and in the midst of peeling away his outer layer to reveal red velvet robes and a jewel-encrusted crucifix.

His smile stretched wide as he beheld Ana, but her gaze shifted as a smaller, wiry man stepped into view, wearing grubby leathers, a thick soiled bandage wrapped around the top of his head and tucked tight beneath his misshapen jaw. He bared black teeth in his battered face and his voice rattled thickly. "Little witch."

Ana grabbed for whatever was lying on the bench seat beside her, not realizing what it was until she brandished it before her. A broken antler. "What the fuck is going on?"

The red-robed priest raised his eyebrows high, spreading his fingers flat over his chest. "Heavens, what a mouth."

"What have you done?" she hissed at Brandt.

The nobleman looked as though his soul was being siphoned out of his chest. Then his face hardened and he became someone else, the man she'd met by the stream. "Silence your tongue, wench."

"You sold me out."

"Have a care, child," the priest said, stepping forward, eyes glittering. "You will do yourself an injury."

"Don't come anywhere near me."

"But we have much to discuss," the priest said, his piercing blue eyes fixed unblinking on hers. "My name is Bishop Angeber."

"I don't care."

His lips curved, revealing white teeth. "She is quite marvelous, Benjin."

"Your Grace," Brandt began, "if we might talk."

"We have no need of talk, boy," the priest said. "You have delivered."

Ana shook her head and scowled at Brandt. "You lying prick."

Angeber laughed shortly, sauntering toward her. "Put it down, girl." He grabbed for the extended prong and Ana whipped the antler upwards, catching his palm and splitting his flesh. The priest hissed and jerked his hand back with a snarl. His guards bounded forward, unsheathing their swords in a glittering sweep of steel.

"Enough!" Brandt shouted, his own men charging to the fore.

Ana shook, looking at the ruby blood dripping from the priest's hand. "Stay back!"

"Ana!" Maudwyn cried behind her. She made the mistake of looking over her shoulder to spy the little girl peering through a crack in the kitchen door.

Angeber's men pounced, a blade catching her bicep in a blaze of pain. The scream caught in her throat as she leaped backwards and swung the antler with all her might. A prong caught in a guard's cheek, sending him careening into his mate with a cry, yanking the antler from Ana's grasp with his momentum.

"Quick," Maudwyn cried, and Ana hurtled through the kitchen door, slamming it closed. The little girl turned the iron key and the lock thunked into place, followed by a crossbar.

Bodies slammed against the heavy wood. "Open this door at once!" a rough voice that was not Brandt.

Ana staggered backwards, Maudwyn clinging to her dress, big brown eyes wide with fright. "It's the bad one," she rasped.

Ana cupped her bleeding arm and dropped to one knee. "Bad one?"

"The red devil," Maudwyn croaked, tears filling her eyes. "Do not let him in, Ana. He set the angel on me."

Ana's head spun; her arm felt like it was burning. She stared around the room. "I have to go. I can't stay here."

"Take me with you," the little girl sobbed as the door rattled against the bar.

"I can't," she said, panting. "There's a worse man out there than the priest. He tried to hurt me. Tried to take me. I have to go."

Maudwyn ran to a curtain in the back corner and shoved it aside, revealing a narrow door. "It goes through the servants' quarters and you can get out from the stable. 'Tis a warren. You will not find your way alone."

Ana's thoughts tumbled toward a landslide. "I can't take you with me. It would be kidnapping."

"What is kidnapping?"

"Abduction," she hissed.

A horrific clang rang against the door and Ana watched the hinges jolt in the frame. "Maudwyn!" Brandt this time. "Open the door at once!"

"Not with *him* here!" Maudwyn shouted. "You said the red devil would not come here again!"

"Red devil?" The priest laughed. "Such a fanciful imagination. You have nothing to fear, sweet girl. I seek only your friend and no harm shall come."

"Bullshit," Ana muttered.

"Bullshit!" Maudwyn bawled.

"Maudwyn!" Brandt cried. "That is foul speech!"

"You say worse!" The girl grabbed again at Ana's dress and pointed to the narrow door. It occurred to Ana that if they didn't hurry, Brandt might send men that way and they would be truly trapped.

"Please," Maudwyn whispered, the little rabbit squirming in her pocket. "I won't be any trouble."

"You have Nibbs to care for."

"Nibbs will stay safe."

"Maudwyn," Ana whispered, despairing.

"I know all the secret paths from here to Ulmenholz, Modeh, and Reinwald," Maudwyn said. "I can show you the way and keep off the main road."

"You have nothing but your nightgown and no shoes on your feet."

"Do not fret." The little girl tugged Ana toward the narrow door and turned the handle as softly as she could. "You shan't come in!" she yelled as the guards pounded on the kitchen door. "We will not let you!"

"Maudwyn!" Brandt bellowed.

Ana snatched a linen cloth from a hook by the door and wrapped it around her bicep, then ran to the table and swept the half-eaten loaf and cheese into her arm, folding up the hem of her dress to carry them.

"Good thinking," Maudwyn whispered, gesturing for Ana to follow her down a dim hall lit by sparsely set oil lamps. The corridor was barely wide enough for a maid to carry a breakfast tray. Steep stone steps took them up and panic twisted her gut. They shouldn't be going upwards—they'd be trapped. Before she could voice her concern, Maudwyn ducked through another curtain into a low hall with doors set in matching pairs on either side. Voices murmured behind some, snoring rumbled behind others. Servants' quarters. The whiff of tallow and tar, leather and moldering rushes scented the air.

She had to stop the girl. Send her back. It was ludicrous, Ana thought, clutching the food in her skirt with one hand, gripping her oozing bicep with the other. It would count against her. Worse than stealing a horse. As bad as murdering a fool. Child abduction. They would cut her throat in the woods if they got hold of her. When they got hold of her. Thief. Kidnapper. Murderer. Witch.

Tears sprang in her eyes. She wanted to go home. She had to go home. She couldn't be here another minute. She had to find Saint Ansel.

Maudwyn slipped around a corner to another steep staircase, thankfully down. It led to yet another corridor and Ana lost all sense of direction. She could hear the distant pounding of the kitchen door. They'd surely give that up. Brandt would tell them about the narrow corridor. Boots would pound toward them any second now. Any second.

The smell of hay grew stronger as they barreled through a dark archway. Maudwyn skidded to a stop and gestured to a clay oil lamp set in an iron sconce, too high for her to reach. Ana released her bleeding arm and the flash of pain made her hiss. The measly lamp struggled to penetrate the thick gloom of a tack room. Horses shuffled in the stables beyond, offering curious snorts.

Maudwyn flung open a trunk and let out a yip of glee, pulling out a tatty pair of little riding boots. "These are my old ones," she whispered, hoisting herself onto the lid of the trunk, pulling grubby socks from the boot sleeve and fighting them onto her feet.

Ana blinked and realized she was dithering, staring at the little girl like a gormless fool. She scanned the hooks and shelves, spotting two thick riding cloaks and a satchel. She swung a musty woolen cloak over her shoulders, and another to swamp the little girl.

"They'll see us on a horse. They'll hear us," Ana whispered.

Maudwyn flapped the edges of the cloak, which were dragging on the ground. Ana took the ends and crossed them over the girl's shoulders, knotting them like a giant toga behind her neck, to let her feet peep out the bottom. She nabbed a woolly cap from the shelf and yanked it down to Maudwyn's ears.

"We will go on foot," the little girl said.

"This is a terrible idea. Your uncle will never forgive me."

"Well, I will not forgive him," the little girl whispered, her lower lip beginning to tremble. "He promised to never let the red devil back in the house. But here he is, and worse, they want to take you."

"Maudwyn, I can't drag you into the night."

"I am dragging you," the little girl said, scuttling to another shelf and grabbing a flint and a coil of twine. She stuffed them in the satchel. Ana scooped up a blanket and a basket of what looked to be carrots. She dumped them all in the satchel and jammed the bread and cheese on top before swinging the strap over her shoulder.

"Maudwyn," Ana began, but the little girl darted to a side door and lifted the latch. Wind stole through the gap. It was freezing. Out in the dooryard, moonlight cast the world in bitter monochrome. Ana felt again that weird sense of dislocation, as if she were in a dream.

"This way." Maudwyn ran toward thick hedgerows. It wasn't until they were halfway across the lawn that Ana looked back and realized they were at the end of the building, the opposite side to the kitchen. She could see none of Brandt's guards but torchlight flickered here and there behind the windows.

When she turned back to follow Maudwyn, the girl had disappeared and Ana stalled.

"Here!" Maudwyn called in a loud whisper. Ana dashed through a break in the hedge, nearly bowling the little girl over. "Through here. You'll have to duck."

The hedge formed a tunnel. Ana had to run half stooped, with only the moonlight at the end of the hollow to guide her.

She stumbled over the uneven ground, marveling at Maudwyn's sure-footedness.

Her back began to ache with the awkward bend of her spine and her saddle-sore thighs burned with the partial squat. Soon they reached the open air and a thick stone wall. The main entrance must be a hundred yards to their left. The wall was high and Ana felt a renewed sense of defeat. "This is ridiculous," she panted. "We can't climb this."

"No need," the little girl said, offering a wild grin.

"This isn't a game, Maudwyn." Ana planted her hands on her hips. "This isn't fun."

"It is better than letting Angeber get his mitts on you."

Ana blinked at the girl. "He laid hands on you?"

The little girl shuddered and spat in the dirt. "In prayer."

A dark surge rolled through Ana and she squeezed her arms too hard and swore at the pain in her bicep. "Maudwyn … Did you tell your uncle?"

"There was nothing to tell. It was just a bad feeling," the girl began. "He kept stroking my hair. When Ma passed. Made me sit on his lap. Stroked my cheek and my neck. Prayed for the angel to watch over me." She hunched her shoulders up around her ears. "It gave me a queer crawling sensation all over. After that, the fainting started."

Ana wished she had slashed the prick's face with the deer antler. "I cut his hand. *Let it rot.*" No sooner had the words formed on her lips than a sharp wind lanced through the hedgerow, stirring the folds of their stolen cloaks. That uncanny tingling zipped behind her ears and she staggered against the stone wall, jarring her sore arm.

"There's a door," Maudwyn said, her eyes popping wide as the wind died. She shivered and spun on her heel. "This way."

They ran alongside the wall, every lunging shadow, every cracking twig setting off sparks of terror in Ana's chest. They must be searching the house now, the grounds. Brandt would have dogs. How long before he set them loose on their scents?

Maudwyn stopped at a stretch of thick ivy and reached through the brambles, feeling her way. A clunk signaled the opening of a latch, sparking the child's fierce grin. Rusted hinges creaked, then she pulled back the leafy curtain, revealing a shadowy gap and moonlight beyond.

Ana had to act fast, darting ahead of the little girl and slamming the door shut.

"What are you doing?" Maudwyn cried. "Let me through!"

"Shhh," Ana hissed, leaning with all her weight. "I can't. It wouldn't be right. It's not safe. Your uncle would murder me for putting you in danger."

"No!"

"Go back to the house. Go to Mrs Pimms. Hide there, till the priest is gone."

"I will scream!" Maudwyn pounded the door. "I will scream and they will come."

"Please don't." She pressed her forehead to the wood. "Please, Maudwyn. If they catch me, they will kill me. If not here, then wherever the man with the black teeth wants to take me. I can't have you caught in the middle of it."

A wrenching sob echoed through the wood and a last thump signaled the child's defeat. "I helped you," Maudwyn croaked. "I helped you but you will not help me."

"I am trying to do the right thing. I want you to be safe."

"The priest is not safe!"

"Your uncle is." She believed it, for the child at least. "Mrs Pimms is. Bryn. Tell them what you told me. Go back to the house. Hide until the bastard is gone."

The pressure on the door released. "I thought you were my friend."

"I am." She drew a shuddering breath, resisting the swell of self-doubt. How had she let the child come even this far from the house? "I'm sorry and I'm grateful. But please, Maudy. You must go back."

There was no reply. She waited, listening intently for the sound of movement. Instinct warned her to bolt but she feared the girl would try to barge through. There were rocks by the wall, a couple of boulders. She risked leaving the door to heave them against the secret entrance. The effort strained her cut bicep and she hissed at the sting. She panted and counted to sixty in her head. Still no sound. *God, let her have gone back to the house.*

Finally, she took off into the forest, the satchel thumping against her hip, her bicep igniting with fiery throbs at every footfall. At first she kept glancing over her shoulder but the strobing trunks of spiny trees made it impossible to spot the door. Besides, she needed to watch where she was going; the ground was slippery with pine needles. Tree roots, boulders, and hollows jarred her steps. The last thing she needed was a twisted ankle or to impale herself on a broken branch.

Wells of moonlight marked a path through the trees. She had no idea where the road was. The river roared somewhere in the distance but she couldn't tell if it was before her or behind her. When her lungs were bursting and her knees began to buckle, she slowed to a walk, heaving to catch her breath.

She tried to picture Brandt's map. Birkenholz House. The river was northwest. But she'd come out on the south side. She needed to veer right? Like a giant U-turn to follow the river up toward Ulmenholz. God, there was no way she'd step foot in that place again, but if she could find somewhere to hide until dawn ... She fumbled in her woolen vest past the blade for the string of Ansel's beads and clutched them to her chest.

"*Help me*," she whispered, not knowing who she begged for help. God? Saint Ansel? Anybody. "*Please.*"

"You're going the wrong way."

Ana yelped and spun. Maudwyn stood beside a bald pine, her nose pink with cold, her eyes pink with tears.

"Bloody hell, Maudwyn!" Ana hung her head and exhaled roughly. "You're going to be the end of me."

"I won't," the little girl pleaded, running forward and throwing her arms about Ana's hips. "I promise. I won't be any trouble."

"How did you get through?"

"There's a bit, further along, where a birch reaches right over the wall. I climbed and dropped down on the other side."

"Are you trying to break your neck?" She hugged the child and groaned. "What if you'd taken a turn? What were you thinking?"

Maudwyn snuffled. "I am supposed to go with you."

Ana huffed.

The little girl peered up at her with pitiful eyes.

"Stop being spooky."

"There's a cave." Maudwyn leaned back. "We can build a fire. Eat the carrots. Wait for dawn."

The forest would be crawling with Brandt's men before then. "Your uncle has dogs, doesn't he?"

The little girl chewed her lip. "My scent is all through the forest. In every direction."

"Mine isn't."

"You came by the road."

"He wouldn't think I was fool enough to take the road."

"Uncle Benjin thinks everyone is a fool."

Ana sighed. "That tracks."

"Let me help."

She clicked her teeth. "Do I have a choice?"

CHAPTER THIRTY-ONE

The morning was icy. Mist from the falls clouded the air, dampening Ana's hair. She knelt on the edge of the deep pool at the base of the waterfall, half deafened by the roar. She splashed water on her face with numb hands, gasping at the cold. The pool glowed emerald green, emptying its flow into the narrow mouth of a toothy gorge. Perhaps she should throw herself in and let the white water pound her to smithereens.

Her whole body hated her as it was. A night sleeping on frozen ground, even curled around Maudwyn and with a fire to warm their little cave, had only multiplied the stiffness in her limbs. Every pressure point along the left side of her body throbbed. Her head throbbed. A leaden dawn had compounded her misery.

She had walked all morning with terror churning her gut, astounded they had made it through the night without Brandt's men hunting them down. They had followed the sound of the falls for water, not speaking. Perhaps the child was rethinking her choice to run away.

Even if they made it to Eadin, Brandt would come and she

would have to answer for her actions. Whatever the extenuating circumstances, she would be held responsible for Maudwyn's removal from Birkenholz.

Horse thief. Murderer. Kidnapper. Witch.

The only consolation she could think of was that Brandt might slit her throat before the man with the black teeth dragged her back to his master and whatever goddamned demon priestess had prophesied her doom in the North. Perhaps she should beg him to do so. If anyone else got hurt because of her ... she dug her fingers into her forehead, pressed her palms against her eyes. She couldn't stand it.

She wondered how far she was from the caves where she and her school friends had emerged. Perhaps she could clear some rubble, crawl inside, and beg the sacred powers to send her back. Perhaps Saint Ansel had already found a way to send her friends back? Perhaps they were back in their proper time being interviewed by the police and Gwen was telling Ana's mother she was still lost. She shoved the thought away, she couldn't let herself think about her mother; it filled her with a desperate ache.

She slipped the beads from her vest and rolled them between her fingers.

"You've been clutching them all night," Maudwyn said, creeping up beside her and sitting cross-legged on the flat rock. She offered Ana the last crust of bread and a curled wedge of sweaty cheese. She had shadows beneath her eyes blue as bruises. She should have been at home in her warm bed, recovering from yesterday's turn. Ana wanted to howl at the sky. The little girl cocked her head. "Are they from a rosary?"

Ana blinked. "I don't know." The bread was stale now and the cheese had a bitter tang but she forced it down. She passed the beads to Maudwyn. "Saint Ansel gave them to me."

The little girl's eyes widened and she cupped the string of beads in her hands like she was holding treasure. "The miracle lady?"

"Apparently."

"What was she like?"

Ana didn't know how to answer that question and shook her head, lifting her shoulders. "I don't know. Nice?"

"Uncle Benjin hates her."

Ana produced a soft snort. "I'm a bit cross with her myself."

Maudwyn pulled Nibbs from her pocket with a handful of watercress she'd collected from the banks. The gray bunny seemed unfazed by its pocket travel, content with its fresh greens, and made no attempt to bolt for freedom. "Stockholm syndrome."

The little girl didn't ask what she meant but heaved a weary sigh.

The whole situation was a disaster.

"How far to Reinwald, do you think?"

"I am not sure. We usually ride and that would take half a day. We have already walked half the night and most of the morning, so..."

"This is like one of those awful word equations. A train leaves the station at 9 am, traveling at a speed of a hundred and ten kilometers per hour. What did the conductor have for lunch?"

"A wagon train? What is a kilometer?"

"I'm not sure I have the emotional strength to explain the metric system." Ana stroked Nibbs' glossy gray back and the rabbit dropped a cluster of turds, which rolled like raisins off the edge of the basin and plopped into the pool. "You'll stick with furlongs and bushels and as the crow flies for a bit yet."

"I don't think I can walk much further."

Ana rolled her lips in a tight line. "I wish we had Precious."

"Did you see Uncle Benjin's face when you called Anubis that?"

Ana snorted. "He will always be Precious to me."

Maudwyn giggled softly, her shoulders bouncing, her eyes welling. The laughter stopped but the tears flowed. No loud sobs.

"You're very brave," Ana said.

The little girl stared at the beads and rolled them between her fingers. "Is Uncle Benjin a bad man?"

Ana bit the inside of her lip. "I'm sure he feels that he's doing the right thing."

"Why would he tell the red devil about you? Let that man with the black teeth take you? That is not what a good man would do."

Crows cawed in the treetops and a cold breeze washed across the basin. Ana hunched in her cloak and sighed. "It's not that simple. The priest is a powerful man. Birkenholz is in the church's debt. I'm sure your uncle felt he had no choice."

"Is he craven?"

Ana cocked her head. "I don't know that word."

"A coward." Maudwyn looked up, her face crumpling.

Ana cupped the girl's cheek. She wanted to bellow "yes" and spit and curse the prick for selling her out. "Sir Benjamin has many people's safety to consider. Tenants whose welfare depends upon him and the clemency of the church. As far as he is concerned, I'm a stranger in his land who stole his horse and brought trouble to his door. He has to be ... ruthless."

"Ruthless?" Maudwyn considered the word. "That means cruel."

"Ruthlessness can be a kind of courage when it's for the sake of others. That's what he's fighting for, Maudwyn, for you and for your people."

"Who will fight for you?"

Ana forced a smile to her lips and balled her fists, pretending to box the air between them. "Me."

It accomplished what she hoped and made the girl smile. Maudwyn offered her the beads. "I think these have kept us safe."

Warmth sparked in Ana's chest and she took the little girl's hand and tied the beads around her bony wrist, drawing the loose threads into a little bow. Maudwyn's mouth popped open and her eyebrows rose.

"I can't," Maudwyn said. "She gave them to you."

"I want you to have them." She rose and reached to help the girl to her feet. Delighted, Maudwyn took her hand, scooping Nibbs with her free hand and fumbling for her apron pocket.

The sound of dogs barking shook the forest close by.

"Nibbs!" Maudwyn squealed, jerking loose. Ana looked down in time to see the rabbit slide from the folds of the little girl's cloak and bounce off the boulder into the pool with a plop. "No!" Maudwyn screamed and dropped to her knees, plunging her arm into the water.

"Shit," Ana hissed, as the little girl pawed at the rippling surface.

"Nibbs!"

Dogs barked and men appeared among the trees. Ana scooped the little girl up and hurtled toward the cover of tall reeds. Maudwyn bawled and thrashed in her arms.

"Stop screaming," she hissed, landing on her bottom in the mud, Maudwyn's weight almost winding her. She clamped her hand over the child's mouth. "Please. They're coming. They're coming."

"Nibbs," Maudwyn's muffled cry vibrated through her fingers. "Nibbs."

"I know," Ana whispered, her eyes pricking. "I know. I'm so sorry."

The girl shook with weeping. Barking rattled the air. Ana breathed shushing sounds in Maudwyn's ear. *Please, God, let them pass. Don't let them stop. Let them walk on.*

A thick brown snout thrust through the reeds, the hound baring its yellow fangs in a low growl. Its bark shook Ana's skull. Maudwyn squealed and knocked Ana's jaw, clacking her teeth, painfully.

"Here!" a gruff voice called. "Rats in a hole!"

Ana recognized the man as one of Angeber's guards, his wind-burned face and grim smile, the slash she'd made to his cheek. He was barrel-chested, thick-necked, and without a sliver of compassion behind his eyes. The hound barked with its whole body, spattering saliva from its jowls. Maudwyn trembled and Ana tried to shield the girl with her arm.

The guard clamped her forearm and yanked them both to their feet. The dog went berserk, snapping at Maudwyn's face.

"Call off your bloody dog," Ana spat. "She's just a little girl."

"Shut your hole, witch." He cuffed her across the cheek, nearly knocking her to the ground.

"Do not touch her!" Maudwyn screamed.

The man snarled at her and she turned to bury her face in Ana's dress. Ana cupped her throbbing cheek, her eyes watering as she looked for somewhere to flee, some means of defense. Then she remembered the knife hidden in her vest.

Four more men, dressed like Angeber's guards, came jogging down the path with swords drawn and more hounds. She searched for the black-toothed Northman, panic heaving in her chest, but he didn't appear. Horses broke through the trees, Brandt and his man Bryn, riding tall, expressions thunderous.

"Call off those fucking dogs!" Brandt bellowed.

Angeber's guards exchanged mutinous looks but grabbed the dogs by their collars, yanking them back.

"Uncle Benjin!" Maudwyn sobbed. "How could you?"

Brandt looked at the child with bleak eyes. "Take the witch."

"Stay!" Angeber's barrel-chested guard pointed at his hound and lunged for Ana, grabbing her by the back of her hair. "The Butcher's henchman is waiting for you."

"Stop it!" Maudwyn screamed, and from the corner of her eye Ana saw the little girl fly at the guard, pounding her fists on his back. Ana slipped the blade free from her vest and rammed it into the man's bicep. He shrieked and released her.

Whether by accident or intention, another of Angeber's guards let slip his hound's collar. The dog bounded forward, barking ferociously, clamping its jaws on Maudwyn's arm.

Brandt shouted, leaping from his mount, sword drawn. Bryn, too, swung from his saddle, scrambling to nock an arrow to his bow. Ana screamed as the girl went flailing backwards, her free arm windmilling, her back foot slipping off the edge of the basin, and she and the dog, still attached to her arm, plunged beneath the water.

A whir and a thud. The guard who'd released the hound collapsed face down, an arrow in the back of his head. The other men cried out and turned to retaliate, blocking Brandt's path to the water, while the barrel-chested guard grabbed Ana with his good arm and yanked her against him. She swung her head back with all her might. The back of her skull cracked against the man's face with a terrific crunch, sending fireworks across her vision. The guard buckled over, blood streaming from his nose.

Before he could recover, she threw off her cloak, kicked off her shoes, and leaped into the pool, plunging beneath the icy flow. All sound and sensation was lost in the cataclysmic cold. The force of the water dragged her toward the mouth of the gorge. She kicked and found no bottom to the basin. Dark forms blurred in the green wash and she reached for them, her pulse hammering in her ears, her lungs already beginning to scream. Maudwyn was in here, swamped by a cloak too big for her.

Claws raked her arm. The dog. It scrambled upwards, using her neck and shoulder for purchase, shoving her lower in the flood. A gray blur wavered beneath her and Ana lunged down, stars popping behind her eyes as darkness crept at the edge of her sight. The cold drilled through her skull. Fire purged her chest. She longed for air but the gray blur was growing still. She struck out with both hands, her fingertips brushing rough wool. She sunk her fingers into the heavy fabric and hauled but the weight only pulled her down.

To her left the water foamed white. Distantly, she realized the mouth of the gorge was before them. A last hope seized her and she let herself fall, pointing her toes down. Maudwyn was there, unmoving among the burden of her woolen cloak.

Ana gathered the limp bundle against her chest as her feet

found the sandy bottom. She let the weight bend her knees, then, with a colossal push, she surged upward with all her might. Through the narrowing aperture of her vision, the water grew lighter above, and just as everything turned utterly black, a frantic hand fisted the back of her hair and dragged her to the surface.

Air thundered through her ears, shattering the silence. She coughed and retched with savage gasps and light opened in pinpricks before her eyes. Brandt scrabbled for his niece among the endless folds of the cloak. Beyond him, Bryn struggled against Angeber's guards and their dogs.

A horrible, broken cry pierced the air. Ana panted and blinked. Brandt was hunched over Maudwyn's still form. He rocked back and forth, pawing her shoulders, begging her to breathe. Ana's ears popped; she coughed roughly and crawled toward them. Maudwyn lay unmoving, the skin around her nose and lips turning as blue as the marks beneath her eyes. Brandt swore and shook her.

Tingling erupted behind Ana's ears and a dizzy swooping sensation made her sway on her knees. She braced, and sure enough a sudden wind barreled through the trees. Ice-barbed and fierce, it lashed her face, and with it, knowing struck her like a cinder block.

"Move!" she cried, scrambling for the little girl. "Move!"

She shoved Brandt aside and lay the child on her back, yanking the folds of the cloak away. She tipped Maudwyn's chin up and depressed the jaw. Then she slid a finger in her mouth and dug about for debris before pressing her ear to her mouth. She couldn't feel breath on her skin but Brandt's shouting was making it hard to hear. "Shut up!" she barked.

He stopped. She listened. Nothing.

She sat up and pressed the heel of her palm in the center of Maudwyn's chest, linked her fingers, locked her elbows, and started compressions, short, sharp, quick, counting under her breath.

"What are you doing?" Brandt demanded.

"Saving her life!" she cried. "Eighteen, nineteen, twenty…"

She hit thirty and paused, pressing her mouth over the child's. She blew, took a breath, and blew again before putting her hands back on Maudwyn's chest to start pumping again. "Count," she commanded. "Count, goddamn it. Tell me when we hit thirty."

Brandt counted the compressions aloud, following the rhythm of her pumping hands. Behind them, a strangled squeal signaled the death of one of the hounds and hellish baying signaled the retaliation of its pack mates. A pained bellow. Bryn was brought to his knees by the dogs. Brandt leaped to his feet, moving out of Ana's peripheral vision. The shrill of singing steel, then the resounding clash of blades. She looked back only for a second. Bryn was flailing beneath the hounds, and Brandt was fighting the guards alone, sword to sword, but still counting.

"Twenty-seven, twenty-eight, twenty-nine, thirty!" he cried with each slice of his blade. Ana paused again to blow in

Maudwyn's mouth, once, twice. She returned to chest compressions. Brandt hacked and slashed behind her. Ana stopped listening and kept pumping. Round after round. Breaths then compressions. Then Brandt cried out and she paused, only to see him fall to his knees, cradling his arm.

Angeber's guards spun toward her.

"No!" she cried, and the wind howled through the forest.

Shouts rose with the pounding of hooves, then horses thundered through the trees. Leon rode at the head of a small company of men, expressions fierce and swords drawn.

A sob broke from Ana's throat; he was alive and somehow, he'd found her. But she didn't miss a beat and kept on—breaths then compressions.

Angeber's guards hesitated, then repositioned themselves and called for their dogs. Snarling, the hounds abandoned Bryn and bounded toward the horses, snapping at their forelegs. The horses reared and Leon and his men fought for control but one by one leaped from their saddles. Blades flashed, Angeber's men charged, and the crash of steel rang in Ana's ears.

She craned her neck to watch as she pumped Maudwyn's chest, shaken by the ferocity of the attack, but Leon's men were unhesitating.

The barrel-chested guard swore, swinging for Leon's head, but Leon ducked and spun away. With a deft pivot, he hefted his long sword, plunging for the guard's heart. The man staggered backwards but parried the blow. Ana could not take her eyes off Leon, the certainty of his movements, the power … he moved like nothing she had seen before, but she knew he could not possibly be at full strength after his fever. Beside him, Brandt was back on his feet, fighting one-handed, fierce as a man possessed.

Ana worked on, yet Maudwyn remained unresponsive, the skin around her eyes and lips now deep violet. The hope that had soared with the appearance of Leon deflated now with each compression. Despair loomed.

How long had it been? Ten minutes. Fifteen? How long could the brain survive without oxygen? A great sob wrenched from her throat but she didn't stop, even as bitter thoughts flooded her heart with defeat.

Water glinted on the string of beads circling the little girl's wrist. Fury fisted in her chest. *My grace is with you*, Ansel had promised. What did that even mean? "What grace?" she sobbed. "What grace? *Show me*." And with a desperate cry she slammed her palm on the girl's chest. "Wake up!"

Maudwyn lay still.

She slammed her hand down again. "Wake up!"

Nothing.

Again and again, raging through her tears. "Wake up! Wake up!"

Nothing.

Ana sank back down on her heels and hung her head. The wind whipped her face, her wet gown near freezing against her skin. That meaningless fucking wind. She'd fooled herself. Let herself get wrapped up in fantasies. This wasn't a miracle. This was real. A little girl drowned. For what?

A roar of defiance burned through her, heat rising in her chest that reminded her again of the blue spark and she rose to her knees and started compressions again. "Wake up," she begged. "Wake up, Maudwyn. Now!"

The little body heaved beneath her hands and Ana reeled back. The wind died, the girl's throat crackled, her chest convulsed, and water gushed from her pale lips.

"Brandt!" Ana cried, turning Maudwyn on her side. She held the little girl's shoulder and pounded her back. "Brandt!" She turned to look for him, in time to see Leon drive his sword through the neck of the barrel-chested guard. Without pause, he intercepted Brandt's assailant, leaving the nobleman free to tend the child.

"Maudy." Brandt staggered across the grass and fell to his knees beside her, hauling the girl onto his lap with no regard for his bleeding arm. She coughed and clung to him, and he held her. "Thank God."

Ana sat dazed as Leon and his men dispatched the remaining guards and hounds. Her ears rang with the stillness. The absence of wind. She had no words for what had happened. No framework to explain it. But she could not deny it meant something.

Leon stalked across the field and dropped to one knee before her, panting in the aftermath of the fight, his dark curls damp with sweat. He examined the gouges on her neck and her bruised face. "Ana," he said, his voice ragged with fury.

"I'm fine," she said, struggling to rise to her feet.

Leon took her arms and helped her up, his brown eyes livid. "Was it this prick?"

"No." She tugged his sleeve. "It was the big guy. You got him."

Leon exhaled and pulled her to his arms. Ana squeezed her eyes closed and leaned into him, wrapping her arms around him. His chest expanded against her as he hauled air in rough grabs. She still couldn't believe it. He was alive. He was here.

He kissed the top of her head. "We went to Birkenholz to rescue you but you had already escaped."

"Sorry."

He snorted and held her close. "How?"

"She had an accomplice," Brandt snapped.

Ana and Leon separated and turned on the nobleman. Maudwyn still lay in her uncle's arms but she had stopped coughing and her expression was baleful. "You did a bad thing, Uncle Benjin," she wheezed.

Brandt cupped her milk-white cheek. "I did not summon the priest. Someone has betrayed my trust. I knew nothing of the Northman nor his agreement with Angeber. Someone told him Ana was being held at Birkenholz."

"You helped them," Ana said, shivering away from the heat of Leon's body, her dress dripping. "You came after us with dogs."

"Not my dogs," he said, fumbling Maudwyn's sopping cloak from her shoulders to wrap her in his own. "I was desperate with worry. What were you thinking, running away in the night? Anything could have happened to you."

"I was afraid he'd make me pray with him again. I was afraid the angel would come."

"I tried to make her stay," Ana said. "I barred the gate to keep her in. She climbed the wall and followed me."

"*She* is a child," Brandt said, his jaw hard. "You should have brought her back."

"That's not fair," Maudwyn cried. "They were going to kill her!"

"You nearly died!"

The little girl shook her head and raised her wrist, water glistening on the string of beads. "Saint Ansel saved me."

CHAPTER THIRTY-TWO

Leon directed Oakin and Edwin to help him weight the bodies and roll them into the gorge with the slain hounds. Micah and Tabor stood watch over Brandt and his man. Bryn sat binding the bite wounds on his arms and legs, swearing under his breath. Brandt pretended to ignore the Eadin Palace guards while he fussed over his niece.

It had alarmed Leon in the extreme to learn of the involvement of Bishop Angeber and the black-toothed man. He could not rest, knowing the Northman was still out there. According to Brandt, Oleg's scout had separated from their party early in the hunt, to follow another set of tracks. Was he watching Ana even now, lying in wait? He scanned the trees, alert for signs of movement, his palm itching for his blade.

Ana took shelter to change her wet clothes, thanks to Oakin's gallant sacrifice. Being the smallest of their company, the young man had offered her his spare kit without complaint. Leon kept track of her bobbing head above the tall reeds, worrying about the desolate look in her eyes, the bruise on her face, the gouges on her neck where a hound had clawed her from ear to collarbone. She had seen too many people killed in the harrowing days since she escaped the caves, suffered too much violence to her person. Again, he pictured running Brandt through.

Ana emerged in Oakin's breeches, shirt, and tunic, and a cloak he did not recognize, with her strange white boots, marred with scuffs, on her feet. Once more the young squire, with her short hair tucked behind her ears. His heart squeezed and he left Oakin and Edwin to manage the last body but stopped short as the little girl ran to greet Ana ahead of him. Brandt, too, stood at a distance, stern-faced and watchful, staring at Ana with an intensity that made Leon grip the handle of his sword.

"You must take these," Maudwyn said, handing Ana the string of beads. "I have Uncle Benjin and Bryn."

"I have Leon and his friends," Ana said.

"But Saint Ansel gave them to you. They will keep you safe."

"Ana saved you," Brandt said, stalking toward his niece. "Not magic beads."

Leon matched his step, unwilling to let him near Ana alone.

"Say goodbye, Maudwyn," her uncle commanded. "I would have a word with your savior before she leaves."

Maudwyn looked at Ana with pitiful eyes. "Promise we will meet again."

Ana made no promise but hugged the girl and kissed the top of her head. "Thank you for helping me. You are brave and kind. Your mother would be proud."

The girl buried her face in Ana's cloak. "I *will* see you again. When Uncle Benjin collects Precious."

"Maybe."

Brandt sent Maudwyn back to Bryn and gave Leon a flinty look. "I wish to speak with Ana. Privately."

Leon's fist cramped around the hilt of his sword. "You may not."

Ana sighed.

"Was it worth it?" Leon demanded.

Brandt looked at him with supreme disdain. "Do not be cryptic, *boy*. Speak plain."

Leon stepped forward, squaring his shoulders. "Taking Ana from the bridge. Threatening innocent people. Dragging her to your castle. Risking her life."

A stiff silence suggested Brandt might reach for his own sword. Leon willed him to do it but Brandt slowly jutted his jaw. "I regret the danger it brought to my niece."

Ana huffed through her nostrils, tugging Leon's sleeve. "Now you're just letting me go anyway. You'll miss out on your compensation."

"He doesn't have a choice."

Ana tugged again and Leon took a reluctant step back.

Brandt made do with needling silence.

"How will you pay the church?" Ana cocked her head.

Leon looked between them, realizing he was missing some important threads.

"That is hardly your concern," Brandt muttered through his teeth. "And shared in confidence."

She looked abashed and Leon hated it; he needed to pummel this prick.

"You really didn't summon the priest?" she asked.

"Certainly not," Brandt said. "Angeber's spies are every-where. His web far-reaching. Likely he had agents posted at the gates of Eadin Palace who reported all that took place."

"Does he know about the prophecy?"

Leon snapped his head toward her. She had spoken to Brandt of the Northmen's prophecy? An uncomfortable sensation squirmed in his gut. To what extent had they conferred at Birkenholz?

"Not that Angeber would give it any credence," Brandt said, a sour turn to his lips. "The man is as spiritual as a turd. His only interest in Oleg's prophecy would come from finding a way to twist it to his advantage."

"What advantage?" Leon demanded.

Brandt glared at Leon with open disdain. "Oleg might be persuaded to raid Eadin Palace if he found out the seven are there. It would save Angeber a great deal of trouble if pagans slaughtered your so-called saints in the process."

Ana looked appalled and turned to Leon. "Brother Ambrose said the sultan would ride to avenge Saint Ansel if Angeber attacked the palace. A holy war."

Leon nodded. "But if Oleg does it, the sultan's fight would be with the Northerners."

"And Angeber could swoop in and claim the palace."

"Precisely," Brandt agreed.

Ana swore and shook her head. "And that's how bishops roll these days?"

Brandt gave a dismissive snort. "Powerful men do as they please when they have no one to hold them to account."

"Is that not the truth," Leon said, crossing his arms over.

Brandt shifted irritably. "I do not regret *any* difficulty taking Ana may have caused Eadin Palace. That is certain."

Ana produced an exasperated sigh.

"I regret that it drew the attention of Bishop Angeber back to Birkenholz."

When Ana's expression softened, Leon couldn't help himself. "Everybody knows you are in the bishop's pocket."

A muscle knotted in Brandt's jaw. "That's the horseshit your saints feed you?"

Leon unfolded his arms and reached for his sword and Brandt's chest swelled ready for a skirmish, but before either of them could draw, Ana stepped between them.

"Leon." She turned her back on the nobleman and pressed a hand to his chest. "It's not worth it."

He blinked down at her pale-green eyes, and swallowed thickly.

"Could I have a moment," she said softly. "With Brandt. Alone."

A sick sinking feeling plunged through his stomach and he fixed Brandt with a murderous glare. "You lay a single finger—"

"Please," Brandt sneered. "If I had wanted—"

"Not helping," Ana snapped, swinging to press her other hand to the nobleman's chest. She was a brief wall between them and only because Leon did not want to see her touch the bastard a moment longer, he stepped away. "Thank you," she said. "I won't be long."

Leon's men were spread out in various states of readiness to intervene but he stalked toward them, his ears hot and his back ramrod straight. Micah gripped his shoulder. "It is well, Leon," he murmured. "Do not let him antagonize you."

"Too late," Leon muttered, staring back at Ana and the nobleman standing close so as not to be overheard. "Much too late."

CHAPTER THIRTY-THREE

Ana peered up at Brandt's stern face. He looked exhausted and worried, and rather like he would have enjoyed an excuse to cross swords with Leon. "About Angeber," she said softly. "Don't let the bastard anywhere near Maudwyn."

He stiffened and stared at her.

"He's a predator."

"What are you saying?"

"I'm saying he … he was creepy with Maudwyn when her mother died, made her sit on his lap, kept stroking her hair and her neck. Made her skin crawl. *He's* the reason she's been having seizures."

His lips formed a grim line and he settled his hand on his sword, his knuckles whitening. "If he touches her again, I shall slit his throat."

She shivered and drew her cloak tighter; she believed him. "Can't you report him?"

He gave a humorless snort. "Shall I write the Pope?"

"Yes," she hissed. "Write the Pope and all his bishop mates and tell them what he's doing."

He sighed. "And why should they believe a word I say, a half-landless lord, drowning in debt to the Holy Roman Church?"

She shook her head. "This fucking place."

He didn't say anything for a moment, then, "You swear a great deal for a miracle worker."

She looked at him sharply. "What do you mean?"

"I mean your speech is more foul than a drunkard swineherd—"

"Not that bit."

His piercing gaze drilled hers. "You brought Maudwyn back from death."

"She wasn't dead. She was—that wasn't a miracle. That was CPR. Cardiac ... cardio ... something, I can never remember what the P stands for, but the R is resuscitation."

"She was not breathing."

"Not breathing isn't dead," she said, aware of sounding desperate.

"Her heart was not beating."

"That doesn't mean—" She suddenly felt very hot. "CPR is real. Where I come from, people use it all the time. Medics. Ambulance officers. Lifeguards at the beach. It's cool, but it's not magic or a miracle or anything like that. It's about getting the heart pumping and clearing the air passages."

"There was an uncanny wind," he said, narrowing his eyes. "It shook me."

She couldn't deny that and she shivered, remembering the

dizziness and tingling, then the sudden blast of knowing what to do.

But that wasn't a miracle, was it?

She wasn't sure if she even believed in God—at least, not in the way she understood organized religion from her days in a Catholic primary school. Spiritual stuff, yes. God in the sense of a greater power, sure. Jesus, she liked the idea of, but what about the deities of countless other faiths?

Besides, weren't miracle workers supposed to be holy people, solid and unwavering in belief? Like Ansel. She thought again of the saint's promise: *my grace is with you.* Is that what happened? She'd experienced the grace of a saint? But it didn't add up. Ana wasn't remotely holy. What faith she had was weaker than partially set jelly. It was all way too deep into the spooky zone.

Yet ... her brain kept tally of the uncomfortable facts: she'd passed through time. She could speak and understand languages that were likely extinct back home. Leon's wound was healed, Maudwyn was alive, and each time she'd experienced the strange sudden wind, something undeniably weird had happened.

"I felt the wind ... then I knew what to do." The admission left her nauseous. A combination of fear and a stomach swollen with river water.

Brandt studied her face, his expression inscrutable. "I would have come for you."

She blinked.

He shrugged and drew a deep breath, his chest expanding. "I needed Angeber's men to believe I was in league with them. I was going to wait until Bryn had Maudy away. Then I was going to track the Northman and Angeber's men and slit their throats in the night."

She swallowed, picturing the throat slitting all too easily. How many dead people had she seen in the last few days? "Why?"

"What sort of question is that?"

"You don't owe me anything."

"I owe you my niece's life."

"You don't, but even before that, I was no one to you."

"You were alone and lost and in need of protection."

She raised her eyebrows. "Didn't seem your concern by the stream or on the bridge."

He exhaled, flicking an annoyed glance back at Leon. "I have explained my behavior already. I shall not waste my breath begging forgiveness."

"I don't recall you apologizing the first time."

"Good God, woman, you have a Jezebel's tongue."

She chuckled and the corner of his mouth gave a reluctant twitch.

"What are you going to tell Angeber?"

He shrugged. "That the Northman killed his men and tried to kill me, that I was knocked into the river and by the time I climbed out, he had escaped with you."

"He won't buy it," she said. "Why would the Northman kill Angeber's men?"

His expression clouded. "Fear not. I am a good liar."

She didn't know what to say to that.

"I will look for the Northman," Brandt said, his manner terse once more. "My men will look for him. We will not let him get back to Angeber."

Her windpipe ached but she breathed through it and whispered, "I just want to go home."

He dug in his pocket and pulled out her phone, handing it to her. "Then I hope your saint can help you."

CHAPTER THIRTY-FOUR

Leon guided his mount along the Roman road, letting his men ride ahead. Ana sat before him, his arm secure about her waist, her fingers fanned over his forearm. Crows squabbled in the canopy of trees, dislodging small flurries of snow from the branches. The sun was beginning to set and long blue shadows raked the path, mist coiling between the trees.

Ana shifted in her seat, trying to get comfortable. He loosened his grip to give her space but she pulled his arm close and he tried to enjoy it. While there was great relief in holding her again, he could not relax. His chest remained tight and his stomach hollow, the unspoken filling the silence with barbs. He churned about the Northman, unaccounted for. Angeber waiting for news. Brandt's claims he would lie to the bishop. The mounting threat to Eadin Palace and Leon's part in it.

His more petty concerns clamored for satisfaction also: he was desperate to know what had passed between Ana and Brandt at Birkenholz. What he said to her beside the gorge. What she said. Why Ana seemed so willing to trust the vicious prick.

And nagging in the foreground of his thoughts: the girl, brought back from death. He'd never seen anything like it before, the way Ana had pumped the child's chest and breathed into her mouth. Another miracle?

The last time he'd suggested Ana had performed a wonder things had gone awry, and he was loath to start a fight. But they would need to talk about it before they made it to the palace. The curiosity in his men's eyes warned him of that. They'd seen her as he had, witnessed the moment the child revived, coughing up water, her face tinged blue. Their usual boisterousness and cocky charm had been restrained on introduction, caution and deference in their manner, and meaningful looks when Ana's back was turned.

He had not told them about her healing his wound. He did not have the words to frame it, and she had made it very clear she did not want him speaking of it. But he might need to convince her otherwise if they were to make amends with the Council of Eadin. The aftermath of battle brought with it the reality of heavy consequence. They would have to give an account of their actions. They must agree on a story and hold fast.

Ana shifted in her seat again and produced a sharp sigh.

"Are you well?" Leon asked.

"I think I swallowed a lot of water. I'm busting to pee."

"We can stop," he said.

"No." She eyed the trees. "I don't want to get down. I don't want to go in there."

"I can come with you."

She scowled up at him. "That would be embarrassing and gross."

He gave her a rueful smile. "I recall your kindness when I was in need."

But she shook her head and faced the road, pressing back against him. "That was different."

"We have many more hours to ride."

"Not yet. I can hold it."

"If you insist."

She leaned her temple against the side of his neck, a sweet and intimate gesture. Perhaps, if he guided them carefully on the road, she might sleep.

"Leon?"

"Ana?"

"Will you be in trouble for coming to get me? Your men? Micah said it was against orders."

"If we manage it with some diplomacy, I trust the council will be appeased," he said, with more assurance than he felt, and pressed his lips to her hair. "You are safe. That is all I care about."

She looked up at him, the fading light catching the side of her face like a master's painting brought to life.

"You came for me," she murmured, so close they shared breath.

"Of course. I had to."

Her pale-green eyes glittered with warning. "Because I'm your responsibility?"

He suppressed a rueful smile, letting his gaze settle on her lips, and whispered over them. "Because I am your friend."

A slow smile lit her face and even though it was undoubtedly foolish to let things between them get any knottier, he kissed her. Soft and unhurried, safe in the nearness of his men. A dream of a kiss. He cupped the side of her face, brushing his thumb over her cheek. Her answering sigh sent heat rushing through his bones. The tension in his chest eased, he forgot the pain in his body, the aching muscles, the cuts and scrapes, the grim work of battle. He wanted to do the same for her, erase the days of grief, kiss her pain and fear into oblivion.

Their breathing became shallow, the kiss growing deeper, restraint slipping. Ana twisted in the saddle, arching to slide her fingers into his hair, pulling him down. He exhaled with a soft moan as her tongue found his, scrambling his senses. The image of Ana from her musical box surged into his mind's eye and he was lost. He gripped her more tightly, his palm sliding over her stomach, and she squeaked.

"I'm sorry," she gasped against him. "I really have to pee."

Ana's cheeks burned with mortification as Leon called his men back and explained the situation. Unfazed, they all dismounted to search the area before spreading out through the trees to form a loose semicircle to guard her while she peed. She scrambled as far back as she dared, torn between the desire for distance so they wouldn't hear her and proximity in case she found herself under attack. One of them started a jaunty whistle and someone else chuckled before joining the melody with their own, providing polite sound cover.

It eased her terror a notch but her hands still shook and she peered through the trees, checking the shadows again. Brandt had insisted she keep the cloak but it was too long and voluminous to manage; she really did not want to pee on the hem, so she unlaced the tie at her neck and lay the heavy garment over a thicket of brambles. She shivered in the cold, wrestling Oakin's breeches down.

She could not help thinking of her first night in Eadin Forest when she had gone for a nature wee, while Gwen and the others lay huddled by the campfire. At least it wasn't pitch-black this time and the men who found her then would not scare her witless now. They would fight for her, defend her, kill for her. An alarming and yet bolstering thought. And, this time, she knew where she was headed. There was something to look forward to. Seeing Gwen. Even Stefan. Friends who knew and understood exactly what she was going through. And the possibility of help.

Her feelings about Saint Ansel ... Mistress Hollinsen were much more complicated. The woman had spoken to her on the bridge—knew who she was and yet let her be taken. Arming her with what? Broken rosary beads? If the blond guard hadn't slipped her the little blade, she would have been completely defenseless. Had Ansel a clue what she had sent her into? She doubted the answer would satisfy her.

Yet, doggedly, her hope fixed on the idea of Saint Ansel. The woman had dreamed of the Kjálka's prophecy, worked a miracle of her own, a gift of understanding. Whether by accident or intention, the power of that wonder had reached Ana and her friends, making the impossible possible.

How many people experienced a single miracle in their lives? Ana had wonders piling up. So many impossible things. Impossible to explain. Impossible to understand. Dizzying and strange. What had Mistress Hollinsen said? *My grace is with you.* Was that truly what saved Maudwyn? The grace of—

A reeking hand clamped Ana's mouth and an arm hooked her neck, yanking her off her feet. She thudded against a bony chest, winded on impact. Stars burst behind her eyes and her arms flopped loose at her sides. The arm at her throat squeezed tight, bruising her windpipe.

There wasn't a thimble of air in her body to make a sound. She struggled to rouse herself as suffocation triggered a bolt of panic, but the man was moving fast, deep into the woods. *No, no, no.* Her feet scrabbled in the dirt, Oakin's breeches tangled around her ankles. Weakness flooded her limbs and her vision narrowed to a dark tunnel, shrinking … shrinking … shut.

CHAPTER THIRTY-FIVE

H er first conscious thought was pain, in her face, her chest, her hands. She tasted blood. The right side of her jaw ached and she explored with her tongue, finding loosened teeth. She swallowed and winced at the agony of her throat. She was lying face down on cold dirt. Her ass was freezing and a gravelly male voice was muttering behind her.

Understanding fired every emergency synapse in Ana's brain and she scrambled to rise, finding her hands bound beneath her. Whimpering, she shuffled onto her knees, turning to face the black-toothed man. He squatted on the ground, holding a flaming torch before him, his eyes wild with loathing … and fear. His jaw still bound, he looked even filthier than when he'd first attempted to abduct her.

Ana fumbled to pull up her breeches, horrified to think she had been dragged there with her pants around her ankles. Had he touched her? Hurt her? But there was nothing in her body that suggested that sort of violation. She yanked the breeches over her hips and her phone flew from the pocket, scudding across the dirt floor with Mistress Hollinsen's beads. A stab of regret pierced her chest but she didn't go after them. Instead, she huddled behind her knees, eyes darting, taking in the rocky formation of a cave.

Her gut shriveled, remembering the Metzger brother's warning that Eadin's cave system stretched for miles through the hills. Was this part of the same caves where her classmates had perished? She wanted to run screaming into the open air.

The black-toothed man picked up the phone, his thumb brushing the screen, and it lit up. Had it turned on in her pocket? When she last turned it off the battery was at 3 percent. He hissed at the photo of her and Gwen and slapped the screen, accidentally activating the camera. He gasped at his reflection and slapped the screen twice more, and the phone took his photo.

He hissed and dropped it. "It is my face!"

Ana knew the script.

"Now I have your soul," she rasped, and her eyes watered with the effort of speaking.

He glowered at her. "Liar."

"It's mine."

He bared his blackened teeth and stomped on the screen.

The crunch made her shudder, but she kept her composure. "Big mistake," she said. "Now your soul is trapped in there forever."

"Foul witch!" He dropped to his knees, his hands hovering over the broken pieces.

"Release me," she said. "And I'll give it back."

Voices rumbled beyond the cave. Her eyes found the passage through which the black-toothed man must have dragged her, and lighter patches that marked an opening. Was it Leon and his men, searching for her? She went to cry out for help but choked in pain. She clutched her throat, the skin raw. The black-toothed man turned expectantly toward the opening and dread sunk deep in her bones.

More flaming torchlight flickered in the entrance of the cave, and several men strode through the passage, ducking their heads. They were huge and terrifying, clad in pelts and cloaks, with long hair, beards, braids, tattoos, their kohl-darkened eyes alive with menace with menace.

Then one stepped forward, not as tall, not as bound with muscle, but somehow worse than all of them put together. The Butcher of the North, head shaved, runes tattooed over his scalp, countless dark marks blanketing his throat. His eyes glittered like coals.

If Ana hadn't already emptied her bladder, she would have pissed herself right there. She scooted backwards until her spine rammed into a rock and she brought her bound arms up to her face and prayed to any god that would listen. *Help me. Help me.*

"One of seven," Oleg muttered, stalking toward her and grabbing her by the hair. He wrenched her head back and she cried out. "I remember you," he said, his eyes raking over her body.

"Don't touch me," Ana rasped. "Don't you look at me."

A grin stretched across his lips and he cocked his head. "I touch and look and take what I want."

"Jarl Oleg," the black-toothed man warned. "She is a witch."

"I fuck witches," Oleg said brightly, his pitiless eyes drilling hers.

"She cursed me," the black-toothed man said. "She cursed my manhood. Now she has taken my soul."

Some of the men sniggered but Oleg finally looked back at his warrior. "Speak more."

The black-toothed man cupped himself between his legs. "I have had time and chance to take my pleasure but ... I could not. I am ... withered."

Ribald mocking rose from the watching ranks. Ana shrank inwardly and sent up another desperate, silent prayer. *Help me. Please. Don't let them touch me.*

"The day after they emerged from the cave," the black-toothed man said, his voice shaking, "I tracked her by a stream. I tied her to a tree while I readied the horse. Her eyes rolled and she began to foam at the mouth. In a wretched voice, she cursed my strength, my sleep, my courage. She said I would waste with fear. She cursed my sex to wither and my tongue to ash. She turned the horse on me." He touched his broken jaw. "I have not slept since. I am plagued with fears. Food has lost its taste. I am unmanned. And now she has trapped my likeness in this box."

Oleg cocked his head again at Ana and shook her by the scalp. "Is this true?"

Ana let her eyes roll back; her voice was already shredded. "Double, double, toil and trouble—"

"Do not let her speak!" the black-toothed man cried.

Oleg cracked his hand across her cheek, splitting her lip; the force almost tore hair from her scalp where his fist still gripped her. She spat blood in his face and Oleg wiped it from the corner of his mouth with his thumb. "Oh," he said, grinning as he licked it clean. He brought his mouth to her ear, his breath hot. "Did you curse my man, tasty witch? Did you take his soul?"

"Yes!" she hissed, and a great rush of tingling swept up her neck. She held her breath, guessing what would come next. A sharp cold wind funneled through the opening of the cave, blasting their faces, sending cloaks billowing and torch flames flaring, and some flickered out. A reckless hope surged inside her. "I curse you," she rasped. "I curse your prophecy! I curse your fucking Kjálka!"

Humor drained from Oleg's face and he clamped his palm over her mouth and squeezed, slow and hard, until the insides of her cheeks cut against her teeth. Ana whimpered and her eyes ran. "Shut your spiteful little hole," he growled, ignoring the howling wind, even as his men panicked. "I did not cross the Hollow Sea or risk the lives of my people to suffer the upstart threats of a filthy slit like you. Do you understand me?" He shook her so roughly it felt like he might snap her neck.

"Kill her," the black-toothed man shouted over the wind,

shielding the torch flame with his body. "Here! Now! In the name of the Kjálka! It must still count as an offering!"

"Her instructions were clear," Oleg said, his eyes boring into Ana's as he dragged her to her feet and gave her a little shake, his hand still fisted in her hair, the other still clamped on her mouth. "They must be brought to her hearth. Alive."

"Why are you doing this?" she said, her voice muffled behind his hand.

He blinked at her, his cruel black eyes boring through hers. "We all pay."

Confounded, Ana wept, struggling for air through her stuffed nose. He gave her a warning look, then uncovered her mouth, letting her draw ragged breaths. He cupped her face, wiping her tears with his thumbs, and spoke like he was gentling an upset child. "Do you hear me, witch? You get to live a little longer but ... if you speak again, I *will* break your arms and your legs."

A warning shout rose beyond the cave but Oleg didn't turn or react while his men ran to the passage opening and quick harsh words confirmed that danger approached.

Oleg raised his eyebrows in a mockery of surprised delight, kissed her on the forehead, and released her. The Butcher unsheathed a black-headed axe from his back and stalked out of the cave with his men, calling to the black-toothed man over his shoulder. "Watch her."

Ana cowered against the cave wall, shaken to the core. She pleaded silently with the wind. *Help me. Saint Ansel. Anyone.*

The sounds of shrieking steel echoed beyond the cave. She pictured Leon and his men, fighting to reach her; it crushed her with desperate hope and fear

The black-toothed man shifted in the torchlight and pulled his dagger from his belt.

"What are you doing?" She brought her bound wrists up before her like a shield.

"I will take back my soul with your life."

"That's not how it works," she cried, her voice cracking, the wind whipping her hair in her eyes. "Only I can release it."

"We will see," he said, taking a step closer.

"Oleg will kill you."

"We have three pilgrims already," he sneered. "Six more sit safe in Eadin Palace, ripe for plucking. We do not need you."

A sick swoop in her stomach left her weak. Three already. *Oh, God.* Who?

Satisfaction sparked in the Northman's bloodshot eyes, and Ana knew that begging was pointless; there would be no mercy. She lurched toward the cave opening but the black-toothed man lunged to block her path. A sudden skid interrupted his trajectory and his foot slid out from under him. He crashed on his back with a mighty whump, the force of his landing breaking his grip on the torch.

It flipped and hit him square in the face. Hungry flames leaped in the roaring wind, catching his hair, and Ana pressed herself against the cave wall, unable to look away.

The man screamed and writhed, dropping his dagger to

lash at his face, but the wind whipped the flames, engulfing his sleeves. The sight and sound were terrible. Ana tried to clamp her ears but her hands were still bound.

The dagger lay in the dirt and she went for it, stopping short when she spotted the broken rosary. It glittered in the firelight by the black-toothed man's flailing feet. Shock delayed her processing, but then it hit her ... he had slipped on the beads.

She grabbed the dagger, backing as far away from the burning man as she could, and crouched against the cave wall. The handle slipped through her sweating palms but she caught it between her knees and squeezed as hard as she could. With frantic strokes, she rubbed her bonds across the blade, trying not to snag her flesh.

She sawed and the black-toothed man screamed. She kept her eyes on the fraying ropes and tried not to breathe in the stench of charring flesh. Soon the screams died. The wind still whipped her face and her eyes ran with tears. *Help me. Help me. Let me live.*

Tingling bloomed behind her ears. The rope gave suddenly and she stabbed the base of her thumb. Bright beads of blood rolled down her wrist and dropped in the dirt. "Shit."

A terrible, familiar sound boomed below her feet and the ground shuddered. Ana's throat closed and terror surged through her as the earth quaked.

She snatched up the dagger and Mistress Hollinsen's beads and scrambled up the passage toward the opening in the cave.

"Leon!" she called. "Leon!"

Heavy rocks crashed behind her and she ducked, stumbling as the ground buckled, slamming her shoulder against the cave wall so hard it knocked the dagger from her grip and left her arm limp. The stone vibrated through her bones and pressure grew in her head. Again, an invisible force compressed her body, like being squeezed through a hard rubber tube. She leaned forward, dragging one foot in front of the other until she had almost reached the entrance of the cave.

Beyond her, men fought in the patchy snow; swords rang and she looked for Leon, but it was hard to tell who was who in the shadows. Behind her, the catastrophe of a collapsing cave gusted dust and freezing air, shoving at her back.

Above the forest the clouds parted and moonlight spilled over the trees. The Eldi Comet streaked the sky like a bright red exclamation mark. She thought she saw a man with dark curls clash his sword with a man swinging a gleaming black axe. She lunged once more toward him and the pressure grew; it was almost unbearable, and then, like a snapped bungee cord, it released and the night became day.

Yet Ana did not tumble into the bright green dawn, nor did her knees crash into dew-damp grass. The scene wavered like a mirage. One moment it was the early morning sun spearing through thick green trees, the promise of heat in its rays, and birds trilling in the forest canopy. Next it was the blinking shadows of a moonlit night, bitter air icing her skin; a bare forest patched with snow and the shrill song of swords.

She blinked, struggling to clear her eyes, willing herself to plunge toward freedom. But something held her motionless between day and night, summer and winter, future and past. It was as though she was caught in the veil itself, that thin place between worlds.

The ambient sound dimmed, growing indistinct like vague noises from neighboring rooms, and the wind died. Her ragged breathing filled her ears, together with the thlack, thlack, thlack of her pulse.

A new fear rose in Ana, a creeping dread that warned her she was not alone in that liminal space. A weight in the atmosphere, a presence thrumming with dark intent. Her mouth dried and she began to tremble.

A cold hand gripped her shoulder, long nails piercing her tunic and puncturing her flesh, whirling her toward the cave passage. Ana screamed and screamed again at the ghostly face looming through the dust. She instantly recognized the mask of thick white paint crusting around the woman's eyes and mouth.

As though plucked from Ana's vision in the hot pools, it was the priestess from the cave hearth, dressed in her pale, blood-spattered gown and with dirty bare feet, her eyes glowing like an animal's in the dark. The Kjálka. Here. Now.

Ana made to reel backwards but found herself pinned in place, adrenaline flooding her system, not fight or flight but freeze. Her vision blurred and the edges of the priestess blurred like a badly projected hologram. Confusion and terror scrambled Ana's brain. Was it real? Or was it another terrible vision? The stinging pain in her shoulder insisted it was real. So, Ana screamed again.

The priestess seized Ana by the neck and squeezed hard. "Little witch," the Kjálka began, her voice a dark and unnatural chorus. "Sneaking witch. Lurking where you ought not to lurk, listening at keyholes."

Ana stood utterly frozen in her terror, arms limp at her sides, unable to make sense of the apparition ... the monster that held her. But her vision swam and though she remained pinned in the priestess's grip, the scene faded into murky gloom before reforming to reprise a different scene. She recognized it instantly—Oleg kneeling before the hearth—the dream from the hot pools.

It unfolded again, as she had seen it the first time, the crowd of warriors, weeping women, and cowering slaves. The priestess stood before the fire, squeezing her fistful of bone shards until the splinters pierced her palm and blood trickled between her fingers. She reached over the flames, and drops sizzled on the hearthstones and the priestess commanded Oleg with a gesture. This was where the dream had warped and leaped ahead last time but not so now ... now Ana saw everything.

The women, weeping softly behind Oleg, were not hugging their arms as she had thought the first time; they hugged small bundles. Gray-faced babes, some malformed, all swaddled and unmoving. Dead. The first woman in the line, in her crown of braided gold, passed her tiny bundle to Oleg. Stone-faced, he fed it to the fire. The remaining women followed in their grief, until all the bundles were placed in the hearth. Seven bundles. *Seven.*

Ana wanted to scream, to throw up, flee her body, but the priestess held her in the chokehold even as the priestess of the first dream gestured toward the cowering slaves, huddling against the cave wall. Two of the warriors in attendance advanced, grabbed one of the shackled figures and dragged them to the hearth. A boy. No older than Maudwyn.

Fresh dread swelled inside Ana, remembering the body she'd seen slumped on the ground the first time. She squeezed her eyes shut but nothing could block out the grisly sounds. When the boy's screams were cut short, Ana looked and his limp body hit the dirt. The priestess had taken his eye.

This is what Ana had seen her swallowing the first time— and she swallowed it again, licked her fingertips, and shuddered, before a stillness settled over her. She drew a long, rattling breath and closed her eyes.

No one moved.

Ana braced, knowing what would come. When the priestess exhaled, she opened her eyes and there was that preternatural creature peering back at them all. This time, when she spoke, Ana understood the words.

"I gave you victory in battle," the Kjálka rasped, many voices braided together, low and unnatural. "I gave your enemies as slaves. I gave you glory, plunder, land. I blessed your crops and your wombs, since the day you set Odin aside and knelt before me." The voice paused, letting the weight of her words settle upon the assembly.

"But you have not been faithful. Now death has come for those who cling to Odin in their hearts. Death has come for those who have spurned the Kjálka. Blight on your wombs, blight in your cradles, blight on your crops, and blight in battle. You are punished for your faithlessness."

Women sobbed and prayers of supplication grew in desperate whispers around the hearth and the thing wearing the priestess finally softened. "Fear not the passing of the red star. The Kjálka is merciful. I will supply what was lost with new offerings. Find them at Eadin's Womb at the closing of the solstice and bring them to my hearth. Seven to appease. Seven to mend. Seven to sow. Seven to rend."

At this the priestess tossed the bones into the fire. A bright red spark rose from the flames. She opened her arms, ushering it toward the hole in the ceiling. Ana counted them as another spiraled high, then another. One by one, until there were seven.

"I seize them from beyond the veil." The priestess reached into the acrid smoke and closed her fist. "I plunder them as chattel from time."

She turned to Oleg and placed her bloodied palm on his cheek. "At the closing of the solstice, I bring you seven from the womb of Eadin. Fetch them for my hearth and your faithlessness will be forgiven. The vine will fruit again. The blight will end. The warrior shall rise in victory. The plunderer will plunder. And the horn of Oleg will be unbroken."

The man conceded a tight nod and the scene dissolved, bringing Ana back to the collapsed cave entrance and the Kjálka here and now, depthless eyes glittering and alien and full of wrath. "Sneaking witch."

"No," Ana whispered. The vision had cut out too soon.

The priestess squeezed. "I heard you. I heard your filthy curse. Did you think your utter nonsense could touch me?" She clicked her tongue, *tsk, tsk.* "Do you not perceive? Do you not feel it in the trembling marrow of your bones? You cannot touch me. I am older than the abyss, older than the deep darkness. I am the maw—"

"*No,*" Ana croaked.

The priestess's eyes narrowed and her lips pulled back, revealing her teeth.

"There was another..." Ana forced the words out, heat igniting in her chest. "Another spark."

The priestess hissed but the weakness that had taken Ana's strength lifted and she scrabbled at the woman's wrist as heat bloomed in her hand and at her neck. The Kjálka's face contorted and there was the sound of sizzling flesh. The priestess screeched, releasing Ana, her hand scorched in two places.

The woman scowled at the imprint of a small cross on the base of her palm where it had brushed the blessed silver hanging at Ana's throat. She turned her wrist, catching the smoldering impression of the rosary where Ana had battered her, still clutching Ansel's beads.

The Kjálka's rage vibrated the air and she bared her teeth, which no longer appeared human but elongated fangs set in an unnaturally distended jaw. "I am going to kill you for that," the many voices rasped like a saw. "But first, I will kill your friends and you will watch the life drain from their eyes. Then you, little witch. Then you."

But the heat in Ana's chest grew, a searing heat, spiraling its way up. It made her sternum vibrate and she pressed her hand to her clavicle. Tingling erupted behind her ears and a fierce knowing gripped her.

"Go to hell!" Ana screamed at the Kjálka, a bright bead of bluish light bursting from her lips, hurtling straight at the creature's face. Ice-cold air roared in her ears and blasted her senses. The Kjálka ... dissolved like an apparition blown away in the wind. She was gone, and the oppressive weight in the atmosphere with her.

She became aware of the distant cry of desperate men, cries of pain cut short, and the thundering of hooves, galloping away.

Ana turned to face the wintry night and stumbled away from the mouth of the cave, only to collide with a heaving male chest.

"Ana," Leon panted. "My God, I thought you were still in there. The dust and the—"

"I'm okay." She couldn't stop shaking, peering past his shoulder at the carnage among the trees. Leon's men were there. Several bodies clad in animal pelts lay splayed and bleeding in the snow, but no sign of Oleg.

"He fled. He was … he was fierce … frightening … then something came over him, like he had changed his mind. He called his men and they—they fled." He pulled her in and hugged her. She was surprised to find he was shaking too, perhaps in disbelief to have survived. "I thought I'd lost you," he said, his voice breaking. "I thought you were gone."

She squeezed her eyes closed and pressed her face into his tunic, too shaken for tears. She had been so close to her world, her own time. It had been right there within reach. Freedom. Life. Familiarity. Security.

She trembled and he held her, and she knew it was bone-deep trauma, the aftermath of terror, the prospect of terror to come … the Kjálka's threats had settled in the deep tissue of her brain. And under it all, beneath the cruel disappointment, the overwhelming confusion, the boiling questions about what the hell had just happened to her, in her, through her, there was a small yet deeply contradictory feeling: relief to still be in Leon's world.

CHAPTER THIRTY-SIX

I t was dawn when they finally reached Eadin Palace. Ana had ridden with Leon, resting against him, eyes closed most of the way, letting him believe she was asleep. Not because she didn't trust him to believe her ordeal in the cave but because she did not have the words for it or the capacity to find them. Only when the palace was in sight did Leon gently rouse her.

The morning was crisp and clear, frost glistening on rolling pasture. The first rays of sunlight gilded the great expanse of the southern wall of the palace, rising on the hill. Her heart swelled with inexplicable longing, like it had when she witnessed the ruins in the moonlight, like it had when she arrived with Brandt's wounded horse. Leon seemed to sense her wonder, gently squeezing her waist. A lump rose in her throat and her eyes welled with an incomprehensible sense of homecoming.

Oakin had ridden ahead to notify the gates of their approach and by the time they made it through the town to the bridge over the dry moat, the portcullis was already open and the guards stood aside, nodding at their returning comrades.

Ana and Leon drew some curious looks and she wondered if any of them had been on the bridge when Brandt had taken her.

But she didn't have the wherewithal to scan their faces and scowl; she was occupied by other matters.

She fixed her gaze beyond the guards and the gate, beyond the wide path before the palace, beyond the mighty arch beneath the bell tower, on the Sacred Grove within. Tears rolled down her cheeks. She knew it was ridiculous. How could a place she'd seen twice in her life feel like home?

It was clearly the influence of exhaustion and trauma, the lingering effects of hunger, pain, sleep deprivation, and utter relief. Relief to have finally made it. Anticipation of being reunited with her friends. The prospect of sanctuary after days of horror.

They rode beneath the towering arch and her eyes couldn't take it all in fast enough. The stonework, the elaborate carving on the mighty double doors set in the walls on either side. The ornate ironwork sconces holding burning torches to illuminate the walk. A sultan had built all this for Saint Ansel. Mistress Hollinsen. The woman in homespun who distributed loaves of bread to pilgrims on the bridge. It made her dizzy.

Leon brought the horse to a halt and dismounted, lifting Ana down. She leaned on his arm, her legs wobbly from lack of use.

"Can you stand?" he asked, his expression etched with concern.

"Can you? You look as exhausted as I feel," she said, and the corner of his mouth hitched in a weary smile.

Micah drew alongside. "Edwin will manage your mount," the handsome lieutenant said. "Best take Ana to the infirmary.

Tabor will notify the captain of our return. I will notify the council."

Leon's brow knotted. "I should speak to the captain and the council. You must not take any blame."

"I told you," Micah assured him. "We only found you *after* you had rescued Ana." He gripped Leon's arm and took the double doors to the left, disappearing inside. Edwin, Oakin, and Tabor took the horses by their leads and led them through the other set of double doors, from where the sounds and smells of the palace stables wafted back to her.

Oakin looked over his shoulder with a sleepy grin at Ana. "Welcome to Eadin, lady."

She smiled at the young man, grateful and overwhelmed by all they had risked to reach her and bring her to the palace. "Thank you," she said in a small voice, deeply aware of how insufficient the words were.

Leon patted her hand where it was hooked over his arm and led her into the bailey, where the great interior of the palace grounds was revealed in its enormity. Ana held her breath as she stepped onto the broad pebbled path that bordered the Sacred Grove, wide enough for wagons, three abreast. She could see all the way to the end, left and right, but the Sacred Grove concealed the opposite side of the palace, trees tall and ancient, pale-limbed silver birches, elegant linden trees, gnarly oaks, and many others she couldn't name. The muted rumble of rushing water reminded her that an arm of the Namen River swept through caves below the palace.

Only the high tree tips that breached above the palace walls were emblazoned by the sun. At the ground level, the paths between the trees were steeped in shadows that seemed to beckon her. Like a magnetic force, she felt herself tipping forward, but a short stone railing surrounded the grove, keeping her from plunging into the interior forest.

She rested her hands on the barrier and stared in wonder. Leon waited, watching her close. "It is an unusual feeling, yes?"

She glanced up at him. "You feel…?"

"I have heard it draws some," he said.

"Yes," she whispered, knuckling away a foolish tear from the corner of her eye. "What is it?"

"The council call it many things—the bower of peace, the breath of heaven, the wellspring of life, and the heart of fire."

"Fire?" She stared at the wood, baffled.

"It depends on your guild," he said. "But some encounter a living fire in the grove."

She shook her head. "I don't understand."

He shrugged. "Others more knowledgeable will articulate it with more understanding than I am able."

"What do you experience?"

He raised his eyebrows, exhaling a resigned breath. "For me, it is a quiet and pleasant place but I have not encountered a particular presence or power among the trees. I do not belong to a guild. I am a palace guard."

She blinked up at him, searching his face, but Leon showed no sign of bitterness or disappointment. Questions were piling up in her brain but noises from the balconies above drew her attention. She looked up at the interior palace walls. There were three stories to the structure. Sections with shuttered arches that opened out on the grove's canopy, and sections of open balconies lit with torches, wide stone stairwells leading to each level, grander arches that let the sun shine through, hinting at large open gathering spaces.

Awe made Ana silent and Leon let her soak it in without interruption. Here and there, people moved about. Shutters opened. Women in pale headscarves and heavy aprons hefted baskets of laundry, buckets of water, bushels of kindling. Men in breeches and tunics extinguished torches, swept balconies, carted crates overflowing with vegetables and loaves of bread. Children hared up and down the stairwells shouting to each other, squabbling, laughing. Ana had to wipe her eyes again.

Leon touched her face, stroking his thumb across her jaw.

"It's just…" Her voice cut out and she swallowed past the lump in her throat. "Amazing."

"Ana!" a voice called behind her. She whirled around to find Gwen running as fast as she could, hampered by a long woolen skirt, waving and crying. Stefan and Olly beside her, Keira and the Metzger brothers behind, calling out and waving, amazement stretching their mouths in broad smiles.

Ana laughed and sobbed and ran to meet them, almost collapsing into Gwen's arms. They held each other and wept.

"Oh, my God, Ana," Gwen gasped. "You're alive. You're here."

"I'm here," Ana choked and sniffed. She opened her eyes to find the others teary and smiling, though Stefan looked concerned and she realized she must look like hell. Gwen did not appear in any hurry to release her so she reached a hand toward Stefan and pulled him into a group hug. The others piled in and they all laughed and cried some more.

"I'm so glad you're safe," Stefan murmured, and Ana produced a watery smile, amazed to find she could hear those words and know he truly meant it and not feel the sting of grief or resentment. She cupped his head and squeezed him close and kissed his cheek, making him laugh.

"Okay, I'm suffocating," Gwen mumbled in the crush.

Chuckles rose around the group and they unfolded and stepped back, pink-faced and crinkled. Ana shook her head at them. "Wow, you guys. You really look the part."

Olly tugged his tunic like the lapels of a tuxedo. Keira fanned the folds of her skirt and gave a little curtsy. "It's cozy and it has pockets," she said, and Ana laughed.

"How did you know I had arrived?"

"We have spies," Conrad said, grinning.

"Spies?"

"We bribe a couple of pages with honey cakes to keep a lookout," Nikolas said, bobbing his eyebrows. Seeing her confusion, he explained. "Children from the School of Orphans take shifts running messages for the council."

"We co-opted their services," Olly said with a wink.

"There's a school for orphans?"

The others nodded but Gwen had stopped smiling, eyeing the claw marks on Ana's neck, the bruise on her jaw, the welt on her cheek and her split lip. "What happened?"

"Vikings," Ana said, hunching her shoulders, suddenly exhausted at the thought of retelling the details of her journey. Leon stepped in beside her.

"There is much to tell," Leon said, with a nod toward Gwen.

Ana realized he must recognize her from her photos. Gwen, Keira, and Olly took in the height and breadth of the handsome young palace guard and gave Ana meaningful looks. Ana bit her lip and Stefan's eyes narrowed. She swallowed and looked up at Leon, who was eyeing Stefan coolly. He definitely remembered Stefan from her phone.

"But as you can see," Leon said, "Ana has wounds that would benefit from a visit to the infirmary."

"I'll come with you," Gwen said, looping her arm through Ana's. "We'll catch you guys at breakfast."

The others stepped aside, letting Leon guide the girls along the path. Ana looked back and spotted Stefan folding his arms, but Keira signaled, mouthing behind Leon's back, *he's hot*. Olly nodded and gave a double thumbs up. Ana rolled her eyes but couldn't help but blush. It felt super weird to have Leon and her friends occupy the same time and space. What would she tell them? Gwen, she'd tell everything, but the others she didn't know so well, and Stefan—well, there was no way she would tell him anything.

Ana never made it to breakfast and lost most of the day to sleep. She'd washed, had her wounds dressed, and been given clean clothes and something to eat. Leon collected her from the infirmary and guided her down a stairwell to a walled kitchen garden beyond the palace. There were sprawling patches of winter vegetables, a pigpen, an enclosure for a couple dozen bleating goats, and a chicken coop. Toward the far wall sat five cone-shaped beehives and a woman working among them. Beside her, a small lad held a bucket.

Ana's heart started to gallop. She was about to face Mistress Hollinsen and she still hadn't decided how she felt about the woman or what she wanted to say.

She was fuming, but questions clogged her processing. She was desperate to ask her about the strange phenomena she had encountered and her terrifying experience with the Kjálka. She wanted answers and most of all reassurance that her chance of returning home wasn't lost forever. For her, Gwen, and their friends.

Leon led her along a set of planks that had been laid in a network of paths through the garden, then stopped at an intersection and waved her on. She widened her eyes, alarmed at the prospect of being left alone with Saint Ansel. He tucked a curl behind her ear and gave her a bolstering smile and walked away.

She wiped her sweaty palms down the hips of her pale-green gown. It wasn't as fine as the one Brandt had lent her but the thick wool was warm and the underdress a sturdy linen. The charcoal shawl she'd wrapped about her shoulders and criss-crossed around her chest was snug, the ends looped under a belt. She needed to tread carefully and not lose her temper.

As she approached, Mistress Hollinsen was bent over and peering through the opening of the central hive, coaxing its inhabitants to surrender their honey. The little boy eyed her approach but didn't alert his mistress. Ana waited, afraid of startling the woman. She wasn't wearing any protective gear and Ana didn't think getting her stung would be a good start.

"Why yes, you have been very busy, majesty," Mistress Hollinsen said softly, plying the bees with compliments and tidbits of palace news while reaching into the hive with a large wooden spatula, scooping out thick chunks of honeycomb. Each time she scooped, she thanked the bees, giving them time to evacuate the harvested comb before depositing it in the boy's bucket.

Finally, Ana cleared her voice and Mistress Hollinsen peered over her shoulder. "Oh, you are soft-footed. You must have heard all my nonsense." She set her spatula in the bucket and turned to face Ana, squaring her shoulders. "I expect you might like to punch me on the nose."

Ana opened her mouth but found she did not know what to say, wrong-footed by the woman's willingness to admit guilt. The little boy did not react to the statement either. Perhaps he was used to people wanting to punch his mistress on the nose.

"I would ask that we first step away from the beehives,"

Mistress Hollinsen said. "Expressions of anger and acts of violence may taint the honey."

Ana blinked. "I hadn't been planning on acts of violence."

Mistress Hollinsen caught her lower lip in a pained grimace. "But you might like to shout a bit."

Ana frowned, her shoulders rising. "A bit. Yes."

They walked back into the center of the garden until the buzzing hum of the hives grew distant. Mistress Hollinsen patted the little boy on the back and he strode away with the bucket, unhurried. She waited until he had reached the kitchen door before turning to face Ana again. Her green and brown eyes scanned Ana's battered face, noting the bandaging on her neck. Her brow crinkled. "How did it go with the beads?"

Again, Ana stalled, surprised by the direct admission of intent. "I think they might have … saved a child's life … killed a Northman … and … repelled an evil spirit."

Mistress Hollinsen's eyebrows rose higher with each confession, her lips forming a tight "o" through which she blew a sharp breath. Ana pulled the little string of beads from a fold in her shawl and offered them to the lady, but the woman shook her head, folding Ana's fingers over them. "Keep them."

"Why? Are you planning to let me be abducted by someone else?" She tucked the beads back in her shawl, her throat tightening. "Perhaps there are other children you would like me to save, or bad guys you'd like me to kill, or demons you'd like exorcised?"

Mistress Hollinsen swallowed. "I had—I *have* no desire to set you in the path of danger."

"You let Brandt take me. You could have led me into the palace. You could have told the captain who I was. You could have—"

"I could have." She nodded sadly. "But I had been prompted to act."

Ana shook her head. "What does that mean?"

"It means ... an inspiration came to me in the moment, an unction to ... allow things to unfold."

Ana tucked her chin back. "Allow things to unfold?"

"For greater purpose."

"Greater. Purpose."

"It is difficult to explain."

Ana's ears burned and she rubbed her brow. She wanted to taint honey. Even punching the woman on the nose seemed reasonable. Yet ... she was aware of the jeopardy ahead and her deep need for this woman's help. For her sake and the sake of her friends, she lowered her voice. "Gwen says the council are investigating our situation. That you're looking for a way for us to go home."

Mistress Hollinsen nodded, relieved and eager for the change in topic. "Yes, there has been much talk and prayer on the matter."

Ana pressed her lips into a tight line. "And?"

"And ... there is yet much to consider. Your summer and our winter solstices. The appearance of the fire comet. The location in the sacred caves."

"And blood," Ana said, staring into the middle distance with haunting realization. "Both times I cut my hand, then the ground began to shake, and when I made it to the cave entrance, that squeezing sensation…" She gestured at her temples.

"Both times? You were … at the threshold … again?"

Ana shivered and hugged her arms around her waist. "I saw it, for a moment. Daylight, summer … but the Kjálka kept me here."

Mistress Hollinsen's lips parted and she stared at Ana. But what Ana saw in the woman's eyes gave her courage. She told her about Oleg and the black-toothed man, the wind and the Kjálka.

"I saw it all again, the vision in the cave."

"The prophecy?"

"There were parts I hadn't remembered, or blocked out … the dead babies."

The woman offered a pained nod.

"I understood her words this time." Ana pressed her fist to her sternum, the place where the saint's spark had ignited in her chest. "Oleg's trying to break a curse."

"Blight on their wombs, blight in their cradles, blight on their crops, and blight in battle."

Ana nodded slowly, weirdly exhilarated and simultaneously creeped out by their shared understanding. "Something about Odin. I didn't really understand that bit."

Mistress Hollinsen tucked her hands in her apron. "Oleg's people worshipped Odin long before the Kjálka revealed herself. The Northerners practice the worship of many gods, yet the Kjálka demanded a singular devotion in exchange for victory, prosperity, and greatness. From what I understand, she kept her promise. Oleg's fame has risen to great heights, his people prospered, his enemies crushed until … recently."

"She said they were unfaithful."

Mistress Hollinsen shook her head. "Odin is deep in the marrow of his people. Difficult to root out."

They fell silent and Ana struggled toward her question. "Why … us?"

The woman's eyebrows rose high and her shoulders lifted. "I do not know."

Ana blinked rapidly. "She wants seven of us, right? As some kind of sacrifice, to lift whatever curse Oleg has brought on himself? Is it seven because it's the same number of dead babies?"

"I do not know. Seven is a powerful number. Biblically, it represents completion. Perfection."

"Perfection? Like we're the perfect sacrifice? Why can't he sacrifice his own people?"

The woman lifted her palms to indicate again that she did not know.

Irritation made Ana tense. "What if we hadn't gone to the caves? What if someone else stumbled in there? What if—"

"Ana." Mistress Hollinsen touched her wrist. "Forgive me. I do not have answers to these questions."

Ana opened her mouth to say it wasn't good enough, but the woman cut her off.

"Please, tell me how you escaped."

She gritted her teeth, exhaled through her nose, and spread her fingers across her breastbone. "Your ... spark." Slowly, haltingly, she began to recount the experience of the heat that rose inside her, the instinct to resist the Kjálka, the blessed silver, and the burns and blue bead of light.

Once she had told Mistress Hollinsen all of that, the sense of relief released the tension in her muscles—a confessional purge—and she found she could keep going, back through the journey, to Maudwyn's near drowning, the holy fool, and the wind again and again.

The details Ana glossed over were Maudwyn's resuscitation and Leon's healing. While she might be willing to admit there were supernatural elements afoot, she was highly uncomfortable with centering herself in the narrative. Hadn't she also cursed the Northmen? She wasn't a saint or a witch and she did not want people thinking she was either.

The woman's eyes glistened. "The wind is special to my guild."

"Does it go with the blue light?" Ana pressed her hand to her chest again, almost expecting to feel the heat rise in her sternum. "The grace of Saint Ansel."

Mistress Hollinsen pursed her lips. "You may call me Ansel. Or Mistress Hollinsen, if you prefer. But I claim no title nor have any interest in such claims."

Ana's scalp prickled. "I think it's a bit late for that."

The woman produced a dismissive snort and cocked her head. "Would you like to visit the Sacred Grove?"

A lump formed suddenly in Ana's throat, familiar longing rising within her. Not trusting herself to speak, she swallowed hard and nodded.

Mistress Hollinsen smiled knowingly and gestured for Ana to join her. The sun had slipped below the hill and twilight bruised the sky, spilling shadows through the furrows of the kitchen garden. There was no sign of the Eldi Comet and Ana shivered as they made their way back to the palace, through a wide corridor, and out into the bailey where the Sacred Grove shushed in the breeze.

The woman led her through an opening in the stone railing onto a path of springy grass. A rush of tingling feathered across her skin and she found herself holding her breath as they stepped between the trees. The ambient sound shifted and changed, the busy sounds of the palace fading into the background. Ana's eyes adjusted to the shadows and she felt small beneath the tall trunks and lofty branches. There were evergreens among the deciduous trees and the greens were deep and lovely.

She was surprised by how quickly the surrounding architecture disappeared and the cool interior forest eclipsed her vision. The lump in her throat swelled and she could not resist the moisture welling in her eyes. The feeling inside her was hard to describe. Again, the profound sense of homecoming. More than what she felt at Brightwater. More than what she felt in her mother's airy flat in Hamburg or any of the flats before that in Ireland, Scotland, or their apartment in Washington DC.

It reminded her, in a way, of her childhood home in New

Zealand, and climbing through the native bush that carpeted the hill behind their house when she was eight years old. Not that the trees were the same. Just the feeling. The rightness of it. Belonging.

She followed Mistress Hollinsen, wending along a path to a little glade where a collection of mossy boulders formed a natural seat. The woman gestured for Ana to sit, noting without comment the tears tracking her cheeks. Ana kept wiping but it didn't stop the tears welling in her eyes.

"Sorry," Ana said, "I'm probably just tired."

"Perhaps," the woman said, her own eyes twinkling with moisture. "Or perhaps you sense the presence of heaven."

Ana bit her lips together, not prepared to comment. She couldn't tell a saint she wasn't sure she believed in God. She believed in something. Something … big. Something good. Something … more. But she didn't have a name for it.

"It matters not," the woman said, her eyes crinkling in the corners with a soft smile, and they sat for some time in silence.

An acute sense of awareness tickled Ana's scalp, like they weren't alone. Strangely, she wasn't alarmed by this. Rather, she wanted to lie on the forest floor and stare up through the canopy and let the soft shushing of the trees wash over her. The peace here was tangible, weighted—not the oppressive weight she felt in the evil presence of the Kjálka but comforting, like a weighted blanket, thick, soft, and so welcoming.

"Ana," Mistress Hollinsen said, finally breaking the silence. "You have spoken of great mysteries and I thank you for your trust. I will keep your account in confidence. But the day is drawing to a close and I am sure you would like to take supper with your friends."

With a slight delay, Ana realized she was being dismissed. The woman had brought her into the Sacred Grove to shut her up? "Yes," she began carefully. "But—"

"I realize you must have many questions and I promise there will be time to speak more in the coming days, but I will need time to think on what you have shared."

"It's just—"

"I would make a request of you."

"Of me?"

Mistress Hollinsen paused, her eyes drifting to the trees. "Everyone who lives here contributes to the life of the palace. We serve where we are able, according to the needs of the community, our gifts, and capacity."

Ana struggled to concentrate, her gaze tracing the branches, drifting toward the treetops and the deepening sky. "We're not … staying," she said distractedly. "I mean, we're very grateful to have a safe place to stay for the meantime, but as soon as we are able, we're going home."

"Of course," Mistress Hollinsen nodded. "But … in the meantime…?"

"You want us to help out?"

"After you have taken some rest and feel you are recovered. Your friends are already contributing."

"Right," Ana said, peering through the shadows toward the

palace balconies where her friends waited somewhere for her to join them. But she couldn't see a trace of the flickering torches lit in their sconces for the evening. It was uncanny. This place was like something from a dream.

Hadn't she fantasized about walking the halls of Eadin Palace in a sweeping gown, of belonging to the place? Here she was, having fallen through time, living and breathing an actual wonder. She wasn't facing the impossible alone. She had friends. Her best friend. Stefan and the others. She had Leon, and her stomach did a little flip at the thought of his embrace and the heady brush of his lips.

She swallowed and met Mistress Hollinsen's intent gaze. Ana wasn't alone. Whatever Ansel liked to call herself, she had a living saint for an ally. And whatever it meant or might mean, this woman had shared her grace with her, and Ana had survived ordeal after ordeal because of it.

She inhaled the clean crisp air of the Sacred Grove, that inexplicable peace seeping into her bones, filling her, holding her, soothing away the cares of days of horror. Home. She was home. Ana exhaled and nodded. "In the meantime, yes."

ACKNOWLEDGMENTS

As always, a book cannot exist without the expertise and kindness of many wise and crafty souls. Thank you first and foremost to my agent Silvia Molteni for seizing hold of this story with both hands and being the very best of champions for its cause. My thanks to Siting Zhao, Allison Moore, Philippa Hudson, Silvia Crompton, Sarah Rouse, and Renata Sweeney in the US and UK, and Jenny Helen, Grace Wang and Leonie Freeman, Nicola Santili and Simon Panagaris in NZ and AU for all their work and support. My gratitude to designer Marcus Pallas for the beautiful cover art. Ismael Gonzalez Grenero for epic character art. To the colleagues and friends who read the early drafts and offered insight, feedback, referrals, or simply kind words and courage to light my path: Rachael King, Hayley George, Steph Matuku, Amie Kaufman, Astrid Scholte, Lili Wilkinson, Fleur Ferris, Nicole Hayes, Gabrielle Tozer, and many more, thank you.

My love and thanks to the "saints" and stalwart cheerleaders: Hayley, Tracey, Ann, Jo and Mike, Audra, Miriam, Olivia, Paulie D, Justin, Steve. And, of course, my beloveds: Ian, Sophie, Izzy, and Evie.

Photo credit: Oliva Spink Photography

AUTHOR BIOGRAPHY

Rachael Craw is an award-winning author of speculative fiction for young adults, including the Spark trilogy and *The Rift*. She completed her Bachelor of Arts in Classical Studies and Drama at the University of Canterbury and a Diploma of Teaching at Christchurch College of Education. She teaches English and Drama, mentors young writers, assesses manuscripts, leads writing workshops, and speaks at festivals and conferences throughout New Zealand and Australia. In her spare time, she walks her dogs, hoards books, and reviews fiction on social media. She lives in the South Island of New Zealand with her husband and three daughters where she teaches part time while working on her latest novel.